A *New York Times* Notable Book

One of the *Chicago Tribune*'s Ten Best Mysteries of 2001

Edgar® Award Nominee for Best First Novel by an American Author

UNPRECEDENTED ACCLAIM FROM CRITICS AND PEERS FOR C. J. BOX'S

OPEN SEASON

"Buy two copies of *Open Season*, and save one in mint condition to sell to first-edition collectors. C. J. Box is a great storyteller."
—Tony Hillerman

"Intriguing, with a forest setting so treacherous it makes Nevada Barr's locales look positively comfy, with a motive for murder that is as unique as any in modern fiction. Pickett is a refreshingly human and befuddled hero. . . . But it's Box's offbeat way of telling the story that puts it on the best-of-the-year track."
—*Los Angeles Times*

"C. J. Box has hit the bull's-eye his first time up. *Open Season* explores an honorable man's love of family and the unflinching measures such a man is willing to take to protect them. Riveting suspense mingles with flashes of cynical back-country humor and makes Box an author to watch. I didn't want this book to end."
—Margaret Maron

"C. J. Box . . . certainly knows the Wyoming territory Pickett covers. . . . Pickett is deceptive and complicated himself, a struggling young husband and father who combines eagerness and ambition, strength and fragility into an interesting, original package."
—*Chicago Tribune*

continued . . .

"Pickett [is] an engaging change from the fast-driving, trigger-happy male heroes of so many contemporary crime novels. . . . What really sets *Open Season* apart, however, is the author's ability to incorporate the viewpoints of his hero's seven-year-old daughter into the story. Box does a very fine job of capturing the heart and fears of a young girl. . . . She is, indeed, an integral part of the story, and she adds a warm counterbalance to the relentless greed of the adults surrounding her. *Open Season* is a very promising debut."
—*The Washington Post Book World*

"A fabulous debut—a great crime novel and a great modern-day western rolled into one. All the elements are here: a tremendous sense of Wyoming's scenic grandeur, vivid characters, and a high-stakes plot that moves like a rifle bullet. Plus, as a bonus, hero Joe Pickett's daughter, Sheridan, is the best-written child character I've read in a long time. C. J. Box is a keeper, and I for one hope he'll write a few more like this one—soon."
—Lee Child

"*Open Season* rings true . . . Box nails the taste and smell of the place, and in the process, creates a sensory experience that can be rare in fast-paced, plot-driven crime fiction—without stalling the plot. He finds a way to weave the mysteries of landscape into the larger mystery at hand . . . Box's yarn is full of the kind of grittiness a reader can expect from a place where blood and bone are not just the stuff of crime fiction, but of sport and survival, too."
—*The Denver Post*

"C. J. Box knows the Wyoming high country inside out, and his protagonist, Game Warden Joe Pickett, is as real and refreshing as they come. This one is a hunting trip and then some."
—Les Standiford

"C. J. Box has written a fast-paced, intelligent mystery that draws us into the wide open spaces of Wyoming and introduces a memorable hero: Game Warden Joe Pickett, unwilling detective and a man with a conscience. A page-turner and a remarkable debut."

—Margaret Coel

"Every few years a first novel appears that immediately sets itself apart from the crowd. As readers, we feel that special shock of recognition that announces, 'Here is something special.' Taking dead aim with his first sentence . . . Box remains square on target throughout this nearly word-perfect debut. . . . Best of all, the soft-spoken Joe Pickett is a Gary Cooper for our time."

—*Booklist* (starred review)

"The unusual setting and flawed characters make for an enlightening, as well as suspenseful, read."

—*New York Daily News*

"*Open Season* is a lean, fast-moving thriller that proves you don't need an urban landscape to make the pages turn. With the exception of James Dickey, I can't think of another writer who has managed to wring so much white-knuckled terror out of rural America. This is a truly outstanding read."

—Loren D. Estleman

"*Open Season* is a western deco, vividly painted and fun as hell. I know nothing of the West, but C. J. Box is a superb guide—and also a very good novelist."

—Randy Wayne White

"[A] debut mystery to be savored . . . Joe Pickett is a modern-day Gary Cooper, soft-spoken and good-hearted . . . [A] clever mix of mystery, western, and scenery-to-die-for . . . Box has created an enduring hero in Joe. . . . Once you stake out *Open Season*, you won't want to turn loose until the limit is bagged and the back cover is closed."

—*The Jackson (MS) Clarion-Ledger*

Titles by C. J. Box

The Joe Pickett Novels

OPEN SEASON
SAVAGE RUN
WINTERKILL
TROPHY HUNT
OUT OF RANGE
IN PLAIN SIGHT
FREE FIRE
BLOOD TRAIL
BELOW ZERO
NOWHERE TO RUN
COLD WIND
FORCE OF NATURE
BREAKING POINT

BLUE HEAVEN
THREE WEEKS TO SAY GOODBYE

OPEN SEASON

C. J. BOX

BERKLEY BOOKS, NEW YORK

THE BERKLEY PUBLISHING GROUP
Published by the Penguin Group
Penguin Group (USA) Inc.
375 Hudson Street, New York, New York 10014, USA

Penguin Group (Canada), 90 Eglinton Avenue East, Suite 700, Toronto, Ontario M4P 2Y3, Canada (a division of Pearson Penguin Canada Inc.) • Penguin Books Ltd., 80 Strand, London WC2R 0RL, England • Penguin Group Ireland, 25 St. Stephen's Green, Dublin 2, Ireland (a division of Penguin Books Ltd.) • Penguin Group (Australia), 250 Camberwell Road, Camberwell, Victoria 3124, Australia (a division of Pearson Australia Group Pty. Ltd.) • Penguin Books India Pvt. Ltd., 11 Community Centre, Panchsheel Park, New Delhi—110 017, India • Penguin Group (NZ), 67 Apollo Drive, Rosedale, Auckland 0632, New Zealand (a division of Pearson New Zealand Ltd.) • Penguin Books (South Africa) (Pty.) Ltd., 24 Sturdee Avenue, Rosebank, Johannesburg 2196, South Africa

Penguin Books Ltd., Registered Offices: 80 Strand, London WC2R 0RL, England

OPEN SEASON

A Berkley Book / published by arrangement with the author

PUBLISHING HISTORY
G. P. Putnam's Sons hardcover edition / July 2001
Berkley Prime Crime mass-market edition / May 2002
Berkley mass-market edition / March 2012

For information, address: The Berkley Publishing Group,
a division of Penguin Group (USA) Inc.,
375 Hudson Street, New York, New York 10014.

ISBN: 978-0-425-18546-9

BERKLEY®
Berkley Books are published by The Berkley Publishing Group,
a division of Penguin Group (USA) Inc.,
375 Hudson Street, New York, New York 10014.
BERKLEY® is a registered trademark of Penguin Group (USA) Inc.
The "B" design is a trademark of Penguin Group (USA) Inc.

PRINTED IN THE UNITED STATES OF AMERICA

30 29 28 27 26 25

To Molly, Becky, Roxanne, and especially for Laurie—
my partner, my anchor, my first reader, my love

And thanks to Andy Whelchel and Martha Bushko, who brought this to life

Prologue

When a high-powered rifle bullet hits living flesh it makes a distinctive—*pow-WHOP*—sound that is unmistakable even at tremendous distance. There is rarely an echo or fading reverberation or the tailing rumbling hum that is the sound of a miss. The guttural boom rolls over the terrain but stops sharply in a close-ended way, as if jerked back. A hit is blunt and solid like an airborne grunt. When the sound is heard and identified, it isn't easily forgotten.

When Wyoming Game Warden Joe Pickett heard the sound, he was building a seven-foot elk fence on the perimeter of a rancher's haystack. He paused, his fencing pliers frozen in midtwirl. Then he stepped back, lowered his head, and listened. He slipped the pliers into the back pocket of his jeans and took off his straw cowboy hat to wipe his forehead with a bandanna. His red uniform shirt stuck to his chest, and he felt a single, warm trickle of sweat crawl down his spine into his Wranglers.

He waited. He had learned over the years that it was easy to be fooled by sounds of any kind outside, away from town. A single, sharp crack heard at a distance could be a rifle shot, yes, but it could also be a tree falling, a branch snapping, a cow breaking through a sheet of ice in the winter, or the backfire of a motor. "Don't confirm the first gunshot until you hear the second" was a basic tenet of the outdoors. Good poachers knew that, too. It tended to improve their aim.

In a way, Joe hoped he wouldn't hear a second shot. The fence wasn't done, and if someone was shooting, it was his duty to investigate. Joe had been on the job for a only a week, and he was hopelessly backlogged with work that had accumulated since the legendary Warden Vern Dunnegan had retired three months before. It was the state's responsibility to keep the elk herds out of private hay, and the pile of work orders on his desk for elk fence was nearly an inch high. Even if he built fence from dawn to dusk, he didn't see how he could possibly get it all done before hunting season started.

There was nothing really unusual about gunshots ringing out at any time of day or night or at any time of the year in Twelve Sleep County, Wyoming. Everybody owned guns. A rancher could be shooting at a coyote, or some of the boys from town could be out sighting in their rifles on a target.

Pow-WHOP.

Joe's eyes swung northwest toward the direction of the second shot, toward the foothills of the mountains where outstretched fingers of timber reached down into the high sage that reflected blue in the heat. The shot had come from a long way, three to five miles.

Maxine, Joe's eight-year-old yellow Labrador, also heard the shot, and bounded from her pool of shadow under Joe's green Ford pickup. She knew it was time to go to work. Joe opened the passenger door with the Wyoming Game and Fish logo on it, and she leaped in. Before he closed the door, he unsheathed his Winchester .270 rifle and scope from its scabbard case behind the seat and fitted the rifle into the gun rack across the back window. His gun belt was coiled in a pile on the floorboard of the truck, so he picked it up and he buckled it on. Even though regulations dictated that he wear his sidearm at all times, Joe hated driving with his holster on because the heavy pistol jabbed him in the back.

As he climbed into the pickup, there were two more quick shots, one after the other. The first shot wafted across the brush and hay. The second was definitely another hit. Joe thought it was likely that at least two—and possibly three—animals were down.

Joe shoved the pickup into four-wheel drive and headed west toward the mountains, driving as fast as he could without losing control of the wheel. There were no established roads, so he kept the left tires in a cow track while the right wheels bounced through knee-high, then thigh-high, sagebrush. Maxine leaned into the windshield with both of her large paws on the dashboard, balancing against the violent pitching of the terrain. Her tongue swung from side to side and spattered the dashboard with dog spit.

"Get ready," Joe told her—although for what he didn't know.

They plunged into a dry wash and ground up out of it, the tires independently grabbing dirt and shooting plumes of dust into the air. Joe nearly lost his grip on the steering wheel as it wrenched hard to the right and left, then he regained control and powered up a brushy slope. His mouth was dry, and he was, quite frankly, very scared.

A game warden in the field rarely encountered anyone who wasn't armed. Hunters, of course, had rifles, shotguns, and sidearms. Hikers, fishers, and campers all too often were packing. Even archery hunters had bows capable of rocketing a razor-sharp broad-head arrow through his pickup door. But that was during hunting season. This was the middle of summer, and there were no seasons open. The only kind of people who would be knocking down big animals now would be poachers or cattle rustlers, and either could be desperate and dangerous if caught in the act.

Joe Pickett topped the small hill and quickly sized up the situation: three large buck mule deer were dead, lying on their sides, on the bottom of the saddle slope. Their throats had been cut to bleed them, but they hadn't been opened up yet to field dress. A bearded man wearing a T-shirt, jeans, and a King Ropes cap straddled the largest of the bucks. He was a big man, built solidly with thick arms and a barrel chest. His T-shirt read HAPPINESS IS A WARM GUT PILE. He outweighed Joe by at least 40 pounds, but he didn't seem menacing, only very upset with the fact that he had been caught. He held a dripping knife in his hand. His rifle was propped up in a tall sagebrush about 50 feet away from him. He appeared not to have a sidearm. His pickup, a battered three-quarter-ton GMC, nosed out of the timber on the opposite slope.

He squinted up at Joe's pickup and his face fell open. "Oh, fuck me," the man said, loud enough for Joe to hear over the whine of the engine.

Joe drove quickly down the hill and positioned his Ford between the man and the rifle so the poacher couldn't lunge for it. Joe got out, told Maxine to stay, and approached the man and the downed deer.

"Please drop the knife," Joe asked, sizing up the deer and the poacher. The poacher tossed the knife aside into the grass. Joe saw no reason to draw his revolver. Joe rarely found a reason to draw his weapon, and even if he did, he doubted he could hit anything with it. Joe was a notoriously bad pistol shot at any range, the worst in his class.

"You're about four months early for deer season, you know," Joe said. He now recognized the man, a local outfitter named Ote Keeley. Joe had seen his photo and a reference request for an outfitter's license on his desk his first day on the job.

Ote sighed. "Meat for the pot, Warden. Just meat for the pot. Some of us got a family to feed." Ote had a deep Southern accent. Joe couldn't identify the state.

Joe squatted over the nearest and largest buck deer and ran his fingers over the soft velvet that still covered the antlers.

"Seems to me you didn't have to kill the only trophies in the herd just to fill your freezer." He looked up at Ote Keeley, his eyes hard. "A meat hunter would have probably been happy with a big dry doe or two."

Joe knew there was a black market for antlers in velvet, and that racks this size would command thousands of dollars in Asia where they were thought to possess healing powers as well as serve as an aphrodisiac when ground up and ingested.

"I'm going to have to write you up. Ote Keeley, isn't it?"

Ote was genuinely surprised. His face flushed red.

"You're gosh-darned kidding me, right?" Ote asked, as if avoiding an additional ticket for cursing.

Joe stood and pulled his ticket book out of his back pocket and flipped it open. "No, I'm not kidding."

Ote stepped toward Joe over the downed deer he was straddling. "Hey—I know you. You're the brand-new game warden, ain't you?"

Joe nodded and began to fill out the citation.

"I heard about you. Everybody has. You're the bonehead who arrested the governor of Wyoming for fishing without a license, right?"

Joe could feel his neck getting hot.

"I didn't know he was the governor," Joe said, wishing he hadn't said anything.

Ote Keeley laughed and slapped his thigh.

"Didn't know he was the governor," Ote repeated. "I

read about that in the paper. Everybody did. 'Rookie Game Warden Arrests Governor Budd.'"

Ote turned serious: "Hey, you're not really going to ticket me, are you? I'm a professional hunting outfitter. I can't feed my family if my outfitter's license gets pulled. I'm not kidding. I'm sure we can work this out."

Joe looked up at Ote Keeley. "I'm not kidding, either. Now give me your driver's license."

It was as if Ote Keeley, for the first time, realized what was really happening. Joe was amazed at the man's almost staggering stupidity. Joe caught Ote glancing toward where he had left his rifle.

"There's more animals in Wyoming than people," Ote spat. "These critters won't be missed by anyone. That herd ran nearly thirty. Vern Dunnegan wouldn't have pulled this *shit*."

"I'm not Vern Dunnegan." Joe said, hiding his surprise about what Ote had said about his predecessor and mentor.

"You sure as hell ain't," Ote Keeley said bitterly, as he pulled his wallet out of his jeans and held it out for Joe. As Joe reached for it, Ote grabbed Joe's arm and jerked it past him, throwing Joe off balance. Ote had Joe's revolver out of the holster before he could recover.

For a brief second, Joe Pickett and Ote Keeley stared at each other in genuine surprise, then Ote raised the pistol and aimed it squarely at Joe's face.

"Uh-oh, look what just happened," Ote said, a little in awe.

"I would suggest you give that back," Joe answered, trying to keep his face from twitching. He was terrified. "Give it back and we'll call it even."

Ote Keeley smoothly cocked the hammer of the revolver. Joe watched the cylinder rotate. Dull noses of lead filled each chamber, and the mouth of the barrel was black and huge, gaping. Ote wrapped his other hand around the grip, steadying his aim.

"Now we're in really, *really* fucking deep," Ote said, more to himself than anybody.

Joe thought of his daughters, Sheridan and Lucy, both at home, probably playing outside in the backyard. He thought of his wife, Marybeth, who had always feared that something like this would happen.

Then Joe's entire consciousness, his entire being, focused on one simple question: would he die with his eyes open or closed?

PART ONE

Findings, Purposes, and Policy

(b) Purposes. - The purposes of this Act are to provide a means whereby the ecosystems upon which endangered species and threatened species depend may be conserved, to provide a program for the conservation of such endangered species and threatened species, and to take such steps as may be appropriate to achieve the purposes of the treaties and conventions set forth in subsection(s) of this section.

—The Endangered Species Act Amendments of 1982
Printed for the use of the Senate Committee on
Environment and Public Works
US Government Printing Office
Washington: 1983

1

Joe lived, but it wasn't something he was particularly proud of. It was now fall and Sunday morning dawned slate gray and cold. He was making pancakes for his girls when he first heard of the bloody beast who had come down from the mountains and tried to enter the house during the night.

Seven-year-old Sheridan Pickett related her dream aloud to the stuffed bear that served as her confidant. Lucy, three and horrified, listened in. The television set was on even though the reception from the vintage satellite dish was snowy and poor, as usual.

The monster, Sheridan said, had come down from the mountains through the dark, steep canyon behind the house very late last night. She watched it through a slit in the curtain on her window, just a few inches from the top bunk of her bed. The canyon was where Sheridan had always *suspected* a monster would come from, and she felt proud, if a bit fearful, that she had been right. The only light had been the moon through the dried leaves of the cottonwood tree. The monster had rattled the back gate before figuring out the latch and had then lurched clumsily (sort of like mummies in old movies) across the yard to the backdoor. Its eyes and teeth glinted yellow, and for a second, Sheridan felt an electric bolt jolt through her as the monster's head swiveled around and seemed to looked directly at her before it fled. The monster was hairy and shiny, as if covered with liquid. Twigs and leaves were stuck to it. There was something white, a large sack or box, swinging from the monster's hand.

"Sheridan, stop talking about monsters," Joe called out. The dream disturbed him because the details were so precise. Sheridan's dreams were usually more fantastic, inhabited by talking pets or magical things that flew. "You're going to scare your little sister."

"I'm already scared," Lucy declared, pulling her blanket to her mouth.

"Then the man walked slowly away across the yard through the gate toward the woodpile where he fell down into a big shadow. And he's *still out there,*" Sheridan finished, widening her eyes toward her sister to deliver the complete effect.

"Hold it, Sheridan," Joe said abruptly, entering the room with a spatula in his hand. Joe was wearing his threadbare terry-cloth bathrobe he had purchased on a lark in Jackson Hole on his and Marybeth's honeymoon ten years before. He shuffled in fleece slippers that were a size too large. "You said 'man.' You didn't say 'monster.' You said 'man.'"

Sheridan looked up quizzically, her big eyes wide. "Maybe it was a man. Maybe it wasn't a dream after all."

Joe heard a vehicle outside, racing up the gravel Bighorn Road much too fast, but by the time he crossed the living room and parted the faded drapes of the front picture window, the car or truck was gone. Dust rolled lazily down the road where it had been.

Beyond the window was the front yard, still green from summer and littered with plastic toys. Then there was the white fence, recently painted, paralleled by the gravel road. Farther, beyond the road, the landscape dipped into a willow-choked saddle where the Twelve Sleep River branched out into six fingers clogged with beaver ponds and brackish mosquito-heaven eddies and paused for a breath before its muscular rush through and past the town of Saddlestring. Beyond were the folds of the valley as it arched and suddenly climbed to form a precipitous mountain-face known as Wolf Mountain, a peak in the Twelve Sleep Range.

With Wolf Mountain in front of them and the foothills and canyon in back, the Pickett family, eight miles from town in their house, lived a life of deep and casting shadows.

The front door opened and Maxine burst in, followed by Marybeth. Marybeth's cheeks were flushed—either from the brisk cold air or her long walk with the dog, Joe wasn't sure which—and she looked annoyed. She wore her winter walking uniform of lightweight hiking boots, chinos, anorak, and wool hat. The anorak was stretched tight across her pregnant belly.

"It's cold out there," Marybeth said, peeling the hat off so her blond hair tumbled onto her shoulders. "Did you see that truck tear by here? That was *Sheriff Barnum's* truck going too fast on that road up to the mountains."

"Barnum?" Joe said, genuinely puzzled.

"And your dog was going nuts when we got back to the house. She nearly took my arm off just a minute ago." Marybeth unclipped Maxine's leash from her collar, and Maxine padded to her water dish and drank sloppily.

Joe had a blank expression on his face while he was thinking. The expression sometimes annoyed Marybeth, who was afraid people would think him simple. It was the same expression, in a photograph, that had been transmitted throughout the region via the Associated Press when Joe, while still a trainee, had arrested a tall man—who turned out to be the new governor of Wyoming—for fishing without a license.

"Where did Maxine want to go?" he asked.

"She wanted to go out back," she said. "Toward the woodpile."

Joe turned around. Sheridan and Lucy had paused at breakfast and were looking to him. Lucy looked away and resumed eating. Sheridan held his gaze, and she nodded triumphantly.

"Better take your gun," Sheridan said.

Joe managed a grin. "Eat your breakfast," he said.

"What's this all about?" Marybeth asked.

"Bloody monsters," Sheridan said, her eyes wide. "There's a bloody monster in the woodpile."

Suddenly, there was the roar of motors coming up Bighorn Road from Saddlestring. Joe was thinking exactly what Marybeth said next: "Something's going on. I wonder why nobody called here?"

Joe lifted the telephone receiver to make sure it was working, the dial tone echoed clearly into his ear.

"Maybe it's because you're the new guy. People here still can't get used to the fact that Vern Dunnegan isn't around anymore," Marybeth said, and Joe knew instantly she wished she could take it back.

"Dad, about that monster?" Sheridan said from the table, almost apologetic.

Joe buckled his holster over his bathrobe, clamped on his black Stetson, and stepped outside onto the back porch. He was surprised how cool and crisp it was this early in the fall. When he saw the large spatters of dried blood between his oversized fleece slippers, the chill suddenly became more pronounced. Joe pulled his revolver and broke the cylinder to make sure it loaded. Then he glanced over his shoulder.

Framed in the dining room window were Sheridan and Lucy. Marybeth stood behind them and off to the side. His three girls in the window were various stages of the same painfully beautiful blond and willowy female. Their green eyes were on him, and their faces were wide open. He knew how silly he must look. He couldn't tell if they could see what he could: splashes of blood on the ancient concrete walkway that halved the yard and crushed frozen grass where it appeared that someone—or something—had rolled. It looked almost like the night nesting place of a large deer or elk the way the grass and crisp autumn leaves had been flattened.

Grasping the pistol in front of him with both hands, Joe skirted a young pine and stepped through the open gate of the weathered fence to the place where the woodpile was.

Joe sucked in his breath and involuntarily stepped back, his ears filled with the *whumping* sound of his own heart beating.

A big, bearded man was sprawled across the woodpile, both of his large hands folded across his belly, palms down, and one leg cocked over a stump. The man's head rested on a log, his mouth parted just enough to show two rows of yellow teeth that looked like corn on the cob. His eyelids weren't completely shut, and where there should have been a moist reflection from his eyes there was instead a dull, dry membrane that looked like crinkled cellophane. His long hair and full beard was matted by blood into crude dreadlocks. The man wore a thick beige chamois shirt and jeans, and broad stripes of dark blood had coursed down both. It was Ote Keeley, and Ote looked dead.

Joe reached out and touched Ote's meaty, pale white hand. The skin was cold and did not give to the touch. Except for the dried blood in his hair and on his clothes and his waxy skin, Ote looked to be very comfortable. He could have been reclining in his La-Z-Boy, having a beer and watching the Bronco game on television.

Clutched in one of Ote Keeley's hands was the handle of a small plastic cooler minus the lid. Joe kneeled down and looked into the cooler, which was empty except for a scatter of small teardrop-shaped animal excrement. The inside walls of the cooler were scratched and scarred, as if clawed. Whatever had been in there had been manic about getting out, and it had succeeded.

Joe stood and saw the extra buckskin horse standing near the corral. The horse was saddled, and the reins hung down from the bridle. The horse had been ridden hard and had lost enough weight that the cinch slipped and the saddle hung loose and upside down.

Joe stared at Ote's blank face, recalling that day in June when Ote had pointed Joe's own pistol at his face and cocked the hammer. Even though Ote had thought better of it and had sighed theatrically and spun the weapon around butt-first with his finger in the trigger guard like the Lone Ranger, Joe had never quite been the same. He had been expecting to die at that moment, and for all practical purposes he *deserved* to die, having given up his weapon so stupidly. But it hadn't happened. Joe had holstered his revolver with his hands shaking so badly that the barrel of the revolver rattled around the mouth of the holster. His knees had been so weak that he backed up against his pickup to brace himself so he wouldn't collapse. Ote had simply watched him with a bemused expression on his face. Without a word, Joe had written out the citation for poaching in a shaking scrawl and handed the ticket to Ote Keeley, who took it and stuffed it in his pocket without even looking at it.

"I won't say nothin' if you don't about what just happened," Ote had said.

Joe hadn't acknowledged the offer, but he hadn't arrested Ote either. The deal had been struck: Ote's silence in exchange for Joe's life and career. It was a deal Joe agonized over later, usually late at night. Ote Keeley had taken something from him that he could never get back. In a way, Ote Keeley *had* killed Joe, just a little bit. Joe hated him for that, although he never said a word to anyone except Marybeth. What made it worse was when word of the incident filtered out anyway.

During the summer Ote had gotten drunk and told everyone at the bar what had happened. The story about the new game warden losing his weapon to a local outfitter had joyously made the rounds, and it even appeared in the wicked anonymous column "Ranch Gossip" that ran in the weekly *Saddlestring Roundup*. It was the kind of story the locals loved. In the latest version, Joe had lost control of his sphincter and had begged Ote for the gun back. Joe's supervisor in Cheyenne heard the rumors and had called Joe. Joe confirmed what had actually happened. In spite of Joe's explanation, the supervisor sent Joe a reprimand that would stay in his personnel file forever. An investigation was still possible.

Keeley's poaching trial date had been set to take place in two weeks, but obviously Ote wouldn't be appearing.

Ote Keeley was the first dead person Joe had ever seen except in a coffin at a funeral. There was nothing alive or real about Ote's expression. He did not look happy, puzzled, sad, or in pain. The look on his face—frozen by death and for several hours—told Joe nothing about what Ote was thinking or feeling when he died. Joe fought an urge to reach up and close Ote's eyes and mouth, to make him look more like he was sleeping. Joe had seen a lot of dead big game animals, but only the stillness and the salt-ripe odor was the same. When he saw dead animals, he had many different emotions, depending on the circumstances—from indifference to pity and sometimes to quiet rage aimed at careless hunters. This was different, Joe thought, because the dead body was human and could be *him.* Joe made himself stop staring.

Joe stood up. There *had* been a monster.

He heard something and turned around.

The backdoor slammed shut, and Sheridan was coming out in her nightgown, skipping down the walk with her hands in the air to see what he had found.

"Get BACK into that house!" Joe commanded with such unexpected force that Sheridan spun on her bare feet and flew right back inside.

On his way through the house and to the phone, Joe told Marybeth who the dead man was.

2

Of course, County Sheriff O. R. "Bud" Barnum wasn't in when Joe called the dispatch center in Saddlestring. According to the dispatcher—a chain-smoking conspiracy buff named Wendy—neither was Deputy McLanahan. Both, she said, had responded to an emergency that morning in a Forest Service campground in the mountains.

"Some campers reported seeing a wounded man on horseback ride straight through their camp last night," Wendy told Joe. "They said the suspect allegedly rode his horse right through their camp while displaying a weapon and threatening the campers with said weapon."

Joe could tell that Wendy loved this situation, loved being in the center of the action, loved telling Joe about it, loved saying things like "allegedly" and "said weapon." She did not get a chance to use those words often in Twelve Sleep County.

"I called out the entire sheriff's office and both emergency medical vehicles at seven-twelve A.M. this morning to respond."

"Did you get a description of the man on horseback?" Joe asked.

Wendy paused on the telephone, then read from the report: "Late thirties, wearing a beard, bloody shirt. A big man. Crazy eyes, they said. The suspect was allegedly swinging some kind of plastic box or cooler around."

Joe leaned his chair back so he could see out of the small room near the front door that served as his office. Both girls were still lined up at the back window, looking out. Marybeth hovered behind them, trying to draw their attention away by rattling a box of pretzels the same way she would shake dog biscuits at Maxine to get her to come into the house.

"Why wasn't I called?" Joe inquired calmly. "I live on the Bighorn Road."

There was no response. Finally: "I never even thought about it."

Joe recalled what Marybeth had said about Vern Dunnegan but said nothing.

"Sheriff Barnum didn't mention it neither," Wendy said defensively.

"The injured man was displaying and threatening a weapon with one hand and swinging a plastic box with the other?" Joe asked. "How did he steer his horse?"

"That's what the report says." Wendy sniffed. "That's what the campers reported. They was out-of-staters. From Massachusetts or Boston or some place like that." She said the last part as if it explained away the inconsistency.

"Which campground?" Joe persisted.

"It says here they was at Crazy Woman Creek."

Crazy Woman was the last developed U.S. Forest Service campground on Bighorn Road, a place generally used as a jumping-off site for hikers and horse-packers entering the mountains.

"Are you in radio contact with Sheriff Barnum?" Joe asked.

"I believe so."

"Why don't you give him a call and let him know that the man on horseback was Ote Keeley and that Ote is lying dead on the woodpile behind my house."

Joe could hear Wendy gasp, then try to regain her composure.

"Say again?" she replied.

Joe hung up the telephone and started for the backdoor.

"You're not going back out there?" Sheridan whispered.

"Just for a minute," Joe said in what he hoped was a reassuring tone.

He shut the door behind him and slowly walked toward the body of Ote Keeley, his eyes sweeping across the yard, taking in the bloodstained walk, the woodpile, the canyon mouth behind the house. He wanted a clear picture of everything as it was right now, before the sheriff and deputies arrived. He didn't want to screw up again.

Squatting near the plastic cooler, Joe drew two empty envelopes and a pencil from the pocket on his robe. Using the tip of the eraser, Joe flicked several small pieces of scat from the cooler into an envelope. He would send that to headquarters for analysis. He gathered several more pieces of scat and put them in another envelope. He sealed both and put them back in his pocket. He left the rest for the sheriff.

Back in the house, Joe dressed in his day-to-day uniform: blue jeans and his red, button-up chamois shirt with the pronghorn antelope patch on the sleeve. Over the breast pocket was his name plate, which read GAME WARDEN and under that J. PICKETT.

When he came downstairs, the girls were sprawled in front of the snowy television, and Marybeth was sitting at the table flanked by dirty dishes. She held a big mug of coffee in her hands and stared at something in the air between them.

Her eyes raised until they met Joe's.

"It'll be okay," Joe said, forcing a smile. He asked Marybeth to gather up the children and some clothes and go into Saddlestring. They could check into a motel until this was over and the backyard was cleaned up. He didn't want the kids seeing the dead man. Sheridan's dreams were already vivid enough.

"Joe, who will pay for the room? Will the state pay for it?" Marybeth asked softly so the children couldn't hear.

"You mean we can't?" Joe replied, incredulous. She shook her head no. Marybeth kept the meager family budget under a tight rein. It was the end of the month. She would know if they were broke, and apparently that was the case. Joe felt his face flush. Maybe they could stay with somebody? Joe dismissed that. While they had made a few friends in town, they were still new, and he didn't know who they could call to ask this kind of favor.

"Can we use the credit card?" he asked.

"Nearly maxed out." She said. "It might work for a night or two, though."

He felt another wave of heat wash up his neck.

"I'm sorry, honey," he mumbled. He fitted his dusty black hat on his head and went outside to wait.

3

After measuring, marking, and photographing, the deputies sealed off the woodpile with yellow CRIME SCENE tape and unfurled a body bag.

Joe stationed himself outside with his back to the window so no one who looked out could see the deputies bend Ote Keeley into the bag, folding his stiff arms and legs inside so they could zip it up and carry it away. Ote was heavy, and the middle part of the bag hummed along the top of the grass as the deputies took the body out of the yard and around the side of the house to the ambulance.

Sheriff O. R. "Bud" Barnum had arrived first and had briskly ordered Joe to show him where Ote Keeley's body was. Despite his age, Barnum still moved with speed and stiff grace. His pale blue eyes were set in a pallid leather face and rimmed with paper-thin flaps of skin. Joe watched as the blue eyes swept the scene.

Joe had expected questions and was prepared for them. He informed Barnum that he had gathered the scat evidence to send to headquarters, but Barnum had waved him off.

"Yup, that's Ote all right," Barnum had said, before returning to his Blazer. "You'll write up a report on it?" Joe nodded yes. That was *all* there was. No questions, no notes. Joe was surprised and felt useless.

From the side of the house, Joe observed the sheriff as he held the mike of his police scanner to his mouth with one hand and gestured in the air with the other. By his movements, Joe could tell that Barnum was becoming frustrated with somebody or something. So was Joe, but he tried not to show it.

Joe went inside the house. Marybeth watched him nervously from her place on the couch.

"Is it gone?" she asked, referring to the body. She didn't want to say Ote's name.

Joe assured her that it was.

She was pale, Joe noticed. Her face was drawn tight. Marybeth rubbed her hand across her extended belly. She didn't realize she was doing it. He remembered the gesture from before, when she was pregnant with Sheridan and then Lucy. It was something she did when she felt that things were on the verge of chaos. She held her arms across her unborn baby as if to shield it from whatever unpleasantness was happening outside. Marybeth was a good mother, Joe thought, and she reared the children with care. She resented it when outside events intruded on her family without her prior consent, permission, or planning.

"He's the guy who took your gun a while back," Marybeth said with dawning realization. "I've met his wife. In the obstetrician's office. She's at least five months along also." She grimaced. "They have a little one about Sheridan's age and I think one younger. Those poor kids . . ."

Joe nodded and poured some coffee in a mug to deliver to Sheriff Barnum out in his Blazer.

"I just wish it wouldn't have happened here," Marybeth said. "I know these things happen but why did he have to come here, to our house? Right to our *house*?"

It's not our house, Joe said to himself. *It belongs to the State of Wyoming. We just live here.* But Joe didn't say that and instead went out the front door after a quick "I'll be right back."

Barnum was signing off from a conversation, and he angrily hung up the microphone in its cradle on the dashboard. Joe handed him the cup of coffee, and Barnum took it without a word.

"What we know so far is that Keeley went into the mountains with two other guides to scout for elk and set up their camp last Thursday," Barnum said, not looking directly at Joe. "They have an outfitters camp up there somewhere. They weren't expected back until tomorrow so nobody had missed them yet."

"Who were the other guides?" Joe asked.

"Kyle Lensegrav and Calvin Mendes," Barnum replied, finally looking at him. "You know 'em?"

Joe nodded. "I've run into them a few times. Their names have come up along with Ote Keeley's in connection with a poaching ring. But nobody's caught them doing anything as far as I know." Joe had once had a beer in the Stockman Bar with both of them. They were both in their mid-thirties, and both mountain-man throwback types. Lensegrav was tall and thin, and he wore thick glasses mounted on a hooked nose. He had a scraggle of blond beard. Mendes was short and stout, with dark eyes and a charming, flashbulb smile. Pickett had heard that Mendes and Ote Keeley had been in the army together and that they had both served in Desert Storm.

"Well, nobody's seen Lensegrav or Mendes," Barnum continued. "My guess is that they're trying like hell to get out of state because they shot their good old pal Ote Keeley right in the chest a couple of times, for whatever reason."

"Or they're still up in the mountains," Joe said.

"Yup." Barnum paused, pursing his lips. "Or that. The word is out to the Highway Patrol statewide to watch out for 'em. Problem is I don't know yet what they're driving. Keeley's truck and horse trailer are up at Crazy Woman Creek where they left it. We're trying to find out if one of them took a vehicle up there as well."

Joe nodded at Barnum and said "Hmmmm." There was an uncomfortable minute of silence.

Sheriff Barnum was an institution in Twelve Sleep County, and he had been in office for 24 years. He rarely had opposition when he ran for election, and in the few times he had, he'd taken 70 percent of the vote. He was a hands-on sheriff, involved in everything from civic organizations to officiating at high school football and basketball games. He knew everybody in the county, and they in turn knew and respected him. Very little got by Sheriff Barnum. Over the years, he had become a storied and colorful character. Specific incidents had become legend. He had put a .357 Magnum bullet into the eyebrow of a ranch foreman who had just used an irrigation shovel to bludgeon to death his own mother, brother, and a Mexican hired hand. He had taken Polaroid snapshots of cows who had apparently been mutilated by alien beings who had arrived on earth in cigar-shaped flying objects. He had arrested a Basque sheepherder in his sheep wagon and confiscated a ewe named Maria that had been dyed pink. He had once turned back two dozen Hell's Angels en route to Sturgis, South Dakota, by firing up a 24-inch chain saw while straddling the yellow line on the highway.

"Your office should have called me this morning," Joe said abruptly. "I was closer to the scene than anyone else."

Barnum sipped the coffee and squinted at Joe as if sizing Joe up for the first time.

"You're right," Barnum answered. Then: "Wasn't it Ote Keeley who took your gun away from you while you were giving him a citation?"

"Yes, it was," Joe replied, feeling his ears flush hot.

"Strange he came here," Barnum said.

Joe nodded.

"Maybe he wanted to take your gun away from you again." Barnum smiled crookedly to show he was joking. Barnum was wily, no doubt about it. Joe hardly knew the sheriff, but Barnum had already tweaked one of his weak spots. There was a moment of hesitation before Joe asked if Barnum planned to investigate the elk hunting camp.

"I would, but right now I'm screwed," Barnum said, banging the dashboard with his fist. "That camp is in a roadless area so we can't get to it. Our chopper's on loan to the Forest Service so they can fight that fire down in the Medicine Bow Forest. Tomorrow night's the earliest we could get it back.

"And my horse posse guys are all in the mountains already because they're all gettin' ready to go hunting." Barnum looked over at Joe, exasperated. "We can't get to that camp unless we hoof it, and I'm not walking."

Joe thought it over for a moment. "I know a guy who knows where that elk camp is located, and I've got a couple of horses."

Barnum began to object, then caught himself.

"Well, I don't see why not, since you're volunteering. How soon could you get going?"

Joe rubbed his jaw. "This afternoon. I've got to fetch my horse trailer and get outfitted, but I'm pretty sure I could get on the trail by about two or three."

"Take my guy McLanahan," Barnum said. "I'll get on the radio and tell him to grab his saddle and some heavy artillery and get his lazy butt out here. You guys might run into some bad business up there, and I want to make sure you've got 'em outgunned."

Barnum grabbed his microphone but halted before he spoke into it.

"Who is it who knows where that hunting camp is?" Barnum asked.

"Wacey Hedeman," Joe replied.

"*Wacey Hedeman?*" Barnum hissed. "He's declared that he's going to run against me in the next election, that blow-dried son of a bitch."

Joe shrugged. Wacey was the game warden in the next district but had patrolled in the Twelve Sleep area temporarily after Vern left and before Joe was assigned the position. Wacey had once mapped out all of the licensed outfitters' elk camps along the Crazy Woman drainage.

"Goddamnit," Barnum spat vehemently. "I hate it when things turn cowboy."

Barnum cursed again, then turned away to radio his dispatcher.

Wacey didn't answer the telephone in his home office and didn't respond to the radio call, but Joe had a good idea where to find him. Before he left in the truck to find Wacey, he kissed Marybeth and his girls good-bye. Lucy gave him a bored kiss. She didn't approve of him leaving the house at any time for any reason, and this was how she showed it. Because she was so much younger and was wise beyond her years—she had absorbed, as if by osmosis, many of the lessons her older sister had learned the hard way—Joe often treated Lucy as a fellow adult conspirator, fighting the many emerging preadolescent forces of her animated older sister.

Sheridan and Lucy were confused by why they had to leave their house. Marybeth was telling them how exciting it would be to stay in a motel, but they weren't yet convinced.

Joe stopped at the door and turned back. Sheridan was watching him closely.

"You okay, honey?" Joe asked her.

"I'm okay, Dad."

"Next time you say you see a monster, I'm going to believe you."

"Okay, Dad."

"You remember who's coming tomorrow night, don't you?" Marybeth asked.

He had not thought about it at all with everything that had happened that morning.

"Your mother."

"My mother," Marybeth echoed. "So we'll be back in the house by then. Hopefully, you will, too."

Joe grimaced.

4

While her mother packed a suitcase in the bedroom, Sheridan did exactly what she had been told not to do and went to the dining room window to watch. However, before she did, she made sure that Lucy was still wrapped in her blanket on the floor watching television. Lucy would gladly tell on her older sister.

The man her dad called Sheriff Barnum stood in the yard near the woodpile, and another man wearing the same kind of policeman's uniform—he was younger than Sheriff Barnum but still old, like her dad—stood near him. The sheriff stood with his back to the woodpile, pointing toward the mountains and talking. His arm swept along the top of the mountains and up the road, and the younger man's eyes followed the gesture. Sheridan couldn't hear what the sheriff was saying. At one point, the sheriff walked from the woodpile to the house. He stopped squarely in front of Sheridan at the window, and Sheridan was too scared to move. Over his shoulder, to the other man, the sheriff called out the number of paces he had measured. Before turning back, he had looked down and grinned at her. It had been a kind of "get out of my way, kid" smile. Sheridan wasn't sure she liked Sheriff Barnum. She didn't like his pale eyes. She didn't like cigarettes, either, and even through the screen in the window she could smell them on his uniform.

As Sheriff Barnum returned to the woodpile, Sheridan thought about how surprised she was that this thing had happened. How could it be that what she had thought the night before was a monster from her "overactive imagination" (as her mom called it) had turned out to be real. It was as if her dream world and the real world had merged for this event. Suddenly, adults were involved. She had had a strange notion: what if her imagination was so powerful that she could dream things into existence?

But she decided this wasn't the case. If it was, she would have brought forth something much nicer than this. Like a pet—a *real* pet of her own.

Sheriff Barnum took a pack of cigarettes out of his shirt pocket, shook them, and flipped one up into his mouth. It was a neat trick, she thought. She had never seen it before. The man with Sheriff Barnum reached over and lighted the sheriff's cigarette for him. A great roll of white smoke grew around the sheriff's head.

Sheridan wore her glasses. She wished now she would have had her glasses on the night before, so she could have seen the man's face in detail when he looked at her. If she would have seen him clearly, she would have trusted her own mind over her imagination and run to her parents' room instead of convincing herself that she had a nightmare about monsters coming down from the mountains.

She loved that she could see clearly now but hated the fact that she was the only student in her class who had to wear glasses. Her first day of school at Twelve Sleep Elementary was also her first day wearing glasses. She would never forget how tall she seemed to be when she looked down or how awkward she felt when she walked. The chalkboard and the words on it were in such sharp focus that they hurt her eyes. It was bad enough that she was one of the new girls in school, and the rude girls had already grouped her into a category called "Weird Country" that was made up of students who lived out of town. Or that she could already read books and say poetry she had memorized while they struggled with sentences. But on top of all of that, she also had to show up wearing glasses.

And she was the new game warden's daughter in a place where the local game warden was a big deal because nearly everyone's dad hunted. It was understood that Sheridan's dad could put others in jail. So far, in the two weeks since school had begun, she had absolutely no friends in the second-grade class.

Sheridan's only friends were her animals, *had* been her animals, and they had all disappeared. The loss of her cat, Jasmine, had devastated her. She had cried and prayed for Jasmine to come back, but she didn't. She begged her parents for another pet to love, but they said she would have to wait until she got a little older. They told her she would have to get a fish or a bird in a cage, something that didn't go outside or into the hills behind the house. She had overheard her dad telling her mom about coyotes (although she wasn't supposed to know), and she had figured out that her cat Jasmine had been eaten. Just like her puppy before that. But while those pets were nice, they weren't what she needed. She wanted a pet to *cuddle* with. She wished she had a secret pet, one that neither her parents, the rude girls at school, or the coyotes knew about. A secret pet that was just hers. A pet she could love and who would love her for who she was: a lonely girl who had moved from place to place before she could make friends and who had a little sister who was too adorable for words and a baby on the way who would command most of her parents' love and attention for . . . *maybe forever.*

Then she saw something outside that quickly brought

her back to earth. Something had moved in the woodpile; something tan and lightning fast had streaked across the bottom row of logs and darted into a dark opening near the base between two lengths of wood.

The sheriff and the younger man were still talking, and they had their backs to the fence and the woodpile. What she had seen was just behind them, only a few feet away, but it didn't look like they had noticed anything. They hadn't even turned around. She could see nothing now. A ground squirrel? Too big. A marmot? Too sleek and fast. She had never seen this kind of animal before, and she knew every inch of that yard and every creature in it. She even knew where the nest of tiny field mice was and had studied the wriggling pink naked mouse babies before their eyes opened. But this animal was long and thin, and it moved like a bolt of lightning.

Sheridan gasped and jumped when her Mom spoke her name sharply behind her. Sheridan turned around quickly but her mom was looking sternly at her and not at the woodpile through the window. Sheridan didn't say a word when her mom guided her away from the window, through the house, and to the car.

As her mom backed out of the driveway and Lucy sang a nonsense song, Sheridan watched over her shoulder through the back car window as the house got smaller. As they crested the first hill toward town, the little house was the size of a matchbox.

Behind the matchbox house, Sheridan thought, was a woodpile. And in that woodpile was the gift her imagination had brought her.

PART TWO

Determination of Endangered Species and Threatened Species

Sec. 4. (a) General.- (1) The Secretary shall by regulation promulgated in accordance with subsection (b) determine whether any species is an endangered species or a threatened species because of any of the following factors:

[(1)] (A) the present or threatened destruction, modification, or curtailment of its habitat or range;

[(2)] (B) overutilization for commercial, [sporting,] recreational, scientific, or educational purposes;

[(3)] (C) disease or predation;

[(4)] (D) the inadequacy of existing regulatory mechanisms;

or

[(5)] (E) other natural or manmade factors affecting its continued existence.

—The Endangered Species Act Amendments of 1982

5

There were 55 game wardens in the State of Wyoming, an elite group, and Joe Pickett and Wacey were two of them. Wacey had received his B.A. in wildlife management while bull-riding at summer rodeos before Joe had graduated with a degree in natural resource management. Three years apart, both had been certified at the state law enforcement academy in Douglas and both had passed the written and oral interviews, as well as the personality profile, to become permanent trainees in Jeffrey City and Gillette districts respectively, before becoming wardens. Each now made barely $26,000 a year.

As Joe drove down the two-lane highway toward the Eagle Mountain Club, he thought of how the morning had violently changed course. Ote Keeley had ridden down from the mountains in the middle of the Pickett family Sunday routine. It was a routine that had moved with them as they relocated throughout the state. It continued to Baggs in Southern Wyoming, then to Saddlestring as he worked under the high-profile Game Warden Vern Dunnegan, then to Buffalo when Joe took on his first full-fledged post as game warden. There had been six different state-owned houses in nine years, five different towns. All of the homes—and especially this one—had been plebeian and small. They were careful at headquarters not to give the taxpayers the idea that their hunting license fees were going toward elaborate homes for state employees. The Pickett house was built into the mouth of a small canyon on a lot that included a barn, a corral, and a detached garage. They had brought their family routine back to Saddlestring district after Vern suddenly retired from the state and Joe finally got the job he wanted most, in the place he and Marybeth liked the best.

It was a job Joe almost didn't get. Vern had recommended Joe and had used his influence at headquarters to get Joe an interview with the director. In what Joe and Marybeth later called "one his larger bonehead moves," Joe had written the wrong date for the appointment with the director in his calendar and simply missed it. When Joe screwed up, he tended to do it massively and publicly. The director had been furious for being stood up and it was only through Vern's intervention that Joe was able to later meet with the director and secure the post.

Both Marybeth and Joe had commented how much bigger the house had seemed to be when Vern and his wife occupied it, back when Joe worked under Vern and he and Marybeth would visit. They both remembered sitting in the shaded backyard, sipping cocktails while Vern barbecued steaks and Vern's attractive wife, Georgia (they had no children), mixed drinks and tossed salad inside. The house at that time seemed almost elegant in a way, and both Joe and Marybeth were envious. The future seemed so bright then. But that was two children and a Labrador ago, and the same three-bedroom home was filled. After only four months in the house it seemed to be shrinking. The baby would make the house even smaller. And everything about it was falling apart. The shelf life for a state-owned and -constructed home was short.

Today was, he knew, likely to be the last Sunday for at least three months that he would be able to cook breakfast for his girls and read the newspapers—and now he hadn't even been able to do that. Big game hunting season in Twelve Sleep County, Wyoming, would begin on Thursday with antelope season. Deer would follow, then elk and moose. Joe would be out in the mountains and foothills, patrolling. School would even be let out for "Elk Day" because the children of hunters were expected to go with their families into the mountains.

Hunters began before dawn, and Joe would begin before dawn. Hunters could legally take game up to a half an hour after dark, and Joe would be out among them until well after that, checking permits and licenses, making sure that the game was tagged properly, that laws weren't broken, and that private land wasn't trespassed on. In Wyoming, the people owned the game animals, and they took their ownership to heart. Joe took his job just as seriously.

He thought about Sheridan saying "Better take your gun," and it bothered him. Sheridan had certainly noticed his Sam Browne belt and the pistol in it when he came home every night. His .270 Winchester rifle rested permanently in the window gun rack of the department green Ford pickup he drove. They knew that his job entailed carrying a gun with him. But never had either child ever suggested he go out and shoot something. Maybe they didn't realize what he really did all day. He had heard Sheridan say in passing that her Dad "saved animals" for his job. He liked that definition, even though it was only partially true.

Joe slowed on the highway to let a herd of pronghorn antelope cross. He watched as they ducked under a barbed-wire fence and continued their journey toward the foothills, toward Wacey Hedeman's district.

Wacey and Joe had both been trained in the field by Vern Dunnegan at different times. Vern told anyone who would listen that they were his "best boys." Because their districts adjoined each other—the warden in the Saddlestring district and the warden in the Basin district—Wacey and Joe often teamed up on projects and investigations. They built hay fences together, shared horses and snow machines when needed for patrol, called on each other for support if necessary, and traded notes. As a result of spending many predawn hours together in one or the other's trucks, Joe had come to know Wacey well. They had even become friends, of a sort. Wacey fascinated Joe at the same time he repelled him. Wacey knew the county and was intimate with ranchers and poachers alike. Wacey was an ex–rodeo cowboy who had an easy, oily charm that worked on just about everyone, Joe included. Even Marybeth seemed to enjoy Wacey, although she startled Joe once by saying that she didn't trust him.

Some of the things Joe knew about Wacey would have confirmed her opinion, but he kept them to himself.

Joe turned his pickup off of the highway into the entrance of the Eagle Mountain Club. A uniformed guard in a white clapboard guardhouse waved at him to go through, and the motorized wrought-iron gate swung wide. But as Joe drove forward, the guard suddenly swung out of the door of the house and approached his window.

The guard was in his late fifties, and his uniform strained across his belly.

"I thought you were somebody else when I waved at you," the guard said, bending his head to the side so he could see into the truck.

"You thought I was Wacey Hedeman," Joe said. "He has a truck just like this. I'm here to see Wacey."

The guard stared hard at Joe. "Have you been here before?"

"Once, with Wacey." Joe let his voice drop. "Now please let me through now. There was a homicide near Saddlestring, and I need Wacey's help on it now."

The guard stepped back but took a moment to wave Pickett through. In his rearview mirror, Joe watched the guard step into the road and write down Joe's license plate number on a pad he took from his pocket.

The Eagle Mountain Club was an exclusive private resort on a hilltop overlooking the Big Horn River. From what Wacey had told him, initial dues to the club were $250,000 and members joined by invitation only. The Eagle Mountain Club had only 250 members, and new members joined only when old members died, dropped out, or were denied privileges by a majority of the members. This had happened only twice to Joe's knowledge, once to the famous televangelist who "baptized" a housekeeper by inserting the neck of a vodka bottle into her and then dunking her in the club-stocked trout pond and the other time when a member, a former astronaut, was found guilty of beating his wife to death with a bronze replica of the Lunar Landing Module. The club had a 36-hole golf course that fingered through the foothills of the Bighorn Mountains, as well as a private fish hatchery, shooting range, airstrip, and about 60 multimillion-dollar homes that had been constructed when a million dollars was an obscene amount of money. The one thing the exclusive membership had in common was a passion for privacy. Few people in the state even knew about the Eagle Mountain Club, and access to it was purposely difficult. It was more than 200 miles from the nearest city of any size—Billings, Montana—and more than 500 miles from Denver.

The Eagle Mountain Club was nearly vacant in the fall, and Joe encountered no vehicles or golf carts on the road.

Few residents stayed during the winter, and most were already gone. As he drove along the wide empty roads bordered by manicured lawns with the Bighorns looming all around him, Joe got the sense of being on top of the country that spread out around him. It was a false oasis hidden away on a mountaintop in Wyoming, a high and dry place where the grass grew only because of nonstop, unrepentant irrigation and where all of the food in the four-star restaurant was flown in from other places. Joe felt that this place didn't belong, and he knew it was there for precisely that reason. The Eagle Mountain Club predated the recent flight to the Rocky Mountains by rich celebrities by about 30 years.

Homes were set back off of the road, and most were hidden by trees. There were no street signs, and driveways to homes were marked by brass plaques imbedded in the pavement with the owners' last names. When he saw the name Kensinger, he turned.

Wacey's muddy green Ford pickup was parked at a rakish angle on the side of the massive two-level log home. Joe parked behind it and got out. His footsteps on the pavement were the only sound he could hear. Joe knocked on the door.

The wide oak front door swung open, and Wacey stood in it and squinted at Joe with a sour expression on his face. Wacey was still thin and compact—a bull rider's body—and his mouth was hidden under a thick auburn gunfighter's mustache. The only thing he was wearing was his red chamois Game and Fish shirt.

"Take your pants off and come on in, Joe," Wacey said in a whisper. "That's what I did." A slow full-face grin started near his corners of his blue eyes.

Someone inside the dark house, a woman, asked Wacey what he was doing.

"My colleague Joe Pickett from the Saddlestring District is here," Wacey said over his shoulder. "I'll just be a minute."

Behind Wacey, in the gloom, Joe saw the form of a very white and naked woman pass. He heard her bare feet slap across the marble floor.

To Joe, Wacey mouthed the name "Aimee Kensinger." Then: "She really does like us wardens."

Despite himself, Joe smiled. Wacey was something else. Wacey had once told Joe that Aimee Kensinger, the trophy wife of Donald Kensinger of Kensinger Communications, had a thing for cowboy-types in uniform. Joe knew Wacey had been spending a lot of time of late at the Eagle Mountain Club. He also knew that Wacey's visits coincided with Donald Kensinger's business trips.

Wacey stepped out on the porch and eased the door closed behind him.

"What's going on?" Wacey asked. "I was right in the middle of something."

Joe knew what. There was a wet stain on the front tail of Hedeman's shirt where his erection stretched out at the fabric like a tent pole. Hedeman followed Joe's eyes.

"That's kinda embarrassing," Wacey said. "Guess I'm leakin' a bit. She'll make a guy do things like that when they aren't used to it."

Joe Pickett told Wacey what had happened that morning. He confirmed that Wacey did know where Ote Keeley's elk camp was located on the Twelve Sleep Drainage. He told Wacey about the cooler, and Wacey seemed interested.

"Ote Keeley. He was that guy . . ."

"*Yup,*" Joe answered sharply.

"When do we need to get going?" Wacey asked.

"Right now," Joe said. "Right now."

"I gotta call Arlene," Wacey replied, referring to his wife.

"Maybe you ought to do it from the truck."

Wacey again started his slow, infectious smile. He winked at Joe and nodded his head toward the door.

"She's gonna finance my campaign for sheriff," Wacey

said in a conspiratorial voice. "And when it comes to sex, she'll try just about anything. She even shaved herself this morning. You ever mess around with a woman who is shaved clean as a whistle? It's weird. Sort of like a little girl, but not a little girl at all, you know? You just don't realize how big and ripe those lips are down there unless you can really see 'em."

Joe nodded uncomfortably.

Aimee Kensinger came out of the house wearing a thick white robe.

Joe said hello. He had met her once at a museum fundraiser dinner Marybeth had taken him to, but he knew she didn't remember him. He hadn't been in his uniform.

"Hello, officer," Aimee Kensinger said. It was a purr, a self-conscious, very obvious purr. Joe was both alarmed and aroused.

Aimee Kensinger had a wide-open healthy face framed by a bell of dark hair. Her feet were bare and her calves were trim. She wore no makeup, but her face was still flushed from whatever Wacey and she had been doing inside.

"Forget it, babe." Wacey said gently to her, giving her a brotherly punch on the arm. "He's married."

"So are you, honey," she said.

"It's different with Joe, though," Wacey answered, shrugging as if he couldn't understand it himself.

"Good for you," she said. Joe couldn't tell if she meant it or not.

6

The command post that had been established at the Crazy Woman Creek Campground had quickly become chaos. The murder of Ote Keeley and the possibility of an armed camp of suspects had ignited the imagination of the entire valley. A crowd had formed in the campground including off-duty Saddlestring police officers, volunteer fire department members, the mayor, the editor of the weekly *Saddlestring Roundup,* even elderly officers of the local VFW armed with Korean War–era M-1 carbines. Two local survivalists had shown up in battle fatigues with specially modified SKS Chinese assault rifles and concussion grenades hung from web belts. Sheriff Barnum didn't mind the crowd; he reveled in it. His makeshift office was established in a stout-walled Cabela's outfitter tent. His desk was a card table. Someone (Joe guessed one of the Korean War vets) told him that when he sat at the table and smoked, he reminded them of General Ulysses S. Grant at Shiloh. Barnum enjoyed the comparison and mentioned it to anyone who would listen.

Joe Pickett and Wacey Hedeman saddled their horses

and shook the hands of well-wishers while they waited for Deputy McLanahan to arrive. Joe had brought up his six-year-old buckskin mare named Lizzie. Joe felt like he and Wacey were star athletes of the local football team. Men clapped them on their shoulders and whacked them on the butt as they walked by. Many said they wished they were going along.

McLanahan arrived armed for a small war, and the gear he had brought would have been fine if the three of them were setting off on a land offensive with four-wheel drives and transport trucks. Unfortunately for McLanahan, this was a designated roadless area of the national forest and the only access was by foot or horseback. In his Blazer and horse trailer, McLanahan had brought hundreds of pounds of bulky outfitter tents, sleeping bags, a propane stove, blankets, cast-iron skillets, Dutch ovens and frying pans, radio equipment and a chuck box filled with plates and utensils that weighed more than 150 pounds by itself. The back of the Blazer was stacked with guns—Joe imagined McLanahan cleaned out the gun cabinet in the sheriff's office. He saw several high-powered sniper's rifles with night-vision scopes, semiautomatic carbines loaded with armor-piercing shells, a couple of MAC-10 machine pistols, M-16 automatic rifles, and semiautomatic riot shotguns. "Typical Barnum overkill," Wacey had scoffed loud enough to be heard by the crowd in the camp. A few people laughed. "Supporters," Wacey whispered to Joe.

Barnum had ordered the three horsemen to "take as much as they could," and McLanahan had loaded down the canvas panniers while Joe and Wacey stared at each other in puzzlement. Barnum made it clear that he was assuming command of the operation and that the two Game and Fish officers were subordinate to the county sheriff, which was officially true in this circumstance. He "strongly advised" that both equip themselves with more firepower. Both had sidearms—Joe had his never-fired-in-anger-and-once-swiped-by-Ote-Keeley Smith & Wesson .357 Magnum revolver, and Wacey had his 9mm Beretta semiautomatic. Finally, Wacey was persuaded to strap to his saddle one of the carbines in a scabbard. Both had pitched in to help McLanahan, who was a boyish-looking former college ROTC officer, to load the panniers on the two packhorses so they could finally leave.

Barnum scoffed when he saw that, instead of digging into the county arsenal, Joe was taking his personal Remington Wingmaster .12-gauge shotgun, which was primarily a bird-hunting weapon. If he had to take a shotgun, Barnum said, at least it should be one of the short-barreled riot guns from the truck. Joe explained that he had had the shotgun since his teens and he was comfortable with it. Joe was known as an excellent wing shot when it came to game birds or, occasionally, clay targets. Strangely, he could rarely hit a target if it was stationary, only if it was moving or flushing from the underbrush. He had the ability to hit a fast-moving target by instinct and reaction, and he never really aimed. If he aimed, he missed. Joe had failed his initial pistol test and had barely passed on his second (and last) attempt. While he was fully capable of bagging his limit of three pheasants with three well-placed aerial shots, he was unable to punch holes in the outline of an intruder on the firing range. Barnum finally persuaded Joe to at least load his shotgun with magnum double-ought buckshot shells so if he had to he could "knock down a house." But Joe thought how odd it was to be loading the shotgun he had used since boyhood for ducks and pine grouse with shells designed solely to kill a man. But he did it, and he filled one pocket of a saddle bag with a dozen extra rounds.

Barnum briefly took Joe and Wacey aside while they waited for Deputy McLanahan to secure his panniers.

"Guess who is on the way to observe this rodeo, boys?" Barnum asked them. Joe and Wacey exchanged glances but neither knew.

"Vern Dunnegan!" Barnum clapped Joe and Wacey on their shoulders. "Your mentor. He called and left a message with the dispatch."

"Why is Vern here?" Joe asked. Wacey shrugged.

"He was in the area and heard about it on the radio, I suppose," Barnum said. "So don't screw up, boys. Not only will the entire valley be watching, but Vern will be watching, too." There was sarcasm in Barnum's voice.

Most of the gear, including the chuck box, they left with Barnum and the bustle of people and equipment. As they finally mounted and had turned their horses to the trailhead, they could hear Sheriff Barnum, flanked by the two retired Korean War vets from the VFW post, on his radio trying to track down his missing helicopter.

"How close are we?" Joe asked Wacey as he nosed his horse through the silent pocket of aspen. In timber this thick, it was best to let Lizzie pick her own way through. He just pointed her in the general direction, which was behind and to the left of Wacey. Wacey was a few yards ahead, and he reined in his mount and leaned to the side of his saddle.

"Coupla hours," Wacey said, also in a murmur.

"That's what I was worried about."

Hedeman nodded. They would not make it to the outfitters' elk camp in daylight, even though getting there before dark had been the purpose of the trip.

Joe walked his horse abreast Wacey's palomino. Two aspens as thin and round as baseball bats stood between them. The grove was heavily timbered, and black roots curled up through a carpet of lemon-colored leaves.

"And here comes the reason why," Wacey grumbled.

It was hushed in the middle of the trees, the light was dappled and muted, but they could hear the clinking of Deputy McLanahan and his packhorse skirting the grove on the outside. McLanahan had fitted the packhorse with hunting panniers, and the bulging canvas bags were so wide that he couldn't follow Joe and Wacey into the grove. Joe and Hedeman caught a glimpse of the deputy down a narrow chute in the trees; it was clear that McLanahan was much less of a horseman than Joe on his worst day.

"When I'm elected I'm going to fire his butt before I even order business cards," Hedeman whispered, looking down the chute where McLanahan had passed. Joe didn't respond. There was no need to.

They waited for Deputy McLanahan in the clear of a saddle slope that was bordered on each side by juniper pine. Commas of snow from that morning lay in long pools of shadow cast by boulders and trees. Groves of aspen were bright yellow with fingers of crimson coursing through them. The evening sun made the colors intense, almost throbbing.

Joe thought of the contrast of the last few hours. At Crazy Woman Creek, he had seemed crowded by admirers and he felt like a member of a powerful force. Here, in the cool darkening stillness of the Bighorns, he felt tiny and insignificant.

"I'm gonna be real sore tomorrow," bellowed McLanahan as he approached.

Joe noticed Wacey shift his weight sharply in his saddle, a familiar sign of irritation.

"When you're sneaking up on somebody, you might consider keeping your voice low," Wacey hissed as McLanahan approached. "It's an old, sly Indian trick. We're assuming that the people we are sneaking up on have ears mounted on each side of their head."

Deputy McLanahan, clearly angry, started to say something but caught himself. Wacey was not fun to argue with.

"You're slow and we're late," Wacey continued in the

low hiss. "We aren't going to get there with any light. We're going to have to cold camp up here and go into the outfitters' camp at dawn to see if we can catch anyone."

McLanahan's jaw was tight, and his eyes glistened. Joe felt sorry for the deputy. Much of the delay had been the deputy's fault but Hedeman was pressing the point.

"Starting late ain't my fault. Barnum read me a list of supplies to bring that was as long as your arm," McLanahan finally said, and his voice caught.

"The hell it ain't," Wacey answered, turning away and nudging his horse forward.

"Don't worry about it," Joe assured McLanahan. "Let it go."

"He don't need to say that," McLanahan answered, his bottom lip trembling. "Not that way."

Don't cry, for God's sake, thought Joe. He clicked his tongue, and the buckskin walked. He left McLanahan alone to compose himself, and he wondered what was with Wacey. Wacey seemed uncommonly irritable. He hoped it didn't have to do with the fact that the success or failure of this venture would likely become an issue in the future sheriff's race against Barnum.

They picketed their horses by the blue light of fluorescent battery lamps and spread out sleeping bags tight against a granite bluff. They were close enough to the elk camp, Wacey said, that a fire was out of the question.

Marybeth had made a half-dozen ham sandwiches, and they ate them in the dark. McLanahan passed around a pint of Jim Beam bourbon, which seemed to improve Hedeman's mood, at least a little.

"I missed my son's football practice tonight," McLanahan said unexpectantly. "I'm the defensive line coach."

"You have a son?" Joe asked. McLanahan was just too young for that, he thought.

"Well, he's not actually my son." McLanahan sounded a bit sheepish. "He's the son of my fiancée. We're livin' together. She's been married a couple of times before. She's quite a bit older."

"Oh."

Wacey snorted. "What in the hell does that have to do with the price of milk?"

"First practice I missed," McLanahan said. "Twelve Sleep plays Buffalo on Friday. Home opener."

"The mighty Buffalo Bison, our nemesis," Hedeman said sarcastically. Then: "Why don't you go find your radio and tell Barnum where we're at and what we're doin'. All those folks down there will want a report so they can spend the rest of the evening second-guessing us. Let him know we'll move on the elk camp before dawn tomorrow."

McLanahan nodded and wandered away to dig through his panniers.

"Jesus," Wacey complained after McLanahan was gone. "Havin' him on the payroll is like havin' two good men gone."

"Take it easy on him," Joe said.

Wacey grunted and chewed his sandwich. "I'll be interested to find out what was in that cooler Ote had with him."

"Yup."

"I suppose it coulda been anything," Wacey continued. "Of course it might not mean a goddamn thing in the end, I guess."

Joe nodded. Then he reeled off the number of ranch houses between Crazy Woman Creek and the Pickett home that Ote Keeley could have gone to for help.

"There was a reason he came to our house," Joe said. "I just don't know what it could be."

"You're gonna send that cooler and those shit pellets to Cheyenne to get it checked out?"

"Yeah."

"Then we'll know," Wacey said.

"Then we'll know," Joe echoed.

"Could be nothin'," Wacey said. "Could be one of those things we just never know, and the only guy who knows is stupid, dead Ote."

"Maybe Ote was bringing you a couple of beers," Deputy McLanahan said from the dark as he approached. "Maybe that's what was in that cooler. Maybe he thought you guys would pop a couple and forgive each other."

"Excuse me, McLanahan," Wacey said. "Did you get Barnum?"

McLanahan told Joe and Wacey that he had talked with Sheriff Barnum and told him of their status. He said Barnum had located the helicopter and the earliest it could get back up to Saddlestring was tomorrow afternoon. There had been no sightings as yet of the other two outfitters, Kyle Lensegrav or Calvin Mendes.

"Guess who else was down there at command central?" McLanahan asked, the light reflecting off his teeth.

Neither spoke.

"Vern Dunnegan!" McLanahan's voice was a mix of excitement and awe.

Joe noted that Wacey had looked sharply at him to check his reaction. Joe didn't flinch.

"Vern says, 'Be careful, boys. Make me proud.'"

"What's Barnum say?" Joe asked.

"Barnum says, 'Don't fuck up and make me look bad.'" McLanahan laughed.

Vern, like Barnum, was a kind of legend—the most popular and influential game warden ever in the area, as well as a force in the community. The kind of guy who had coffee with the city councilmen at 10 each morning in the Alpine Cafe and who was not only tougher than hell on poachers and game violators but was also known to fix a few tickets and let a few locals off the hook. Even though he was primarily a state employee, Vern always like to think of himself as an entrepreneur. He boasted that he had 31 years of business experience. Vern was always involved with something in town, whether it was the local shopper newspaper, a video store, satellite dishes, or a local radio station. Vern always owned a share and had a partner or two. For whatever reasons, the partners always left town and Vern ended up with the enterprise. Then he sold it and moved on to the next venture. Some said he was a good businessman. Most said he was nakedly greedy, and he systematically looted each company until the partners left out of disgust and fear. Vern Dunnegan had cast a big shadow. So big, Marybeth had said, that Joe had yet to see much sunlight in the Twelve Sleep Valley as far as the community went. Vern had supervised both Wacey and Joe, and he had tutored them both in the ways of the field. No one knew more about the ways and means of poachers and game law violators—or about the vile side of humans out-of-doors—than Vern Dunnegan.

It was Vern's shadow that had probably prevented Joe from being notified that morning about the incident in the campground at Crazy Woman Creek. Vern had resigned six months earlier to go to work for a large energy company as a field executive in "local relations," whatever that was. The rumor at the time was that Vern had more than tripled his salary.

They discussed the plan and the possibilities. They would move in on the elk camp in the predawn from three directions and close in. Wacey said he would communicate with Joe and Deputy McLanahan with hand signals. If anyone was in the camp, they would surround and disarm them as quickly as possible.

"We don't know if these two had anything to do with Ote getting shot," Wacey said. "Ote may have wandered out of camp on his own, run into some kind of trouble, and made the midnight run to Pickett's house. These two might not even know where he is or what's going on."

"On the other hand . . ." interrupted McLanahan, barely able to contain his excitement of the possibility of being part of some real action.

"On the other hand, they may have gotten drunk with old Ote and got in a fight and shot him a couple of times," Hedeman finished. "So we've got to be prepared for just about anything."

"If they're involved they might not even be there," Joe said. "They might have cleared out last night and they're in Montana by now."

Joe lay in his sleeping bag but couldn't sleep. He doubted the other two could either. The stars were out, and it was colder than he had expected it to be. He could see his breath in the starlight.

His revolver was within reach on the side of his sleeping bag, and he reached down in the dark and felt the checkered grip.

Joe thought of his girls. It was only 9:30, although it seemed much later. Both girls would be in bed, but probably not asleep. More than likely, they would be pretty wound up in that motel room. Sheridan would be reading or gabbing to her bear. She used to do that at night with her kitten, and before that, her puppy. Marybeth would be reading Lucy a story or cuddling her until she drifted off. Sheridan would no doubt be checking the motel window for the approach of more monsters.

He wondered how this incident would affect his girls, especially Sheridan. It was one thing to look for monsters and another thing to actually see them. Ote's sudden appearance had somehow thrown a new curve on things, and Joe knew Marybeth would be thinking about that. The sanctity of their little family had been violated. Ote's blood would remain on the walk for months—and in their memories forever. Joe wondered what kind of cleaning substance he could buy that would remove bloodstains from concrete. How would Lucy remember this day? Would it make her more cautious, more suspicious? Would Sheridan wonder if her parents—especially her dad—could actually protect her from harm after all? The relationship between a father and his daughters, Joe had discovered, was a remarkably powerful thing. They looked to him to accomplish greatness; they expected it as a matter of course because he was their dad and therefore a great man. Someday, he knew, he would do something less than great and they would see it. It was inevitable. He wondered at what age his luster would dim in Sheridan's eyes and then in Lucy's. He wondered how painful it would be for them all when they recognized it.

Joe Pickett had two passions. One was his family and the other was his job. He had tried as best he could to keep them separate, but that morning Ote Keeley had forced them together. Joe now looked at both differently and what he saw pained him. Marybeth had never actually complained about the way her life had gone since marrying Joe Pickett. Her frustration appeared in random sighs and sometimes hopeless facial expressions that she probably didn't even recognize as such—but Joe did. Marybeth had been on a career path—she was a bright and attractive woman. But by marrying Joe in college, having children, and moving around the state with him from one beat-up house to another, her life had turned out differently than she, or her hard-driving mother, imagined. Marybeth deserved a certain standard, or at least a permanent home of their own; Joe had not been able to provide either. It was eating at him, taking a million tiny bites. When she talked on the telephone to her old college friends who were traveling and managing businesses and enrolling their children in private schools, she would be blue for weeks afterward, although she wouldn't admit it. While he loved his job—he was, after all, nature boy—the guilt he felt this morning when he learned that they couldn't even afford a motel room in town still shrouded him. The exhilaration of the mountains right now brought a hard-edged sense of regret and confusion. His belief that what he did was *good*—and that he was good at it—would not put his daughters through college or allow his wife to ever take a real vacation.

Joe shifted to try to get more comfortable. He tried to think of other things but he couldn't. Joe tried to imagine what Marybeth would think if she could see him now, on a manhunt with his hand on his revolver and two (heavily armed) men sleeping next to him. It was a boyhood dream coming true; good guys pursuing bad guys. He couldn't deny the excitement that was keeping him wide awake. It would be hard to describe to Marybeth how he felt right now. He wasn't sure she would understand.

He wondered what Marybeth, the protector of his career who had never understood what Joe saw in Vern (or Wacey, for that matter), would think of Vern being back in Saddlestring. Joe tried to stave off the resentment he felt toward Vern. Vern had been good to him and had recommended him for the Saddlestring district. It wasn't Vern's fault that everybody seemed to think Vern hung the moon when it came to setting the standard for a local warden.

Too much to think about, and no conclusions to be reached.

He raised up on an elbow and in the faint light of the stars, could see Deputy McLanahan walking away from the camp to relieve himself. McLanahan couldn't sleep either.

As he stared up at the hard white stars—there were so many of them that the night sky looked gauzy—Joe realized that if things were to change for him and his family, *he* probably would have to change. Marybeth and his girls deserved better than what they had; to give them more, he would have to give up the other thing he deeply loved.

But first there was the matter of a dead man in his backyard and an elk camp a few miles away.

Wacey sighed deeply. He was snoring. He seemed to be exhausted. Joe wished he could sleep like that.

At six a.m., they had rolled up their sleeping bags in silence, saddled up, and followed Wacey up and over the summit into the creek bottom where the elk camp was. No one had brought breakfast.

Joe was alert but not completely awake. Although he knew he must have slept, he could not recall actually waking. He had slipped in and out of a kind of cruel half-consciousness that was vivid with dreams and episodes that didn't connect.

Joe followed Wacey down a horse trail toward the camp. It was still dark enough that Wacey's worn denim jacket was out of focus. Deputy McLanahan followed Joe. No words had yet been exchanged that morning.

They tied up their horses in a stand of lodgepole pines. Wacey poured dusty piles of oats into the grass for the horses to eat and to distract them and keep them quiet while the three men walked the rest of the way up the trail to the camp. It was an hour before dawn and the mountain air was crisp. The cold that had settled in for the night was just beginning to retreat through the trees and up the slopes.

They were upon the camp in less than thirty minutes. Canvas outfitters' tents came suddenly into view, blue-gray smudges against the dark grass and trees, and when they did, Wacey dropped into a hunter's squat and Joe and McLanahan followed suit. They kept hidden from the tents by a hedgerow of three-foot young pines.

Wacey leaned into Joe and McLanahan and whispered that McLanahan should flank left and Joe right. Wacey would continue down the horse trail and hide behind a granite spur just inside the periphery of the camp. When they all found good cover where they could see into the camp, they would wait until it was light. Wacey said he would ask the outfitters to come out with their hands behind their heads. If only he spoke, he said, the outfitters wouldn't know how many men were out there. Joe was impressed by Wacey's take-charge attitude and command of tactics. Wacey seemed to be a natural and comfortable leader, and he had led them straight to the elk camp without a map. He had taken command and was not shy about it. Joe had not seen this side of Wacey before.

"Did you see the horses?" Wacey asked, in a low whisper. "There's two of 'em in a corral." Joe shook his head no. He had dropped too quickly to see anything more than the tents.

"There's probably somebody in camp after all," Wacey said, looking to both Joe and McLanahan. "Those horses are likely to notice us before the outfitters do, so keep quiet and close to the ground and out of sight."

McLanahan let out a long breath that rattled at the end of it and mindlessly caressed the stock of his shotgun with his thumb. He was anxious and probably scared. McLanahan's face no longer had the kind of whiz-bang enthusiasm for action in it that Joe had seen the night before. Joe understood.

* * *

Joe kept low and picked his way through the trees to the right side of the camp. He kept his shotgun parallel to the ground, glad he had it with him. He slid along the trunk of a thick, downed pine tree until he reached the root pan. It was there, for the first time, that he really raised up and looked at the camp.

There were three tents constructed in a semicircle, with the opening of each aimed at a fire ring. They were permanent tents with stoves inside and probably wooden floors. Black stovepipes poked from the top of each tent. A thick wooden picnic table with benches was near the fire ring, as well as stumps for the elk hunters to sit on while they drank and watched the fire at night.

The ground around the tents was hard packed by years of boots and horses' hooves during hunting season. A blackened coffee pot hung from an iron T near the cold camp fire. It was impossible to tell when the campsite had been used last.

Behind the tents, directly opposite the horse trail they had entered the camp on, was the area used for hanging elk and deer. The crossbeams for suspending the carcasses as they were skinned and cooled were wired high in the trees, as well as rusty block-and-tackle for winching up 500-pound animals. Joe could now see the makeshift lodgepole corral through the trees.

The camp was still. Only the gentle tinkling of a foot-wide creek—the headwaters of the north fork of the Crazy Woman—made a sound. They had somehow surrounded the camp without raising warning chatters by squirrels, and the horses apparently hadn't seen them either because there was no nickering. Joe looked at his watch and waited. The fused warm light of dawn was now creeping down the summit. It was a clear morning, and the camp would soon be bathed in sunlight.

He shifted to get more comfortable and tried to imagine who might be inside the tents and what they might be doing. As he did so, he noticed a quick movement.

Suddenly, there was a shiver of the canvas on the side wall of the nearest tent. Joe eased the barrel of the shotgun through the roots of the tree so it pointed in the direction of the camp. He looked down the length of it toward the tent and the side wall.

There was another shiver, then a sharp tug from the inside. Joe watched both the side of the tent and the door for any sudden movement. Joe held his breath. A low muffled grunt came from within the tent. He raised himself up hoping to catch the eye of either Wacey or Deputy McLanahan to indicate to them there was movement in the tent but could see neither. Joe settled back down and located the safety on the shotgun and clicked it off. The beating of his own heart now rivaled the sounds of the creek.

A distinct round bulge appeared in the canvas, about a foot from the floor of the tent. The bulge slid slowly down the wall, straining at the material and pulling the canvas tight until the bulge rested near the ground. Joe kept the front bead of the shotgun on the middle of the bulge. He thought about his historic inability to hit anything that was stationary, and it worried him.

He had never been in a situation like this before. How would he react?

Then the bulge pushed its way outside and what emerged was the black-and-white bicycle-seat head of an enormous badger. The badger's head darted from side to side, and it sniffed the air.

Joe lowered the shotgun and briefly closed his eyes. He let his breath out in relief. Then he studied the badger as it grunted and struggled its way out from under the wall of the tent. The badger was massive, the largest he had ever seen. As it scuttled away from the tent, rolls of fat shimmered under its coat, and its belly nearly dragged along the ground. Before it crossed the creek and entered the brush, it froze and noticed Joe for the first time. The badger swung its head at him and bared its teeth, and Joe noticed the pink tint of its head and mouth, the bright red of the piece of meat in its jaws. The badger had been feeding on something inside the tent. There was a brief, chilling moment when Joe and the badger stared into each other's eyes.

Then things happened too quickly. Nearly out of his field of vision, Joe saw the door of the middle tent flap open and a man step out wearing old-fashioned long-handled underwear. Someone yelled—McLanahan or Wacey—and the man reacted by turning toward the sound. A rifle barrel raised from the side of the man, and suddenly there was a rapid series of deafening explosions that split the stillness of the morning wide open like an ax to a melon.

Something struck Joe hard in the face and he found himself sitting down, his gloved hand covering a vicious red-hot sting under his right eye. He pulled the glove away and saw his own blood smeared across the leather. There were several more explosions and then a ringing in his ears. Joe scrambled back to the roots of the tree. The middle tent was now collapsing under the sprawled weight of the man who had raised the rifle. Flowers of dark red bloomed on his thermal shirt. The man was still and his arms outstretched, and his rifle was on the ground near his feet. Wacey was screaming for McLanahan to stop firing.

Then Wacey turned toward the camp: "Anybody in that tent throw your weapons out first and come out with your hands behind your heads!" Wacey shouted. "There are twelve armed U.S. marshals out here and one of your party is already down!"

Joe brought the shotgun to his cheek and pointed it toward the nearest tent. The butt of the shotgun was instantly slick with his blood. His face was now numb; he would assess his wounds when this was over.

In the camp, nothing happened.

Wacey barked out another warning. Both Joe and Wacey shot nervous looks at the body on the middle tent, and neither saw any movement. The tent was now down, and the man was partially covered by thick folds of dirty canvas that collapsed over him.

Wacey stepped from behind the rocks and slowly walked into the camp, his carbine held loosely and ready in front of him. Wacey had fired at least one shot from the carbine, because he jacked an empty brass shell into the grass with the lever action. McLanahan stood up from where he had hidden directly across the camp. He was reloading stubby shells into his shotgun.

You shot me, Joe thought. *One of your pellets ricocheted and hit me right in the face, McLanahan.*

Wacey had quickly determined that no one was in the tent nearest to him and had now crossed over the fire ring and approached the tent the man had come out of. Wacey squatted for a moment over the body of the man who had just been shot, apparently confirming that he would be no further trouble. Joe crossed the creek and neared the closest tent, the tent the badger had come out of, from the side.

"Anybody home?" Wacey called toward the last tent.

Joe smelled it before he saw it; when Wacey threw open the tent flap, Joe gagged and turned away.

Kyle Lensegrav and Calvin Mendes were still in the sleeping bags where they had been shot and killed two nights before, their pale naked arms and parts of their faces chewed to the clean white bone by the badger.

8

Sheridan sat in the shade of the big cottonwood tree in her backyard and ate a bowl of dry cereal with her fingers. She still wore her blue school dress but had kicked off her shoes and socks. She ate and watched the woodpile, waiting and hoping for something to happen.

Someone from town had called her mom to tell her that her dad was okay and would be on his way home soon, and now Mom was calling Sheridan's grandmother to give her the good news. When Mom talked to Grandmother Missy, she talked for a long time. Unlike other grandmothers, Sheridan's insisted that her grandchildren call her by her proper name. Likewise, Missy never referred to her grandchildren as grandchildren. Sheridan felt that Missy was embarrassed that she even had grandchildren. Sheridan always felt a little silly calling a lady of her grandmother's age "Missy." It seemed like such a lightweight name.

Mom said that the bad guys had been caught and that Dad had been hurt a little but that he would be all right. Dad would have to spend the night in the hospital in Saddlestring and answer a lot of questions and then he'd be home. So that would be good.

The hotel had been okay for a night but Sheridan was glad to be back home. It had been fun. For dinner, she and Lucy had eaten popcorn shrimp that was delicious, and there were more than 30 television channels in their room. There was an elevator to all five floors, and she and Lucy had spent hours going up and down on it. There was a game room where she begged her mom to play pinball with her, and her mom had agreed. Her mom could actually be kind of fun when she wanted to be, and it surprised Sheridan that Mom had played pinball before. She even knew how to bump the console with her hip to manipulate the steel ball. It was nice not to have to make the bed in the morning, and Mom said it was okay to leave the towels on the floor of the bathroom, which was a treat. But by then Sheridan was ready to leave and go to school. Lucy wanted to stay. Mom said Lucy liked luxury, just like Grandmother Missy.

In school, the rude girls had gathered around her and asked her questions about the dead outfitter and her Dad and what had happened in the mountains. Sheridan was for once the center of attention, and she liked that. The girls who had called her Weird Country now wanted to be around her because she had seen a real live dead man. They asked her what the dead man looked like, how is eyes were. The monster, in a strange way, had brought Sheridan not only a secret but a lot of luck. She liked the new good luck her secret had brought her. One girl, named Melanie, who was popular and had never spoken to Sheridan before, asked Sheridan if she wanted to be her best friend.

She had almost told her mom about what she had seen in the woodpile while they were in the hotel but had decided not to do it. Sheridan reveled in her secret, and wanted to see the animals again. She knew somehow that what she had seen in the woodpile was important. If seeing a dead man caused all of this attention, what would happen if people knew about the secret pets?

When Sheridan got home from school, it looked like Mom had tried to scrub the blood off of the sidewalk and had thrown away the lengths of wood from the top of the woodpile that had blood on them. Sheridan could still see some of the stain on the walk but she had to look hard to do so.

A small sound pulled her attention away from the walk. Sharp black eyes looked out at her from the woodpile and she held her breath, afraid even the slightest movement would scare the little creature away. She didn't know how long it had been watching her, and she had not seen it poke its head out from between the ends of two thick logs. The creature was perfectly still and hard to see at first.

The little animal had a round knobby head and large, black shiny eyes. Its ears poked up straight and round from its head like a cartoon Mickey Mouse. It had a tiny pink nose at the end of a slim snout, and it looked chinless. The animal was light brown with a dark stripe that came over the top of its head and down between its large eyes. She could see a long, thin neck behind its head but couldn't see the creature's body in the shadows of the logs. All that was visible was one small foot with slender fingers and nails poised around the bark of the log it stood on. The creature's hands were delicate and well-formed, and they looked capable of grasping and picking up small objects.

Sheridan was delighted that the creature had not retreated into the logs yet, but stayed and let itself be looked at. She liked the creature's big, dark eyes, and thought that the animal not only looked cute but smart as well. Its eyes were intelligent and sparkling.

Without breaking her gaze with the animal, she reached down into the fold of her dress and grasped a handful of Cheerios. Trying not to make her movements too quick, she threw the cereal toward the woodpile. Cheerios rained on the logs and the creature popped quickly back inside.

She was starting to regret what she had done—she thought she had scared the animal back into hiding—when the little round head reappeared. This time, Sheridan sat still, trying to quiet both her heart and her breath. She was so excited that she wanted to shout, but she didn't dare.

"Hello again, little guy," Sheridan whispered.

The creature was now leaning farther out of the logs than it had been before. She could see its tiny shoulders and clawlike front feet. Its long, narrow body was now several inches out of the hole in the wood. The dark stripe ran down its back as far as she could see. The creature focused on a Cheerio directly below it in the joint of a branch. It looked from the Cheerio to Sheridan and back to the Cheerio. Suddenly, in a lightning movement, it shot completely out of the hole, stuffed the Cheerio in its cheek, turned like a little, brown tornado, and vanished back into the woodpile.

Sheridan let out a long whistle. "Wow," she said. "*Wow.*"

She scooped the rest of the cereal from her dress and the grass and tossed it in handfuls toward the woodpile. She hoped the creature would now know the sound for what it was—food.

And then there were three. Their heads popped out of the side of the woodpile. *Pop, pop, pop.* She instantly recognized the first creature she had seen as the biggest and darkest. There was also a lighter brown animal with a smaller head. And the smallest one was almost light yellow in color and with a sleeker look about it. She felt happily overwhelmed by the six shiny eyes on her, and she giggled and covered her mouth.

One by one, with the large, dark animal leading the way, the creatures shot out of the woodpile, gathered cereal, crammed their cheeks, and zipped back into holes in the logs. By the third trip, they all seemed more comfortable, and not as manic in their movements. The big, dark one ventured the farthest from the woodpile. It stood straight up on its hind legs. Then it used its front paws to stuff a Cheerio into its now-fat cheeks. It looked alert—and comical. Now it stood just a few feet away from Sheridan.

"What are you doing, Sherry?"

Lucy's voice scared Sheridan as much as it did the animals. All three creatures disappeared quickly back into the woodpile.

"What were those things?" Lucy asked. Lucy sat down in the grass next to Sheridan. Lucy could be so annoying.

Sheridan explained in a finger-pointing, big-sister way that the animals were their secret pets. She told Lucy not to say anything to Mom about them. Lucy didn't really understand. She kept asking if she could play with them now.

"If you tell Mom and Dad about those pets, they'll die, and we'll be in A LOT OF trouble," Sheridan hissed. "All of my pets die when people know about them!"

"Can they be my pets, too?" Lucy asked.

Sheridan fought the impulse to say no and made a decision to bargain instead. "They can be our pets," she said. "But they're a secret."

"Can we name them?" Lucy asked. She always wanted to name everything. Sheridan agreed.

Then she sent Lucy back inside with the empty bowl to ask for more dry cereal.

9

The helicopter finally arrived at the outfitters' camp late in the afternoon to airlift bodies both alive and dead to the Twelve Sleep County Memorial Hospital. Sheriff Barnum as well as officers from the State of Wyoming's Department of Criminal Investigation (DCI) were waiting at the hospital to talk to Joe. He was interviewed at least five different times by different men, including Sheriff Barnum. Although Joe could not say he actually saw the man point his rifle at Wacey or Deputy John McLanahan, he could say that he saw the man raise the weapon. Was it possible the shooting victim was raising his hands above his head to surrender at the time? Joe said he didn't think so. The state investigators didn't press that line of questioning.

By the time they were done, Joe hoped he had told the same story to each investigator, that there were no inconsistencies. It was apparent though, by the tone and questions of the last interviews, that the shooting was considered justified.

Remarkably, the man who had been shot at the elk camp was still alive and had been airlifted to Billings for massive surgery. The last Joe had heard, the man was reported to be in critical condition and not expected to live through night. The victim had been shot seven times, including five partial and somewhat reckless shotgun blasts (McLanahan) and two .30-caliber rifle bullets (Wacey).

The man who had been shot was Clyde Lidgard, a local from outside of Saddlestring who lived in a wreck of a house trailer on the road to the landfill. Lidgard was a mentally unbalanced modern-woodsman type who lived on a disability pension from the lumber mill as well as fees he collected for looking after summer cabins in the mountains. Lidgard was not an outfitter, and as far as anyone knew, he had never associated with any of the three murdered men. Joe had once been to Lidgard's trailer after someone had called the office and reported a wounded mule deer limping around near the dump. Joe couldn't find the deer, and he went to Lidgard's trailer to see if Lidgard had seen the animal. Clyde Lidgard was not inside the trailer at the time but was instead hiding in the outhouse. Joe heard him in there and waited for him to come out. Joe had heard from someone that Lidgard didn't like visitors and that his outhouse was his hideout of choice. After nearly fifteen minutes, Lidgard had stuck a gray, craggy face outside the door.

"Ain't no sick deer here," Lidgard had bellowed.

"How do you know I was looking for a deer?" Joe had asked back.

"Go away," Lidgard had croaked. "You is on private property!" He had pronounced it "propity."

Lidgard had been right, and since Joe hadn't seen any sign of a deer, dead or alive, he had left. As Joe had driven his pickup along the rutted trail toward the road, he had watched in his rearview mirrors as Clyde Lidgard had scuttled from the outhouse into his trailer. The next time he would see Clyde Lidgard would be as he came out of the tent in the elk camp and walked into a firestorm of shotgun blasts. But in the confusion at the elk camp, Joe had no idea who the man was.

Lidgard was considered crazy but not dangerous, despite the fact that he was rarely seen in the mountains without his ancient .30-.30 lever action rifle. No one had ever seen the 9mm semiautomatic handgun they had found stuffed in Lidgard's coat pocket, but few people knew Lidgard well at all. It would be a couple of days before the pistol could be confirmed to be the murder weapon of all three outfitters. Why Lidgard had stayed in the camp after shooting the men—two while they slept in their tent—was unknown and the subject of much speculation. Maybe he wanted the camp for himself, one of the state investigators said. Maybe he just didn't know what to do, McLanahan guessed. Or maybe he was waiting for someone, Barnum said.

Joe thought about the fact that men like Clyde Lidgard were not the aberration in places like Saddlestring that many might think. Mountain towns and out-of-the-way rural communities all had men like Clyde Lidgard in and around them. Stops at the end of the road collected Clyde Lidgards like dams collected silt.

Wacey came into Joe's hospital room that night after Marybeth had left. Wacey looked even more exhausted than Joe felt. Wacey said the investigation was continuing, but it would probably be wrapped up soon. All of the evidence indicated that the shooter was Clyde Lidgard. All they were waiting on was the report from DCI that the gun found on Lidgard was in fact the gun that had been used on the outfitters. Wacey said he had talked to reporters not only from the local papers but to radio and television reporters as far away as Denver. He told Joe, not without a hint of a sly grin, that he, Joe, and unfortunately Deputy McLanahan were being thought of as heroes. Wacey said the whole story was being treated as quite a big deal and had made all of the wire services. A stringer from CNN had interviewed him on camera, and the piece was supposed to be broadcast that night. Barnum, though, was being questioned as to why he sent the small party into the mountains without backup and why it took so long to airlift them all out with a wounded suspect.

"I'm looking good and Barnum's looking bad," Wacey said. "I can live with that."

"I bet you can," Joe said. "Now answer one question for me."

"Fire away."

"Was Clyde Lidgard raising his rifle to shoot at you?"

Wacey shook his head no. "Not at me. He was aiming it at McLanahan. That's why McLanahan started blasting."

"Then why did you shoot him twice? McLanahan was shooting buckshot, but you nailed the guy twice in the lungs with your rifle."

Wacey shrugged. "Wouldn't you want me there and ready if Clyde Lidgard had raised his rifle at you?"

Not long after Wacey left the hospital room, Joe felt another presence near his bed. When he opened his eyes, someone was looming over him in the dark. He hadn't realized that the lights in his room had been turned off. And he didn't understand how anyone other than a doctor could be in his room. For a moment, he forgot to breathe. But then he recognized the silhouette as belonging to Vern Dunnegan, his old supervisor, the man who cast the big shadow. Vern clicked on the bedside lamp.

"Hello, son," he said gently.

Joe could see Vern clearly now. Vern had gained some weight, but he'd been portly to begin with. Vern had a trimmed, dark beard flecked with gray that bordered a round, jovial face. He had a round nose and probing, dark eyes. His movements, despite his bulk, had always been swift, and he gave the impression of a man who carried himself well. Vern had a quick, jolly chuckle that would burble out at any time, in any situation. The chuckle often disguised what Vern was really thinking and what he might say or do. It was one of the things Marybeth had never liked about him. She found Vern patronizing, especially toward Joe. She said he was calculating and manipulative, and she didn't like her husband to be manipulated. As warden, Vern had an extremely high opinion of himself and his influence in the county and the state. Generally, he was right. People knew him and respected him. Many feared him. But he had always considered himself to be a mentor to Joe. Vern's dealings with Joe had always been fair, and to Joe's advantage. It was Vern who had fought for Joe's moving back to the Saddlestring district, and he had made it happen. The fact that Joe was one of Vern's favorites didn't do him any harm within the agency either.

Vern sat down on the bed near Joe's knees. Joe felt the mattress sag. "I just talked to Wacey," Vern said. "My boys did all right up there. How's your cheek where old Deputy McLanahan shot you?"

Joe nodded and said he was okay, just tired. Absently, he touched the bandage on his face.

"Need a drink? I've got my flask in my pocket. I'm drinking Maker's Mark these days instead of that old Jim Beam I was used to. I've moved up the bourbon hierarchy."

Joe shook his head no. He remembered how angry Marybeth used to get when he returned home late after drinking with Vern, pretending he'd "just had a couple of beers."

Vern seemed to read his mind.

"How many kids do you and Marybeth have now?"

"Two. Sheridan and Lucy. And Marybeth's pregnant."

Vern chuckled and shook his head. "A loving wife, two

wonderful kids. A house with a picket fence. Literally a picket fence. D'you still have your Lab?"

"Maxine. Yes."

Vern continued to shake his head and chuckle.

"Tell me about Ote Keeley," Vern said.

Joe told him all of the details that Sheriff Barnum had never asked him about. Dunnegan waved his hand when Joe began to recount the actions of the EMTs.

"Interesting," Vern said. "You sent the shit pellets in?"

Joe nodded.

"Heard anything?"

"Not yet. I plan to call tomorrow."

"Let me know, will you? I'm still interested in this kind of stuff."

"Yup."

"How's Georgia?" Joe asked.

"She's fine, she's fine. She's living pretty well on the alimony I pay her," Vern said.

"I hadn't heard," Joe said, taken aback.

"You know, Joe, I came to a realization. That realization is that I'm a promiscuous man. I wasn't doing her any favors staying with her and chasing women on the side, as you know. One morning about eight months ago, I just woke up and rolled over and looked at her puffy face and decided I didn't want to ever do it again. Simple as that. I wanted to wake up next to other bodies—younger bodies, older bodies, bodies with big lips and big breasts. I wanted to hear other women's voices. So I packed my stuff and I didn't see her again until court."

Dunnegan smiled and shrugged, showing Joe palms-up and his 10 stubby fingers. "It could happen to anyone," Vern continued. "Men are promiscuous. That's what we are. We try to pretend otherwise, but deep down we know it's true. We wake up with hard-ons and don't really care who's next to us as long as we can poke her."

Vern let out his trademark happy chuckle but his eyes

were on Joe's face. In fact those eyes never left Joe's face as Vern talked, as he changed subjects from this to that, as he prodded and tested for what made Joe react. It was this probing, mildly sarcastic, offbeat quality that had made Vern such a good interrogator when he was a game warden.

"I mean it could happen to anyone except Joe Pickett, who is clean and pure and good," Vern said.

"I'm not sure exactly what you mean by that," Joe said.

Vern leaned forward and rolled the bed tray to him so he could put his elbows on it. "Marybeth is a fine woman, I'm sure," Vern said. "But wouldn't it be fun to get a piece of somebody else? Did you ever meet Aimee Kensinger? Don't you think about that? She likes guys like us. Guys in uniforms, who carry guns and work outside."

Joe looked away. He didn't like where this was going.

"Look at you, Joe. Tall, rangy. Gold-flecked brown eyes. Babes love solid guys like you."

"You didn't come here to talk to me about that," Joe said.

Vern chuckled and slid a paper napkin out from beneath a water container on the tray. Joe watched as Vern unfolded the napkin, then refolded it until it was in the shape of a rectangle. Vern drew a pen from his shirt pocket.

"This is the state of Wyoming." Vern said, sketching the border of Yellowstone Park in the northwest corner and the ranges of the Rocky Mountains from top to bottom on the napkin. Vern found the motorized bed control and raised up the head of it so Joe could see clearly.

"Joe, what we've got here are two pipelines currently under construction." Vern drew two heavy black lines from north to south on the east side of the mountains. "The idea is to start at the natural gas fields in Alberta, cross Montana and Wyoming, and be the first to hook up to the energy system in Southern California. InterWest Resources, my new outfit, are the good guys. CanCal, our competitors, are the bad guys. Each pipeline costs about a million dollars a mile to build. Whoever gets there first is going to spend a fortune in order to make a gazillion dollars. Whoever gets there second just spends a fortune."

On the napkin, Vern drew the CanCal pipeline as it ran through the Powder River Basin to Central Wyoming near Lander then took a sharp left through the Wind River Mountains.

"CanCal is working on environmental and regulatory approvals to take their pipeline over South Pass and on to L.A." For Los Angeles, Vern drew a set of dollar signs. "The hoops these companies have to go through to build the line are fucking insane. There's environmental impact statements, federal and state easements, private property easements. It's unbelievable. InterWest has as many lawyers on the payroll as it does pipe fitters. The capital outlay is unbelievable to accomplish something of this magnitude."

Joe simply nodded. The race to California by the two companies had been a fixture of state news for more than a year. He watched as Vern lowered his pen to the end of the InterWest line on the napkin.

"I met the InterWest boys when they first came to Saddlestring about two years ago. They contacted me because I knew everybody and everything." Vern chuckled and his eyes moved to Joe's face. "The InterWest boys had been looking at the topo maps, and they saw where if they could take their pipeline through the Bighorns that they might gain six months on CanCal and be the first to California. They asked me if it was possible to do this. I told them it could be done if they had the right front guy working the landowners, the Feds, and the state land guys. 'Give the right guy a checkbook,' is what I told them."

Joe reached out and spun the napkin around. The pipeline ran straight through the mountains and through the Twelve Sleep Valley.

"The right guy was me, of course," Vern said. "I negotiated with them for a real salary for the first time in my life and one percent of the stock in the company. I promised them I would deliver a route for their pipeline and by God if I didn't get it done."

Joe looked up from the napkin. "You have?"

Vern sat back triumphantly. His eyes seemed to glow. "Private easements are done, state lands are cleared legally, and all we're waiting on is the final approval from the Forest Service on the environmental impact statement and approval at a few town meetings, and we'll be bringing the pipeline over the top," Vern said. "Saddlestring is dying, Joe. This pipeline will bring in a bonanza for the whole county. It'll be like the oil-boom days of the early eighties once again. People around here will have good paying jobs again."

Joe shook his head. What a gamble Vern had taken with the community and environment.

"InterWest needed someone who knew these people so they came to me. They needed someone who was trusted—and clean as a whistle-pig. You're that same kind of guy, Joe."

"Are you offering me a job?"

Vern leaned forward and spoke softly. "I'm testing the water."

"What's the job pay?"

"Three times what you're making, Joe. For the life of the project. Five to ten years, maybe more. Who knows after that." Vern slipped the flask from his hip pocket and poured some in a water glass. He offered it to Joe, who shook his head no, then sucked on it himself. "Maybe some stock options, too."

Joe sat back in the bed. He felt hot. It was as if Vern had somehow read his thoughts while he had been in the mountains the night before.

"You've got a wife and kids, Joe. You're a nice, wholesome guy. You're a goddamned hero right now. No one could ever doubt your sincerity when you talk to them. You deserve a lot better. You're working for nothing. You have a family, and a picket fence, and a dog. You," Vern said, letting the chuckle start low in his belly, "are an endangered species. There ain't many like you, Joe."

Vern slipped his pen back in his pocket and pulled out a business card. Joe read it:

VERNON S. DUNNEGAN
Land Manager
InterWest Resources

"Call me," Vern said, standing up. "Do it soon."

10

At Joe's insistence, the doctors grudgingly released him not long after Vern Dunnegan's visit. They had strongly suggested Joe stay in the hospital and rest but Joe had no intention of following their advice. I'm fine, he said. As much as he wanted to call Marybeth and have her come pick him up, he didn't. It was late and the girls would be in bed—he didn't want to wake them. He signed off on the insurance paperwork and located his pickup in the parking garage. As he swung the truck out onto the street, one thought kept repeating over and over in his mind: *eight miles on the right-hand side and we're home.* As he swung off of the Bighorn Highway onto the narrow gravel strip near his house he thought: *my wife and my girls, my anchors, will be inside.* The discussion with Vern had left a bad taste in his mouth.

The simple acts of turning off the headlights, pulling the keys from the ignition, and crawling out of the pickup were difficult in themselves. He was worn out and almost drunk from fatigue. He rubbed his eyes as he let himself in the front gate. The only thing that had kept him going for the last few hours was the prospect of getting home. Now that he was home, it was as if he were imploding. They had kept him overnight in the hospital for observation, and Marybeth had come alone to confirm that he was all right. The double-ought buckshot had chipped his cheekbone and stopped there, and it was easily removed. He would have a scar there for the rest of his life.

The first person he saw when he stepped inside his home was his mother-in-law, Missy Vankeuren, curled up on the couch with dozens of glossy magazines splayed like a massive poker hand on the floor beneath her. She was wearing a cream cashmere sweater and black stirrup pants. Her dark hair was cut close to her face and, as usual, she didn't look her age. She was and always had been an attractive woman. When she looked up, there was no doubt she read him like a book, because he was too tired to feign a hardy welcome. In fact, in all that had happened over the last three days, he had forgotten she was coming.

"I never get a chance to read at home," was what she said by means of a greeting. "So I brought my magazines with me, and it's wonderful to have the time."

"That's great," Joe said, because he couldn't think of anything else to say. Missy lived in Phoenix now, Marybeth had told him, dating a wildly rich and influential cable television magnate who was part of the Arizona political glitterati (Missy dutifully sent Marybeth society page clippings from the Arizona *Republic* and Phoenix *Gazette* that mentioned her name). She no doubt had little time between functions to read all the back issues of *Glamour, Gourmet, Southern Living, Cosmopolitan, Vanity Fair,* and Condé Nast *Traveler* that were arranged on the floor.

Marybeth arrived from the hallway and had on her perfect hostess face with the big grin.

"The girls wanted to stay up, but I finally put them to bed. They're awake right now and want a good-night kiss."

"That I'd be glad to do," Joe said.

He squeezed Marybeth's hand as he walked past her and opened the door to the girls' bedroom. The light was on and they were reading. He kissed Sheridan in the top bunk and Lucy in the bottom bunk.

"What happened to your face?" Sheridan asked.

"Just an accident," Joe said, involuntarily reaching up and fingering the large bandage beneath his eye.

"That's not what I heard," Sheridan said, propping herself up on her pillow. "At school they said you got shot."

"It was an accidental shooting," Joe said.

"Will you tell us about it tomorrow?" Sheridan asked.

Joe paused. "You girls get to sleep," he said. Lucy rolled her eyes and covered herself with the sheet.

"I've been looking out this window," Sheridan told him. "I haven't seen anything. No more monsters."

"You won't," Joe assured her. "That's all over now."

Lucy was faking sleep. It was something she did to punish her father for being away. He kissed her and told her good night, but she held firm and wouldn't acknowledge it, except for a hint of a smile.

Joe poured himself a bourbon and water in the kitchen. He had not taken any of the painkillers the doctor had prescribed for him, saving them for tomorrow.

"It says here that fat grams aren't everything," Missy Vankeuren said from the other room. Joe assumed she was talking to Marybeth. "You still need to watch calories. Just because something is low in fat doesn't give you license to eat like a pig."

He drank a quarter of the drink, then topped off the glass with more Jim Beam. Joe was not much of a drinker anymore, although he'd done more than his share in college and when he worked with Vern. But his intake of alcohol always increased proportionately when his mother-in-law was around.

He came into the living room and sat down. Marybeth had just come from tucking in Lucy. She frowned at Joe, and then smiled at her mother. She offered to get her mother something to drink, and Joe realized he was being scolded for not asking her himself.

"Do you have any red wine? That would be nice."

"Joe, would you open a bottle?" Marybeth asked.

"Where is it?"

"In the pantry," Marybeth said. "And I'd like a glass also."

Joe found the wine on a shelf in the pantry. There were a half dozen bottles to choose from. All must have been purchased within the last couple of days, anticipating her mother's visit, because normally the only thing on that shelf were boxes of breakfast cereal.

Marybeth, Joe grumbled to himself as he located the corkscrew, was a wonderful strong woman with strong opinions . . . except when her mother was present. When Missy flew in to visit, Marybeth shifted from being Joe's wife and partner to Missy's daughter, the one with unrealized potential, according to Missy. Her favorite child, according to Missy. Marybeth's older brother, Rob, was a loner who failed to keep in touch, and her younger sister, Ellen, had devoted her life to following the alternative rock band Phish on their never-ending concert tour. Marybeth was the one, Missy had once said while she was drunk and sobbing, who married too early and too low (she may have forgotten about those comments by now, but Joe hadn't). Rather than being the well-dressed, wealthy corporate lawyer she should have been, Marybeth was the wife of a game warden in the middle of Wyoming who made less than $30,000 a year. But, Missy no doubt felt, *it still may not be too late.* At least that's what Joe read into many of the things Missy said and did.

They had discussed all this before, and Marybeth thought Joe was too hard on her mother. Marybeth said that yes, she did sometimes assume the role of daughter when Missy was around, but after all she *was* Missy's daughter. Her mother just wanted the best for her, which was what mothers did. And Missy was proud of Joe in a way, Marybeth had said. Joe appeared to be faithful and a good father. Marybeth could have done much worse, Missy felt.

Joe's mood was sour when Marybeth came into the kitchen. He poured two glasses and handed them to her.

"Cheer up," Marybeth said. "She's trying to be pleasant."

Joe grunted. "I thought I was being the model of propriety."

"You're not being very accommodating," Marybeth said, her eyes flashing. Joe stepped up close to Marybeth, so that what he had to say couldn't be heard in the next room. He had just been through three of the strangest days of his life, he told her, from finding Ote's body, to the shoot-out at the outfitters' camp, the finding of the mutilated bodies, to the barrage of questions afterward, to the hospital. His mind was reeling, and he was beyond tired. The last thing he needed upon finally getting home was Missy Vankeuren. The Missy Vankeuren who at one time resented the hell out of her daughter for having the gall to make her a *grandmother,* of all things.

Real anger flashed in Marybeth's face.

"It's not her fault all of this happened," Marybeth said. "She's just here to visit her granddaughters. She had nothing to do with a man dying in our backyard. She has a *right* to visit me and her granddaughters, who think she's wonderful."

"But why does it have to be now?" Joe asked lamely.

"Thomas Joseph Pickett," Marybeth said sharply, "go to bed. You're tired and disagreeable, and we can discuss this tomorrow."

Joe started to say something, then caught himself. Her tone was similar to what he heard when she was mad at the children and used their formal names. It was fortunate she was right because Joe didn't have the energy for an argument.

Joe entered the living room, and Missy looked up from her magazine. Her eyebrows were arched in an expectant way. Joe found this annoying. She obviously knew there had been words in the kitchen.

"I'm going to bed," Joe declared. He knew he sounded simple.

"You should do that," Missy said, purring. "You are probably just dead with all you've gone through."

"Yup."

"Good night, Joe. Sweet dreams." Missy dropped her eyes back to her magazine and, with that gesture, dismissed him.

When Marybeth came into the bedroom later, Joe woke up with a start. He had been dreaming he was back in the mountains, back at the elk camp, reliving what had happened. In the aftershock of the shooting, time had become fluid, and Joe had drifted with it, like a raft on a river. The bodies of the outfitters were still in their tent where they had been found. Clyde Lidgard was still wrapped in the folds of the tent. He was moaning. They covered him with blankets. Pink bubbles formed and popped from a hole in his chest as he breathed. Deputy McLanahan was getting violently sick in the bushes from the tension and the release. The stench from the tent drifted to Joe and Wacey when the wind shifted.

In his dream, they were still waiting on the helicopter to arrive. They were all hungry.

"What time is it?" Joe asked.

Marybeth was scrubbing her makeup off in the bathroom adjacent to the bedroom. She was scrubbing hard. She was still mad.

"Midnight," she said. "Mom and I were visiting. I didn't realize how late it was getting."

"Honey, I'm sorry," Joe said. "I just need sleep."

"So sleep."

"I will, if you'll get me that bottle of pills from the counter."

Marybeth brought him a glass of water and the bottle of painkillers and returned to the sink. She had stripped to her bra and panties to scrub her face. Joe thought she looked good standing there. She stood on her toes to get her face closer to the mirror, and he admired her legs. Marybeth was not extremely thin, but she was firm and still looked athletic. The only place she looked pregnant was her belly. Marybeth carried her babies high and straight out as if she were already proud of them. She looked perfect as far as Joe was concerned. She could be fun in bed, and Joe suddenly wanted her there.

"What are you thinking?" she asked, looking at him from the mirror.

"I'm thinking you look pretty good."

"And . . ." Marybeth said, "aren't you too tired?"

"And I want you."

Marybeth stopped scrubbing and turned toward him. "Honey . . ." she said, almost pleading and gesturing toward the closed bedroom door.

"She can't hear us," Joe replied dryly. "I'll make a point not to shout."

Marybeth glared at him. "It's not that. You know I don't like to do anything when my mother is in the house."

Joe knew. They had had this discussion before, many times. But he continued, "Do you think she thinks the kids were conceived by divine intervention?"

"No," Marybeth said, "but I'm just not comfortable when I know she's in the house, under the same roof. If I'm not comfortable, how fun can it be?"

Joe conceded the point, as he had conceded the point before.

"Okay," he said, covering up. "No hard feelings."

"Good," she said. "I'm glad you understand. I know it's irrational, but it's the case here."

When she came to bed, he was still awake.

"Do you want to know who came in and saw me last night in the hospital?" Joe asked as she snuggled into him.

"Wacey."

"Well, him, too," Joe said. "But after Wacey, Vern Dunnegan came to call."

He felt her stiffen.

"I really hate hospitals," Joe said.

"I know you do. What did Vern have to say?"

"He just wished us well and said he thought I had done a good job up there in that camp with Wacey. He said he was proud of his two boys."

"You're my boy, not Vern's," Marybeth said. Then she cautioned him. "Be careful with that man. I don't trust him. I never have."

Joe chuckled at that. The pills were beginning to work. He felt numbing waves slowly wash over him. "He just stayed for a minute, but he said he wanted to meet with me later this week. He said he wanted to talk about my future."

"What did he mean?" Marybeth asked haltingly.

"He kind of offered me a job with InterWest Resources," Joe said. "For a lot more money."

"You're kidding," Marybeth said, sitting up and turning to him.

"I'm not," Joe said, patting her.

"Well, my goodness, Joe," she said. *"My goodness."*

PART THREE

Lists

(c) (1) The Secretary of the Interior shall publish in the Federal Register [, and from time to time he may by regulation revise,] a list of all species determined by him or the Secretary of Commerce to be threatened species and a list of all species determined by him or the Secretary of Commerce to be an endangered species. Each list shall refer to the species contained therein by scientific and common name or names, if any, specify in respect to such species over what portion of its range it is endangered or threatened, and specify any critical habitat within such range. The Secretary shall from time to time revise each list published under the authority of this subsection to reflect recent determinations, designations, and revisions made in accordance with subsections (a) and (b).

—The Endangered Species Act Amendments of 1982

11

The triple funeral for the three dead outfitters was unlike anything Joe Pickett had experienced before. Ote Keeley's wish that he be buried in his 1989 Ford F-250 XLT Lariat turbo diesel had caused complications with the staff of the Twelve Sleep County Cemetery in that they were required to dig the biggest hole in the ground they had ever dug. The rental of an earthmover was necessary, and the size of the hole created a fifteen-foot mound of fresh soil at the head of the grave. The ceremony had been organized by the widows of Ote Keeley and Kyle Lensegrav (Calvin Mendes was unmarried) and the "unconventional" Reverend B. J. Cobb of the First Alpine Church of Saddlestring.

Joe Pickett stood soberly in his suit, hat, and bandage on a hillside listening to Reverend Cobb give the eulogy as he stood perched on the hood of the pickup. The Keeley and Lensegrav widows and children flanked the crowd and the truck. Behind the families, a blue plastic tarp hid a large pile of something.

It was a beautiful day at the cemetery. A very light breeze rattled the leaves of the cottonwoods, and the sun shone down brilliantly. Dew twinkled in the late fall grass, and the last of the departing morning river mist paused at the treetops.

Although Reverend Cobb's eulogy covered the short history of the outfitters—boyhood friends who hunted in Mississippi, joined the army together, served the country well in Operation Desert Storm, and relocated to the game-rich mountains and plains of Wyoming—Joe couldn't stop looking at the massive hole in the ground in front of the pickup and wondering what was under the blue tarp behind the families.

The mourners consisted of a few fellow Alpine Church members and several of the outfitters' drinking buddies. Joe noticed that there were no other outfitters present, and when he thought about it, he wasn't that surprised. Keeley, Lensegrav, and Mendes had been drummed out of the Wyoming Outfitters Association for their radical views and tendency to commit obvious game violations.

"They were salt-of-the-earth types," intoned the Reverend Cobb, a pudgy bachelor with a crew cut, who was known for his survivalist tendencies and small but fervent congregation. "They loved their trucks. They were throwbacks to a time when men lived off of the land and provided for their families by their outdoor skills and cunning. They were prototypes of the first white Americans. They were frontiersmen. They were outdoorsmen. They were sportsmen of the highest caliber. And these boys knew their calibers, all right. They ate elk, not lamb. They ate venison, not pork. They ate wild duck, not chicken . . ."

The three mahogany-stained pine caskets were in the bed of the pickup, two side-by-side on the bottom and the third laid across them on top. Joe couldn't tell which casket contained whom. The weight of the caskets made the four-wheel-drive pickup list to the rear. The Reverend Cobb finally finished up his comments about what the outfitters ate.

Ote Keeley's wife wasn't hard to pick out as she was the only pregnant woman there. She was thin and small and severe. Joe guessed that normally she wouldn't weigh more than 100 pounds. She had short-cropped blond hair and a pinched, hard face. Her mouth was set around an unlit cigarette. She tightly held the hand of a small girl who wanted to go look at the big hole instead of stand there respectfully with her mother. The girl—Joe would later learn that her name was April—was a five-year-old version of her mother but with a sweet, haunting face.

Joe had introduced himself to her before the services began and had said he was sorry about what happened and that he had children, too, with another on the way.

She had glared at him, her eyes narrowing into slits. "Aren't you the motherfucking *prick* who wanted to take my Otie's outfitting license away?" Her Southern accent made the last word sound like "uh-why."

The little girl didn't flinch at her language, but Joe did. Joe said he was sorry, that this was probably a bad time, and scuttled back to the loose knot of mourners on the side of the pickup.

The Reverend Cobb ended his eulogy by saying that there were certain sacred items that the families of the deceased wanted their loved ones to have with them in the afterlife. At his cue, Mrs. Keeley and Mrs. Lensegrav peeled back the blue tarp to reveal a large pile of objects.

"Kyle Lensegrav would be lost in heaven . . ." the reverend paused until Mrs. Lensegrav turned from the pile with her arms full, ". . . without his Denver Broncos jacket."

Mrs. Lensegrav approached the pickup and draped the jacket over one of the coffins on the bed of the truck.

"Where Kyle will be, the Denver Broncos will always be predominantly orange and blue, as they were in the seventies, eighties, and mid-nineties before they changed into their new hideous uniforms," thundered the reverend.

Joe watched in fascination as Mrs. Lensegrav placed Kyle's favorite hunting cap, spotting scope, Leatherman tool bag, meat saw, Gore-Tex boots, and saddle scabbard on the coffin.

Mrs. Keeley was next.

"Not every man has the skill, determination, and acumen to bag a moose that will forever be listed as one of the top five Boone and Crockett–sanctioned trophies of North America!" the reverend said. "But Ote Keeley can make that claim and these massive beauties . . ."

Mrs. Keeley struggled under the weight of the huge moose antlers—rumor had it that Ote had actually shot the animal illegally within Yellowstone Park and sneaked it out—and Joe felt an urge to step forward to help her. He caught himself because he wasn't sure that she wouldn't attempt to skewer him. Somehow, she summoned the strength to place the antlers over the top coffin.

". . . will forever be mounted above Ote's celestial easy chair."

There were more items for Ote, including a television, VCR, tanned hides, his HAPPINESS IS A WARM GUT PILE T-shirt. Calvin Mendes was probably shortchanged in the ceremony overall because the only items the women put on his casket were his bound volumes of *Hustler* magazine and a case of Schmidt's beer.

Then the Reverend Cobb started up the pickup, eased it into drive, and leaped from the cab. Joe watched, as did the rest of the small crowd and the families, as the Ford inched forward and descended into the massive hole. It settled to the bottom with a solid thump, and no one wanted to look down to see if the caskets had jarred loose and broken open.

Joe wondered, as he walked down the hill through the cemetery, how long the engine of the pickup would keep running and whether or not the cemetery staff would choose to shut it off before they filled up the grave with the earthmover.

12

After the funeral, Joe went to work. It felt good to get out of town and away from the cemetery and go to work. He had packed his lunch that morning in the kitchen and filled a Thermos of coffee. Maxine had been waiting for him in the back of the pickup, her heavy tail thumping the toolbox like a metronome as he approached.

He patrolled a Bureau of Land Management (BLM) tract to the west of Saddlestring, a huge, nearly treeless expanse that stretched from the river to the foothills of the Bighorns. It was deceptive, complicated country, and he had always liked it. From a distance, it appeared to be simply a massive slow rise in elevation from the valley floor to the mountains. In actuality, it was an undulating, cut-and-jive high-country break land of hills and draws and sagebrush. The landscape had folds in it like draped satin, places where shadows grew and pronghorn antelope and large buck mule deer thrived. A spider's web of old unnamed ranch roads coursed through it. Herds of deer and antelope had long learned how to take advantage of the land and the landscape, to live within its folds and draws and literally vanish when pursued. The antelope especially used the starkness of the break land for defense, and they often frustrated hunters by silhouetting themselves on the tops of hills and rises so that they were so much in the open there was no way to sneak up on them. The only trees in the area were the silent markers of hundred-year-old failed homesteads and cabins.

It was opening day of antelope season, the only day there would be real hunting pressure, and it was Joe's job to check the licenses and wildlife stamps of hunters. Most of the hunters he had checked that morning were local and out for meat, although he did visit the trailer camp of an outfitter with four hungover Michigan auto executive clients who were wearing state-of-the-art outdoor gear and were struggling through a Dutch-oven breakfast. Everyone was legal, with the correct licenses and stamps. They planned to go hunting later in the day when they sobered up.

Joe idly wondered how Missy Vankeuren would react when Marybeth told her about Joe's job offer with Inter-West Resources. Joe harbored a feeling of sweet vengeance and secretly wanted to be there when Marybeth gave her the news. It had been a special time in bed after he told Marybeth, and they had both been a little giddy. Marybeth had even broken her rule about not having sex while her mother was under the same roof. Neither before or after had Marybeth said she wanted Joe to take the job, and Joe didn't say he wanted to take it. But the possibilities electrified them both. He wondered now if Missy would warm up to him, now that she knew that his salary could soon triple. In his experience, the women in his life were brutally, honestly practical. Maybe she would think that her daughter had done all right after all.

As he left the camp, he heard the booming of rifles in the distance, and he drove toward the direction of the shots. There was the closed-in *pow-WHOP* sound rather than an open-ended explosion, and he knew that whoever had been shooting had hit something. They had; three local hunters had killed four antelope, which was one too many. The hunters explained to Joe that a bullet had passed through a buck and hit a doe unintentionally. Although Joe believed them, he gave them a speech about shooting into the herd instead of selecting specific targets, and he ticketed the hunter who had killed two. Joe asked the hunters to field dress all four animals and to deliver the extra animal to the Round Home, a halfway house in Saddlestring that fed and housed transients and local alcohol and drug addicts. More than half of the Round Home population consisted of Indians from the reservation, and they preferred wild game meat.

Throughout what remained of the morning, Joe moved from camp to camp, stopping periodically to survey the landscape through his spotting scope. He liked working outside, in the break lands and in the mountains. He liked working outside and coming home and taking a shower before dinner. When he went to sleep most nights, he was physically tired. He knew there were not many jobs left like his anywhere in the world.

Joe vividly remembered, as a 10-year-old, when it first came to him that being a game warden was the thing he wanted to do. He and his younger brother, Victor, had been sleeping outside in the backyard like they did most nights in the summer—in sleeping bags spread out on the trampoline. The stars were bright, and there was a light night breeze. Inside the house, his parents were yelling, fighting, and drinking, which was not unusual for a Friday night. Outside in his sleeping bag, young Joe Pickett read the latest issue of *Fur, Fish, and Game* magazine under a flashlight. He couldn't wait until the magazine was delivered every month, and he read it from cover to cover, even the advertisements in the back that sold animal traps and urine lures and do-it-yourself boats. Victor slept next to him in his sleeping bag, or at least Joe hoped he did. It was worse than usual with his parents that night. Inside, there had been a loud crash of glass, and he had heard his father scream "Goddamnit, woman!" and then his mother was crying and his father was consoling her. It went back and forth like this a lot, only usually it wasn't this loud. While he read and hoped his little brother slept, he heard the clattering rattle of ice in a shaker. His father was the last of the great martini drinkers, and this was the eighth time he had heard the shaker that night. The hollering and crashing was punctuated by periods of silence marked by ice rattling in a shaker, as if both parties had agreed upon time-out while they refueled. Joe knew the neighbors had probably heard the commotion as well.

His flashlight was dimming but he hadn't finished reading yet, so he climbed down from the trampoline and tried to sneak through the house to his bedroom where he kept fresh batteries. He didn't want to be seen and he didn't want to see his parents, but he stepped on broken glass in his bare feet in the kitchen and trailed bloody footprints down the hall carpet, all the way to his room. On the way back outside, with two D batteries in his pajama pockets, he met his mother in the hallway. She was drunk and sentimental, the way she sometimes got, and she rained sloppy kisses on him (which he preferred, considering that if she were sober, he'd have gotten a violent rage and open-handed slaps because of what he had done to the carpet) and guided him into the bathroom. While she tried to pull slivers of glass from his feet (she said she was sorry for breaking the glasses on the floor earlier), he watched her and winced. Her makeup was smeared with tears, and a cigarette danced in her mouth as she talked. It reminded him that she thought of herself as an early sixties hipster. Because she was in such bad shape, she tended to drive the slivers deeper into his foot with the tweezers before regaining her balance enough to pull them out. He told her he was okay even though he wasn't, and he bandaged his own feet while she went out to rejoin his father and the pitcher of martinis.

With new batteries, the flashlight glowed white and strong and he lay on his stomach in his sleeping bag and wished he lived somewhere in the mountains, anywhere other than where he was. It was then that he read the advertisement in the back of the *Fur, Fish, and Game* magazine:

HOW TO BECOME A GAME WARDEN

Don't be chained to a desk, machine, or store counter.
This easy home-study plan prepares you for an exciting career in conservation and ecology.
Forestry and wildlife men hunt mountain lions, parachute from planes to help marooned animals, or save injured campers.
Live the outdoor life you love. Sleep under pines.
Catch your breakfast from icy streams.
Live and look like a million!

Under the text was a photo of a rugged and smiling proto–game warden in a six-point hat holding up what appeared to be a bobcat. The game warden had indeed looked like a million.

"I want to be a game warden," Joe had said aloud.

"Me, too," Victor mumbled from deep in his sleeping bag, surprising Joe. "I want to go where you go."

Joe reached in Victor's sleeping bag and found Victor's hand. They shook on it. The next day, Joe sent in his five-dollar fee. It had set him on this course.

Victor never followed. Ten years after that night, while Joe was in his second year of college and Victor Pickett was a senior in high school, Victor broke up with his girlfriend, got drunk, and drove his car into the massive stone arch to Yellowstone National Park's north entrance. It was three in the morning, and he was going 110 miles per hour.

No one ever knew why Victor had traveled for two hours to get to Yellowstone to do what he did. Joe could only speculate that it had something to do with a vicious emotional brew of alcohol and violence and the dream escape from both that a place like Yellowstone seemed to offer.

Joe parked his truck on a hilltop that allowed him to see most of the break land, and he ate his lunch and drank coffee. He mounted his spotting scope on his window and left the radio on. The sun had burned off the early morning damp and the day was warm, dry, and cloudless.

From this vantage point, Joe watched as a scenario developed far below him. A large herd of nearly 80 pronghorn antelope were spread out along the top of a plateau, warily eating grass and moving east to west. To the west, snaking along a four-wheel-drive road, was a single white vehicle. The occupants of the vehicle were below the rim of the plateau where they could not be seen by the herd. From the movements of the antelope, Joe could tell they had not yet noticed the white vehicle.

Chewing on a chicken salad sandwich, Joe focused on the white truck through his spotting scope. He recognized the vintage International Scout and the two older hunters who were driving it. Joe watched as the hunters stopped their vehicle and slowly walked up the side of the plateau. It took nearly a half an hour for the hunters to get to the top. Once there, they hunkered down behind a reef of tall sagebrush to take aim.

Joe leaned away from the scope and watched the herd in

its entirety. The herd, as a single unit, suddenly jerked to life and rocketed east along the plateau, each animal trailing a thin plume of dust. Then the delayed sound of two heavy shots, one a definite hit, washed up to him over the distance. He lowered his eye to the scope again and could see at least one downed antelope in the distance. One of the hunters was now walking toward it, and the other was going back to get the Scout.

Joe washed down the last of his sandwich with coffee, then started the pickup and began to move over the hill. The herd was now a long way away, still running fast. He could no longer make out individual animals, just a rapidly retreating white cloud of dust. Pronghorn antelope were the second fastest mammals on earth—only an African cheetah could outrun them.

By the time Joe drove his pickup over the rim of the plateau, the hunters had completely field-dressed the pronghorn and were in the process of attaching the back legs of the animal to a hook tree. He recognized the men as Hans and Jack, a retired ranch hand and retired school teacher from Saddlestring. Hans now ran a janitorial business part-time, cleaning downtown commercial buildings such as the drugstore and the video rental store. Hans and Jack had hunted together for more than 30 years, and they had developed antelope hunting into an annual craft. Their Scout was a customized traveling meat-processing plant. The older they got, the more refinements they made to compensate for their age and the more their appreciation for taking care of and eating game meat grew. First it was the old freezer they packed with ice that filled most of the bed of the small pickup. They had learned to cool down the meat as soon as possible to prevent any spoilage from the warm days of September. Then they had added the winch and the crane to elevate the carcass from the ground in order to skin it and further cool it out.

They showed Joe their newest invention, a five-gallon

gravity-based water tank with a hose that they could use to wash and scrub the carcass down once it was skinned. Joe watched as the hunters quartered the animal into sections and rotated each section on the winch to the icebox. Hans's movements were getting shakier with each year, Joe noticed, and Jack kept his distance when both of them were skinning with their knives.

Then Hans asked Joe a strange thing.

"You ever heard anything about endangered species being found up in the mountains, Mr. Pickett?"

"What?" Joe asked, suddenly paying more attention to what the two old men were saying.

"Hans," Jack said, eyeing his partner.

"Just wondering." Hans said with a bemused, holier-than-thou expression on his face. Hans and Jack exchanged glances, and went back to their work. Joe waited for more that finally came.

"It'd probably be best for everyone if nothing was ever found," Hans said, looking up at Joe. "My guess is that we wouldn't be able to hunt out here anymore if someone thought there were endangered animals out here."

"Damned right," Jack said.

"Why'd you bring this up?" Joe asked. "Do you know something?"

"No reason," Jack said.

"Just bullshitting you," added Hans.

"If you know something, you need to report it," Joe said looking from one to the other. He couldn't tell whether he was being fooled with or not.

"And that's what we would do," Jack assured Joe. "Indeed we would."

"Indeed," Hans echoed.

It had been a strange interlude, Joe thought.

When they were done and the Scout was hosed down and cleaned, Jack and Hans offered Joe a cold beer from the cooler. He thanked them but declined, and he wished them luck for the rest of the day. He knew that if Hans and Jack didn't get their second antelope today, they eventually would, so he would see the Scout out in the break land every day until that happened. Hans and Jack had the patience of the retired, and they were both known as good hunters and good cooks.

Joe had no problem with hunters hunting for meat. He felt, compared with buying it at the supermarket in cellophane-wrapped parcels, that hunting was basically more honest. He had never understood the arguments of people who opposed hunting on principle while eating a cheeseburger. He thought it was important for people to know that animals died in order for them to eat meat. The process of stalking, killing, dressing, and eating an animal was much simpler and easier to understand to Joe than having a cow killed by a sledgehammer-swinging meat-processing plant employee and having the eventual results appear as a small packet in a shopping cart. He appreciated people like Hans and Jack.

For Hans and Jack, hunting for meat was still a way of life and not really a sport. The greeting of "Got your elk yet?" was as common as hello in the small mountain towns, and the health and size of game herds was a matter of much public concern and debate.

Joe figured this was why the murders in the elk camp were the talk of the town. The killing of three outfitters realized every hunter's nightmare: that out in the field someone may be hunting for *them.* No one had ever heard of such a thing happening before. Sure, there were accidental shootings and incidents of fistfights and threats—the kind of things that would inevitably happen when men (there were very few women in the elk camps) left their jobs for a week or two and got together in the mountains to hunt. But considering the number of guns and the gallons of alcohol available, deliberate killings during hunting season were incomprehensible to the people of Saddlestring.

And the more Joe thought about it, the more he realized that the killings were incomprehensible to *him.*

Feeling good about the day and the job he had done, Joe worked his way through the break land toward the road that would take him back into town. Vern Dunnegan had called him early that morning, before the funeral, and asked Joe to meet him at five in the Stockman's Bar. If it was like the old days, Vern would be in the last booth on the right, past the pool table. That was Vern's booth.

13

The Stockman's Bar was a dark place where they served shots and beer under the dusty heads of local game animals and where the walls were covered with black-and-white photos of local rodeo contestants from the 1940s and '50s. No matter what day or hour it was, there seemed to always be the same number of patrons. Joe walked past a dozen men on stools, toward the pool table in the back. A hanging Coors beer lamp illuminated the green felt of the pool table and highlighted the side of Vern's face. Vern was in his booth, and he had company.

"You're early." Vern said as a greeting, extending his hand toward Joe. "Joe Pickett, this is Aimee Kensinger." She was in shadow. Joe's eyes had not yet adjusted to the dark bar.

Joe took off his hat. "We've met."

"See, I told you that," Aimee said to Vern.

Vern chuckled and gestured for Joe to sit across from him in the booth.

"Will you drink a beer with me?" Vern stated more than asked. "Aimee's got to get going."

"Oh, yes, I had forgotten about that," Aimee said sarcastically. Joe liked her voice. As his eyes adjusted, he could see she was wearing some kind of fuzzy, black sweater and a thin gold necklace. She was smiling at him. "I'll see you around, Joe Pickett."

Vern stood and let her out of the booth. She tousled Joe's hair as she left, which embarrassed him. She was a beautiful woman, no doubt about that. Vern followed her as far as the bar and returned with four shots of bourbon and four mugs of beer on a tray.

"Happy hour," Vern said. "Two for one." He downed a shot and chased it with beer. "You're looking good, Joe. How's the pellet wound?"

Joe told him it was fine and took a long drink from a mug. The cold beer tasted good. The afterimage of Aimee Kensinger hovered next to Vern.

"She still likes me," Vern said, smiling. "Even though I don't wear the uniform anymore."

Vern threw another shot down his throat. "She likes you, too." He wiped his mouth with the back of his hand. Joe didn't respond. He didn't want to go there.

Joe tried to gauge how much Vern had been drinking. This certainly didn't seem to be his first shot of the afternoon, judging by how flushed his face was. Vern had always been a hard drinker, and there had rarely been a night after work when Vern didn't suggest they stop for one or two. But since Vern had returned, Joe had yet to see him without bourbon within his grasp.

"Have you given what we talked about any thought?" Vern asked.

Joe nodded.

"Well?"

"I need to discuss it with Marybeth," Joe said. "We really haven't had a chance to talk it over yet."

Vern's eyes never left Joe's. "She's a smart woman,"

Vern said. "She'll steer you in the right direction. D'you want me to talk to her?"

"That won't be necessary." Joe felt a twinge of resentment toward his former boss. Vern obviously thought he could talk Marybeth into making Joe take the job. Vern thought he could talk anybody into anything. Usually, he could. Vern was a highly intelligent man and very persuasive. But for a reason Joe couldn't quite articulate, he found himself resisting the job offer.

"I know one thing," Joe said, drinking at the beer. "I know I won't be ready to make any big moves until these outfitter murders are finally solved."

Vern sat perfectly still. He looked at Joe with disbelief.

"What in the hell is there to solve, Joe?" Vern asked, his voice low and tight. "Clyde Lidgard shot three local white trash outfitters, and you guys shot him. Case closed."

"There are too many unanswered questions," Joe said quickly. "Why did he do it? Why was he up there? Why did he stay there if he did it? Why did Ote Keeley come to my house? What was in that cooler? In my mind, there are a lot of things that have to be answered."

Vern sat perfectly still with a look of outright contempt on his face, his eyes boring a hole in Joe. Although he felt his resolve weakening, Joe looked back and did not flinch. He steeled himself against Vern, determined to not let him talk him out of continuing the investigation.

"Joe," Vern said, his voice barely over a whisper. "Let's you and me take a couple of minutes and talk about the *real fucking world.*" Vern bit off the last three words with a vehemence that caught Joe completely off guard and unnerved him.

"I don't know the answers to those questions, and I frankly don't give a shit," Vern hissed. "Murders are messy. When the killer is shot before he can talk, there are all kinds of loose ends. This is not an exact science—you should know that by now. These things aren't always wrapped up neatly. Sometimes when it's too neat, an innocent man goes to prison, but usually the guy is scum and should be in there anyway. Don't beat yourself up trying to put every piece together. Forget about it and move on with your life, Joe."

Joe thought about what Vern said. And he thought about Vern. There was an urgency there Joe couldn't understand and hadn't expected.

"What about the cooler Ote brought to my house?" Joe asked. "What was in it?"

Vern brought his hand down on the table with a wet slap.

"Again, who the fuck cares?" Vern asked, reaching over and taking one of Joe's shots. "Let it go."

"I talked to a couple of hunters today who asked me if I knew anything about an endangered species being found in the mountains," Joe said. "They wouldn't elaborate, and I don't know if they were kidding or not."

"Who were they?" Vern asked. He knew everybody.

"Hans and Jack."

"Fuck 'em," Vern said, dismissing them. "Coupla gossipy old hens."

"I don't know about that," Joe said. "I always thought they were all right."

"Joe . . ." Vern sighed.

"I've got an obligation to find out and report on it," Joe said. "You know that."

Vern sneered back. "An obligation to whom?" he asked. "The Wyoming Game and Fish Department? The U.S. Fish and Wildlife Service? The Sierra Fucking Club? The president of the United States?"

"Vern," Joe reasoned. "You know what we're supposed to do if we find something like this. Or even suspect it. And what if it's tied to the outfitter murders in some way?"

Vern rolled his eyes. He used to do the same thing when he thought Joe had said something incredibly naive.

"You know, Joe, what I'm about to say will shock you," Vern said. "But I know good men who have found an endangered species on their land and shot it and buried it without a second thought rather than announce it to the world. I know a rancher over by Cody who cornered some kind of wolverine-type creature that he *knew* was supposed to be extinct. He blew that little sucker away and fed the pieces to his dogs. That rancher knew that if he had reported it, he would have been kicked off of his own land so that a bunch of bark-beetle elitists could claim they were saving the world."

One of the men from the stools at the bar weaved near their booth as he made his way toward the bathroom. Vern leaned across the table to Joe and kept his voice down.

"Do you realize what would happen to this valley if it got out that there might be something in the mountains? Even if it was nothing more than a silly rumor started by a couple of gossipy old hens? Even if there was no more to it than a couple of future Alzheimer's candidates blabbering into the wind? Or even if you, as the game warden, announced that you thought there was something up there?

"Think of the people who work in the lumber mill," Vern said. "Think of the logging truck drivers, the cowboys, the outfitters, the fishing guides. They'd be unemployed while the Feds roped off the entire valley for the future. Environmentalists from all over the country would move in with their little round glasses and sandals and start giving press conferences on how they're here to protect the innocent little creatures from the ignorant *locals.* Whether or not anything was ever found up there, the environmentalists would keep things tied up in the courts for decades just so that they can tell their members they're actually doing something with their dues.

"Third-generation ranchers would lose their ranches. Support people—teachers, retailers, restaurant owners—would lose their jobs or move on eventually. All because

Joe Pickett, master game warden extraordinaire, suspects that there might be some rare *thing* in the mountains.

"Half the people in this town would hate your guts," Vern said. "Some would lose their jobs. Your cute little girlies would catch all kinds of horrible crap in school. They would bear the brunt of it, Joe, and it would all be your fault."

Joe found himself breaking his gaze with Vern and looking down at the table, but thinking, *InterWest Resources and their pipeline wouldn't do too well either.*

Vern continued, "It might be different if the endangered species laws either made any sense biologically or if they weren't just political mind games. But neither is true. Listen."

Vern went on to recount how there were more than 950 plants and animals listed as either "endangered" or "threatened" and an additional 4,000 species that were candidates for future listings. And how 20 years and billions of dollars later, fewer than 30 species have come off the "endangered" list. He said the laws were hypocritical, that species considered "cute," like wolves and grizzly bears, fared better than species that were ugly to human eyes, and no rational scientific basis was used. He said he had looked at the numbers and figured out that more than $190 million had been spent on bald eagles, northern spotted owls, red-cockaded woodpeckers, grizzly bears, West Indian manatees, Florida scrub jays, and whooping cranes. Then he spoke in broad, global terms and stated that at least 99 percent of all species that had ever lived on earth had become extinct naturally, without man's "interference." Mass extinctions had happened since the dawn of time. Snail darters, Colorado squawfish, spotted owls, and Mount Graham red squirrels wouldn't be missed by anyone or anything.

"Animals die, Joe," Vern said. "Species go belly up. It

happened before the first fish crawled on land and figured out lungs, and it will continue to happen. What gives us the right to be so arrogant that we think we can control what lives and what dies? We aren't as almighty as we like to think when it comes to affecting the real world, the natural world. All of the nuclear bombs on earth have about one ten-thousandth the power of the asteroid that slammed into the planet and killed all of the dinosaurs. What humans can do to change the planet is puny. We're deluding ourselves if we think we're so fucking smart that we can either save or create a species. How do we know that by saving some little dickey bird that we aren't preventing a new and improved dickey bird from evolving? Who do we think we are?" Vern asked. "Who the hell are we *to take on God*?"

Joe sat back. He felt as though he had been pummeled.

Vern noted the reaction and, obviously thinking he had persuaded Joe, drank the last shot of bourbon and smiled.

"Speaking of God," Vern said. "Have you ever heard of the God Squad?"

Joe shook his head no.

"It's a real thing. I didn't make this up. It's composed of the secretary of interior, the secretary of the army, the secretary of agriculture, and a couple of other guys. It is their job, when it comes down to the nut cutting, to decide which species live or die in the national interest. Can you believe the incredible arrogance of that?"

Joe and Vern finished their beers in silence. As Joe got up to leave, Vern reached out and held his arm. Their eyes locked.

"There is an offer on the table, Joe. The window of opportunity for that job offer is starting to close. If you choose not to take advantage of it, you will be making a mistake."

Joe was unsure whether he was being advised or threatened.

"I'll let you know, Vern," Joe said. "Seems like there are a lot of things I need to decide."

"You'll do the right thing," Vern said, patting Joe on the hand. "You're a good man, Joe, and you'll do the right thing."

14

Sheridan and Lucy named the largest creature—the first one they had seen—Lucky, the smaller, brown creature Hippity-Hop, and the long, thin creature Elway. They decided the animals were a family, and a happy one. Lucky was the dad, Hippity-Hop was the mom, and Elway was the son. The names, they thought, matched their personalities. And boy, could they eat.

They ate everything. Not only would they emerge from the woodpile for Cheerios, but they would stuff bits of hot dog, luncheon meat, and vegetables into their cheeks. The only thing they didn't seem to like were jelly beans, and that upset Lucy because she had a whole plastic purse full of them.

During dinner, Sheridan had learned to hide bits of food in her napkin to take out to the backyard later. Lucy ate all of her dinner, but she would gladly sacrifice her snack because she wasn't much on sweets. Together, while Mom was clearing dishes or talking on the telephone or visiting with Grandmother Missy, Sheridan and Lucy would ask to play in the backyard (the wish was always granted) and then go feed the secret pets.

Lucky, Hippity-Hop, and Elway weren't silent after all. They could chirp and chatter and make a trilling sound like a muted baby's rattle when they were annoyed or playful. Sheridan sometimes thought the animals were so loud that there was no way Mom or Grandmother Missy wouldn't hear them, but they never seemed to.

Lucy would eventually give the secret away, Sheridan thought. She was just too little to keep her mouth shut. Just that evening after dinner Lucy said she wanted to go outside and "feed Lucky." Sheridan explained that Lucky, along with Elway and Hippity-Hop, were their imaginary pets. Mom complimented Sheridan for playing so nicely with her little sister. Grandmother Missy beamed at them both.

When the creatures were done eating or didn't emerge from the logs, Lucy wanted to "play animals" with Sheridan. Sheridan went along, which meant Lucy pretended she was one of the creatures and Sheridan was feeding her. Sheridan would throw imaginary food on the grass and Lucy, a good mimic, would replicate the creatures as they picked up the food in their claws and stuffed it into their cheeks.

Sheridan knew it wouldn't last. Something would eventually happen. It always did.

But while the creatures were alive and playful, and while they just belonged to Sheridan (and Lucy), she would enjoy it. Having the secret and seeing those little faces pop out of the woodpile was a wonderful treat—and something she looked forward to every afternoon on the bus ride home.

While it lasted, it was magic.

15

Joe went back to the break lands before sunrise. He drove there in a heavy, wet mist and had to use the four-wheel drive to get to the top of his lookout hill. The day broke wet and dark, and the rain increased. The clouds were low and filled the sky, and the water pooled on the slick bentonite clay of the plateaus or created chocolate brown ponds or streams that foamed through draws. The valley was socked in, and from what he could see through his spotting scope, the antelope hunters had stayed in their camps. The roads had already deteriorated and were either marble-slick or mushy, depending on the terrain. He decided to get out of the area while the option was still available. On the way back he winched out a crew of hunters stuck in a ditch and followed them down to the main road.

Once he reached home, Joe left his boots and yellow slicker in the mudroom, put his hat crown-down on his desk, and called Game and Fish Headquarters in Cheyenne and asked for the Wildlife Biology Section. He told a technician about the package he had sent them and asked whether the contents had been examined yet. He was asked to hold.

From his chair, he could smell coffee from the kitchen, and he could hear the murmuring of Marybeth and her mother at the table.

At last a man identifying himself as the chief biologist came on the line. Joe had heard of him but had never met him. Joe listened to him and felt his scalp twitch.

"What do you mean you don't have it?" Joe asked.

"Exactly that," the biologist said, the righteous annoyance of a higher rank apparent. "No one here has seen it or recalls receiving it. How did you send it to us?"

Joe described the small box wrapped in brown paper and tape.

"You sent it regular mail? Not UPS? Not Federal Express? Not registered mail?" the biologist fired at Joe. "So there's no receipt. You sent it so there was no way to trace it?"

Joe felt his temper rise. He kept his voice low and even. "I called ahead and was instructed to send it by mail," Joe said. "I was told that in these days of limited state budgets, we were to avoid extravagances like Federal Express."

"Who told you that?" the biologist asked flatly.

"I think it was you," Joe said. The voice sounded the same. "I called you the day I found it."

There was a long, frustrated sigh over the telephone. "Well, we don't have it."

"Can you look again? It's important," Joe said. "Nothing I've had examined has ever been lost before, either from there to here or from here to there."

There was a long silence. "Sure, we can look. But no one here recalls getting it."

He asked Joe to confirm the address he sent it to and the section. He asked Joe if he had put enough postage on the parcel.

Joe started to answer when the biologist asked him to hold again because he said someone might have found it. Joe sat back in his swivel chair with the receiver up to his ear. He recalled how the boys in Cheyenne often felt about the wardens in the field and vice versa. Vern had warned him about it years ago—how the agency directors sometimes felt that field wardens would go native and forget they were state employees, that the wardens would start to think of themselves as advocates for local ranchers or hunters or boosters. Some of the Cheyenne brass thought of the field wardens as prima donnas out there with their fancy trucks, guns, and badges. Like they were local celebrities rather than subordinates. But the resentment could be mutual. Joe had never placed a call to headquarters before 8 A.M. or after 5 P.M., knowing that anyone he needed to talk to would only be in during those hours. He might start the day by patrolling the Bighorn break lands at 5 A.M., but things were different in Cheyenne. Biologists got paid the same whether they found a package or didn't find it.

Out of the corner of his eye, he could see Sheridan and Lucy playing in the living room. Lucy was being a dog or something and was raising up on her hind legs for an invisible treat that Sheridan was giving her. *It was cute.* Marybeth had said the night before that the girls seemed to be doing extremely well and that the Ote Keeley incident had not seemed to upset them. Marybeth said both girls had spent the last two days playing near the woodpile in the backyard and never even mentioned what had happened there. She said Sheridan, Miss Emotional, had even been consistently sunny. Marybeth said she was beginning to feel that maybe there would be nothing to worry about after all.

"Nope, sorry," the biologist said as he came back to the telephone. "We found a package and opened it, and it was a piece of a dead eagle a warden sent us from Ranchester to see if it had been shot."

Joe cursed under his breath. The biologist agreed to call him if the package ever showed up.

* * *

Joe walked into the kitchen for a cup of coffee. Marybeth and Missy were sitting at the table and stopped talking when he walked in, confirming that they had been talking about him. He filled his cup and turned and leaned against the counter. Marybeth looked radiant, and she smiled at him. Missy was smiling, too, and she looked at him with a kind of detached respect he had not seen from her before. Neither was about to ask him about the job offer or what he thought about it. Yet. They were both trying to gauge his mood.

Lucy crawled into the kitchen on all fours and propped up on her haunches near the table with her mouth open. Missy fed her a piece of a waffle from a plate. Joe guessed this routine had been going on most of the morning.

"There's your treat, little doggie," Missy said.

"I'm not a doggie," Lucy said over her shoulder as she scooted back into the living room to be with her sister.

"I don't know what's going on, but the girls are being angels," Marybeth told Joe. "Maybe their grandmother brings out the best in them."

Joe laughed, and Missy gave Marybeth a look.

The telephone rang in the office, and Joe excused himself to answer it. There was silence on the other end after Joe identified himself. The barely perceptible hiss in the line indicated it was long distance.

"You don't know me." It was a woman's voice. "I work at headquarters in Cheyenne." Her voice was steady, but nervous. She was barely audible.

Joe reached behind him without looking and closed the office door. It was now quiet in the room. He sat down at his desk.

"You called about a package today," the woman said. "I saw it come in Tuesday and it went to Game Biology. Then it disappeared."

"What do you mean it disappeared?" Joe asked.

"It disappeared."

Joe thought about it, saying nothing. The woman again said that it had disappeared. She clipped her words, and he could sense the caution in her voice, as if someone might walk in on her any minute.

"Who are you?" Joe asked.

"Never mind," she said. "I've got two kids and a husband who's out of work. I'm a state employee with benefits. I need this job."

"I've got a couple of kids, too," Joe said. "And another one on the way."

"Then you had best just forget about that package," the woman said sharply, not wanting to establish any kind of common interest. "Just forget about it and go on with your life."

Joe frowned. It was the second time he had received that advice. While she talked, he slid open his desk drawer. The other envelope, the one with the last few pieces of scat, was still there.

She paused briefly, then continued. "Let me put it this way: anything you send us will get lost."

"Why are you doing this?" Joe asked.

There was a hint of exasperation on the other end of the phone. "I don't know," she said. "I just felt that I had to. I have to go now."

"Thank you," Joe said but she had already hung up.

Joe thought about what to do. Still holding the receiver, he sifted through his desk until he found his old address book and then dialed his friend Dave Avery. Joe and Dave had gone to college together and Dave now worked as a game biologist for the Montana Fish and Game Department in Helena. After they had caught up (Dave had divorced but was engaged again), Joe asked him if he could send him a sample for an independent analysis.

"Where was it found?"

"My backyard."

"And my Wyoming colleagues can't decide what squeezed it out?"

"There's some dispute," Joe hedged. He didn't want to go into the story of the lost sample. There wasn't any need to.

"Sound's like you're challenging me," Dave said. "Name That Shit."

"I am," Joe said, forcing a laugh. Dave agreed to take a look at it, whatever it was, and to keep both the sample and the results in confidence.

Joe sat back in his swivel chair. He thought about what the woman at the lab had told him. He wondered how he could go about finding out who she was and if he even should. He believed she had told him the truth about the missing sample. He wished she hadn't, because things had suddenly become a lot more complicated.

16

The tires of Joe Pickett's pickup made a sizzling sound as he drove through the wet streets of Saddlestring to the county sheriff's office. It was still raining, and there were very few people out on the streets. Those who were out were scurrying from one door to another holding their hands on top of their heads. Joe thought how strange it was that the rain had continued throughout the day. Rain was a rarity this time of year; in fact, it was a rarity, period. Wyomingites, Joe had observed, didn't know what to do when it rained except get out of it, watch it through the window, and wait for it to go away. The same people who chained up all four tires and drove through horizontal snowstorms and bucked snowdrifts just to go have lunch in town during the winter had no clue what to do when it rained. A few ranchers stretched plastic covers, sometimes referred to as "cowboy condoms," over their John B. Stetsons but few people owned umbrellas. Fewer yet would let themselves be seen with an umbrella open because it would appear urban and pretentious, and the only rain slickers he ever saw were rolled up neatly and tied to the backs of saddles, where they generally remained. But Joe liked rain and wished there were more of it.

Vern had been right. Saddlestring was dying. A decade ago the coal mines in the county were operational and the Twelve Sleep Oil Field was pumping, but now both were silent. Only a reclamation crew still worked at the mine, and the oil wells had since been capped, waiting in vain for the price of a barrel of oil to rise. Even the agricultural jobs had shrunk as out-of-state wealth bought local ranches for tax write-offs and in some cases took them out of production. Cattle prices were the lowest in a decade. A quarter of the storefronts on the main street were boarded up. In the past five years, the population of the town had decreased by 30 percent. Houses were available in all parts of town, and the prices were cheap. Saddlestring's one radio station had announced it was going off the air as of the first of next month. Unemployment was high and getting higher. Vern's pipeline would pump not only natural gas but new blood and dollars back into the community.

Saddlestring was a classic western town borne of promise due to its location on the railroad, but that promise never really played out. In the 1880s, a magnificent hotel was built by a mining magnate, but it had faded into disrepair. The main street, called Main Street, snaked north and south and had a total of four stoplights that had never been synchronized. The two-block "downtown" still retained the snooty air of Victorian storefronts designed to be the keystones of a fine city, but beyond those buildings, the rest of Main Street looked like any other American strip mall, punctuated by gun shops, sporting goods stores, fishing stores, bars, and restaurants that served steak.

Joe entered the sheriff's office and hung his jacket and hat on a rack.

"Still raining?" asked Deputy McLanahan from his desk behind the counter. Joe said it was and asked if Sheriff Barnum was available. Wendy, the receptionist/dispatcher, eyed Joe coldly, long enough to remind him that she still didn't like him after their telephone conversation on Sunday. But then she relented and buzzed Barnum on the intercom, saying "Game Warden Joe" was here to see him.

Sheriff Bud Barnum sat behind a desk stacked with mountains of paper and mail. He was sipping from a large white foam cup that he appeared never to put down. Although Barnum's office was good sized, there were stacks of magazines and documents everywhere, and the untidiness of it gave Joe a claustrophobic feeling. There was a single, brown Naugahyde chair across from Barnum's desk, and Joe moved a few pieces of unopened mail from it and sat down.

Barnum sipped loudly from his cup. Joe could smell the strong coffee.

"You ever been to that new coffee place down the block?" Barnum asked. Joe nodded that he had. Marybeth liked to meet him there for coffee and oversized muffins when he took a morning break.

"It's a pretty good place," Barnum said quietly. "The people who own it are a little goofy, though. It's kind of a hippie establishment. They moved here from California, and she doesn't wear makeup or shave her legs, which I don't understand the significance of. He was some kind of computer engineer before he sold his stock and moved out here. All their food is vegetarian."

To Joe, Barnum looked very tired. His pallor was grayish, and there were bags under his eyes.

"They've got all these different kinds of coffee these days," Barnum said, looking at the big foam cup. "This is Ethiopian Jaba-Java. All my life I thought there was only one kind of coffee and that it came out of a big red can with a little Mexican or Colombian farmer on it. Then all of the sudden there are a hundred kinds of coffee. They feature a new kind of special coffee every day in that place. I've been trying a different one every day to try and make up for all of those years I was sheltered. I don't know why it is that alcohol and tobacco are now bad, but jolts of caffeine are suddenly good. It is beyond me, and it makes me feel old."

He handed Joe the cup for Joe to try it. To be polite, Joe had a sip. Barnum had a disarming and likable way about him.

Joe nodded.

"Pretty good, eh?" Barnum said. "Who'd a thought there could be coffee from Africa? Plain old American coffee just isn't good enough for us anymore, I guess."

Joe felt awkward. Then he came right out with it: "Can I ask you a question about the outfitter murders?"

"Pertaining to what?" Barnum asked, sitting a little straighter in his chair, his heavy-lidded eyes fixed on Joe.

Joe started to answer, but Barnum spoke again.

"First I need to know whose camp you're in," Barnum said.

"Whose camp?"

"Wacey Hedeman's or mine," Barnum said. "The guy who is running against me. Your pal."

"I'm neutral," Joe said truthfully. "I don't have a position on that."

Barnum's expression never changed. Joe had no idea what Barnum was thinking. It was unnerving.

"Stay that way," Barnum warned.

"I intend to," Joe replied.

"I'm going to lose the election," Barnum said flatly. "I've been around long enough to know this is the last one, even if no one else realizes it."

Joe had no idea how to answer that. He couldn't imagine Bud Barnum not being the sheriff of Twelve Sleep County. Clearly, Barnum couldn't either.

"I don't know what the hell I'm going to do after that," Barnum said. "Maybe the governor will give me a job, but then I'd have to move to Cheyenne. Probably I'll just stay here and drink a lot of coffee."

Joe lamely suggested that there was still a month and a half until the election and that anything could happen in that time. Barnum nodded wearily.

"You had a question."

"I'm wondering what the status of the investigation is."

"The *status of the investigation,*" Barnum mimicked, his expression theatrically perplexed, "is obvious. The state crime-lab ballistics has proven that all three Mississippi yahoos were shot with the same nine millimeter semi-automatic pistol at close range, and that pistol was found on Mr. Clyde Lidgard by Deputy McLanahan and yourself and Mr. Hedeman. Lidgard is in critical condition in the Billings hospital, having never regained consciousness, and the doctors up there say every day that he won't live through the night but he has so far. Unless Mr. Lidgard regains consciousness and tells us a story that is different from what we already know, the case is all but closed."

Joe waited for more. No more was coming.

"So when Clyde Lidgard dies, the investigation ends," Joe said.

"Unless there is some kind of new evidence to open it back up," Barnum said. "Simple as that."

Joe nodded. "His trailer was searched?"

Barnum's tone was mildly sarcastic. "It was searched both by the sheriff's office and by the state boys. Nothing could be found that either implicated or exonerated Lidgard. The report is in the file if you want to read it over. Lidgard was a strange bird, and his trailer was a strange place. He liked to take a lot of pictures with his Kodak Instamatic. There are thousands of photos out there. He also liked to collect pictures of Marilyn Monroe, including that first-ever *Playboy* magazine with her in it. That magazine's probably the only thing Clyde owned that was worth anything. If that magazine is still out there, it will amaze me because more than likely it ended up in the briefcase of one of the state investigators. But aside from the magazine, everything that was in the trailer is still in the trailer, and the unit has been sealed and locked."

Joe took it all in and waited for Barnum to finish.

"Do you mind if I take a look on my own?" Joe asked.

Barnum again resumed the perplexed look. Then he smiled slightly as if Joe amused him. "You going to do some investigating?"

"Just curious."

"Can I ask why?" Barnum said, his eyebrows arching.

Joe shrugged. "I guess I'm taking this whole thing a little personal because Ote Keeley died in my yard. This whole thing has affected my family."

"What's there to solve?" Barnum asked. "In my twenty-odd years of experience dealing with things like this, I've come to the painful and sometimes unpopular conclusion that many times things are exactly what they seem to be."

"Maybe so," Joe said. "But I need to convince myself."

The sheriff studied Joe for what seemed an inordinate amount of time. "Go do what you need to do," Barnum finally said. "Lidgard's trailer keys are in the file. Just don't take or disturb any of the evidence, because we might find a next of kin who wants some of that crap out there."

Joe thanked him and stood up.

"Joe," Barnum said, as Joe reached for the doorknob, "shouldn't you be out there in the woods catching poachers or counting gut piles or whatever it is you boys do?"

That stopped Joe and turned him around.

"Yes, I should be," Joe said quietly. He did not say what he was thinking, which was, *Shouldn't you be out there following up every last possibility instead of sitting here on your butt, drinking coffee and worrying about the election?*

Joe got a copy of the crime report and the trailer keys from Deputy McLanahan.

"Depressing, ain't he?" McLanahan asked Joe. "This is a really fun place to work these days. When I try and make a joke or even smile about something, he tells me to quit trying to act like Jerry Lewis."

Joe nodded and got his jacket and hat.

"Jerry Lewis," McLanahan echoed as Joe stepped outside. It was still raining.

Written with a felt-tipped marker, the cardboard sign on Clyde Lidgard's trailer read: Anyone caught vandalizing or attempting to enter these premises will be prosecuted to the full extent of the law by order of the Twelve Sleep County Sheriff's Department.

The rain had caused the letters on the sign to blot and run, and there were several long rivulets of black running the length of the door.

It was dark inside the trailer, the heavy rain only allowing a meager amount of light to filter in through the grimy louvered windows. Joe searched for the light switch but discovered that the electricity had been cut off. It smelled musty, and there was the sharp stench of rotting food from the refrigerator and garbage. He decided to check them last, on his way out, because he guessed that the smell would be overpowering once he opened the doors. Joe drew his flashlight from his belt and turned it on. He felt wary and voyeuristic standing in the middle of the dead man's home. The investigations Joe conducted were usually done outside, more often than not over the carcass of a game animal shot and abandoned. In the trailer, Joe felt closed-in. He believed that he didn't know Clyde Lidgard well enough to be in his home. Plus he had no idea what he was looking for in the trailer.

The trailer was small and filthy, years of grit coating the floors and counters. He stood near the kitchen table in the middle of the trailer, trying to decide where to look first.

He shone his flashlight around the room, exposing a hallway that branched off of the room he was standing in. All the doors were wide open, the result, Joe guessed, of the sheriff's search. At the end of the hall, Joe could just make out the foot of a bed in a large bedroom. There were two rooms off of the hallway. One led to a tiny bathroom and the other to a small room that appeared to have been used for storage.

Joe started down the narrow hallway, and his holster caught on an exposed nail. He stepped back and unbuckled his cumbersome belt and put the holster on the table. He kept his flashlight.

Joe stepped inside the bathroom. Old Marilyn Monroe pictures, puckered from steam, covered the walls and ceiling. The staples that secured the pictures were rusty. Shelves against the corner were filled with dozens of brown, prescription drug bottles. Most of the bottles were dusty and hadn't been used in some time. Joe read the labels and saw most had been prescribed by doctors at the local VA hospital. The most recent had been filled by Barrett's Pharmacy in Saddlestring. Joe recognized the names Thorazine and Prozac but knew little about either drug.

The small bedroom was filled with boxes, clothes, and junk. So much had been haphazardly piled into the room for so long that the room couldn't really be entered without taking boxes out. Joe shone the flashlight into several of the closest boxes and found them filled with envelopes of photographs. As Sheriff Barnum had said, there appeared to be thousands.

Joe then entered Lidgard's bedroom and found that the twin bed nearly filled all of the floor space. Joe had to turn sidewise and shuffle around the bed to look around. There were a couple of yellowed posters of Marilyn Monroe stapled to the wall along with an army photo of a younger Clyde Lidgard and a calendar from Lane's Feed and Grain in Saddlestring. The sheets on the bed were not beige as he had first thought, but were white sheets so dirty they appeared beige. There was a stale smell in the room.

Joe slid back the closet doors. Lidgard had a surprising quantity of clothing—they completely filled the closet rack—but none of them looked to have been worn for years. Dust covered the shoulders of the shirts and jackets. On the shelf above the clothes, Joe saw a dozen boxes for .30-.30 rifle cartridges. The price tags on the boxes ranged from $8.50 to $18.00, indicating they had been purchased over at least 20 years. Joe reached up to find that the older boxes were empty but for whatever reason Lidgard had chosen to keep them. Judging by the photographs, junk, pill bottles, and cartridge boxes, Lidgard had been an obsessive collector of things. Joe stood on the end of the bed to make sure he had seen everything on the shelf. The heavy coat of dust was tracked with recent finger smudges, and Joe assumed they had been left by the other investigators. But Joe didn't see what he looking for.

Joe closed the closet and drew a small notepad from his shirt pocket.

"Lidgard's trailer," Joe wrote. "No nine millimeter cartridges."

It took Joe several trips to bring out all of the boxes of photographs from the junk room to the kitchen table where the light was better. It appeared that the thick envelopes full of photos were not really arranged in any manner. But in general, the top envelopes contained more recent photos than those at the bottom of the boxes.

Joe took out the newer sets of photographs, looked at them, and was careful to return them into the proper envelopes. The most recent photos had been developed at Barrett's Pharmacy, the same place Lidgard filled his prescriptions.

If Joe had hoped that the photos would reveal anything other than the fact that Lidgard was a poor if prolific photographer, he was quickly disappointed. The photos were generally of bad quality, and of mundane and inane things. Lidgard apparently carried his camera with him everywhere and from his car window took a lot of photos of things that only Lidgard could explain. Most were crooked, with a left-hand tilt to them. There were trees, lots of photos of trees and bushes. Joe squinted to see if there was anything in those trees and bushes, but he could not find anything of note. There were landscapes: sagebrush, foothills, mountains, the river valley. Sometimes there would be a photo of a part of Clyde Lidgard. There were several pictures of Lidgard's shoes taken as he apparently just stood there and shot down. There were a couple of photos of Lidgard's unfocused face as he held the camera away from him at arm's length and triggered the shutter. Joe studied Clyde Lidgard's face for any kind of clue, but what he saw was a dark, pinched, almost tortured scowl obscenely lit and shadowed by the flash. There was an eerie photo of Lidgard taken into the bathroom mirror with the flash obscuring most of the frame. There were pictures of the cabins Lidgard looked after in the mountains and photos of buildings in downtown Saddlestring. There were two entire rolls taken of snowdrifts. In one of the winter pictures, Joe could discern a herd of elk traipsing across the plains in the far distance, the animals no larger than flyspecks. And occasionally there were unfocused photos of Lidgard's shrunken penis.

Joe reached down into the box for a handful of envelopes from past years. Many of the pictures were taken inside a VA hospital. There were nurses, doctors, light fixtures, other patients, tile floors, and again, Clyde Lidgard's penis.

Joe went through photos until the light got so poor he could hardly see. The most recent photos were from the summer before, and they had been taken in and around Saddlestring. That left a gap of at least two months from Clyde's last photos until he was shot in the outfitters' camp. Joe noted the time lapse in his notepad. He wondered what had made Lidgard stop taking pointless photographs.

When he finally took the boxes back to the junk room, he realized he had given himself a headache. The drumming of the rain on the roof had toned down to sporadic pings. He had been trying to see things that weren't there in the photos, trying to find something in them that would give a clue to who Clyde Lidgard was and how he ended up in the camp. He had found nothing, and the photos had only depressed him. There was something intimate in looking at the photos, as useless as they turned out to be. Lidgard, for whatever reason, had chosen to take the photos, have them developed, and stored them away. Lidgard might see things in the pictures that no one else could see, Joe guessed. Or he might see things out there that he felt compelled to photograph, only to get the photos back and to discover they weren't really there after all. Joe concluded that he knew no more about Clyde Lidgard than when he entered the trailer, but because of the penis photos he now knew more about Clyde Lidgard than he cared to.

Joe took a deep breath and opened the refrigerator. A thick roll of stench washed over him and stung his eyes. He squinted as he moved the flashlight around—putrid hamburger, spoiled milk, oozing cheese. He reached up and flipped down the door to the freezer compartment and the stink was even worse although the compartment was nearly empty.

Joe blew out a breath and kicked the trailer door open to get some air. Then he turned back to the freezer. The freezer pan was full of congealed blood and fluids. Tufts of brown hair were stuck in the blood and to the sides of the compartments. Until recently, Clyde Lidgard had stuffed his freezer with animal parts. And now they were gone.

Joe stood outside the trailer with his hands on his knees, breathing deeply, fighting back nausea. His head pounded and his eyes still stung. Eventually, he was breathing crisp clean air. There was the strong, sweet smell of wet sage, and Joe inhaled gratefully. Dusk brought a red-smeared sunset over the foothills.

Joe straightened up and wiped his eyes with his sleeve. Then from behind him came a powerful *whump* sound. He turned in time to greet a ball of flame as it rolled out of the trailer, scorching his face.

It was remarkable how fast the trailer burned. Already the walls were gone, exposing the black skeleton frame.

He watched helplessly. Whatever evidence there might have been inside was being destroyed. How could this have happened? He hadn't smelled gas.

He remembered that he had left his holster inside and he cursed out loud. Then something made him turn around.

On the road leading toward Saddlestring, a pair of brake lights flashed. If a small herd of antelope hadn't crossed the road and forced the vehicle to slow down, Joe probably wouldn't have seen what looked like the back of a dark Chevrolet Suburban.

Vern Dunnegan drove a Suburban, but so did lots of people. Vern had also once taught Joe the trick of waiting until dusk to sneak up on hunters and use no lights because that was the hardest time to be seen in a moving vehicle.

Joe wondered if that had been Vern, and, if so, what Vern would be doing out at the Lidgard place.

17

When Joe got home, Wacey's mud-splashed pickup was parked in the driveway. Joe pulled in alongside it and, as he walked toward the house, sniffed his shirtsleeves. There remained a strong odor of smoke from Clyde Lidgard's trailer. Maxine met him at the door and trailed him into the house, a gold shadow not three inches from his leg. Lucy and Sheridan were playing in the living room. Lucy was again playing the role of an animal and Sheridan was feeding her invisible treats as Missy looked on, amused. Wacey was leaning against the door frame of Joe's office and Marybeth was inside, looking through Joe's desk calendar.

"Want one of your beers before I drink them all?" Wacey asked.

"Sure."

Wacey returned with a cold bottle. "You don't smell good, Joe," Wacey whispered out of the corner of his mouth as he brushed by Joe and handed him the beer. "I heard about Clyde Lidgard's trailer burning down. How in the *hell* did that happen?"

Joe was in a dark mood. He had radioed the Saddlestring

Volunteer Fire Department (they had arrived ten minutes after the framework of the trailer sighed and collapsed in on itself into a sizzling pile) as well as Sheriff Barnum (who rolled his eyes skyward and moaned ruefully) about the ball of flame. The fire department recovered what was left of his gun and holster; the black fused-together mass still smoldered in the back of his pickup where he had thrown it. Rarely had Joe Pickett felt as stupid as he did right now.

"Did you ask him yet, Marybeth?"

"Ask me what?"

Marybeth had a curious smile on her face. Joe looked from Marybeth to Wacey, puzzled.

"Wacey has a proposition for us," Marybeth said.

Wacey stepped forward and shut the office door behind him. It was a small room. Wacey grinned. Marybeth grinned.

"Aimee Kensinger has to go to Venice, Italy, for three and a half weeks with her husband," Wacey said. "She asked me if I knew anyone who would be trustworthy enough to stay in her house and keep it up and walk her dog every day. You know, that little rodent Jack Russell terrier of hers."

Joe nodded slowly, waiting for more.

"He suggested us." Marybeth added in a way that indicated to Joe that she liked the idea. "Our whole family. Even *Mom.*"

Wacey jabbed his thumb over his shoulder in the direction of Missy in the living room. "That way she could live more *in the style to which she is accustomed,*" he said, affecting enough of a pompous lilt to make Joe smile in spite of himself. "It's going to be like a family vacation without really going anywhere."

Joe turned to Marybeth. "So you want to do it?"

Marybeth spoke practically. "We're out of room, Mom's sleeping on the couch, everything seems to be falling apart, and it would be a good time to get some repairmen in here when they're not bothering everybody. It seems like we're *always* here. It *would* be kind of like having a vacation."

"Which, as far as I know, you two have never had," Wacey chimed in. "Hell of an opportunity. *Hell* of an opportunity."

"We move in Thursday," Marybeth said.

"Then I guess the matter is decided," Joe said flatly, then drained his beer.

Marybeth asked Wacey if he wanted to stay for dinner. But Wacey said he had to get home. On the way toward the door, Wacey stopped suddenly and watched Lucy and Sheridan play.

"That's a cute little dog," Wacey said.

"I'M NOT A DOGGIE!" Lucy yelled back, arching up on her feet with her chubby arms curled under her chin while Sheridan fed her an invisible treat.

"What are you, then?"

"I'm not a doggie," Lucy said, folding back down to her haunches.

Joe walked with Wacey out to his pickup. Wacey stopped and stood in the dark before he got in. Wacey had brought an unopened beer with him and Joe heard the top being unscrewed.

"Joe, do you know how it's going to look when word gets out that you burned down Clyde Lidgard's trailer?"

"Another bonehead move," Joe admitted, reaching into the bed of the pickup to see if his weapon was cool enough to touch. It was still warm. He tersely described what happened and said he couldn't understand how the fire had started. He left out the part about maybe seeing a Suburban.

"What a stroke of bad luck," Wacey said, looking at the now-useless gun. "I bet Barnum's having a good laugh about it. By tomorrow half the town will know."

Joe sighed. He couldn't believe he had lost his gun again.

Wacey took a swig of beer. "Are you sure this is something you ought to be pursuing?"

"Ote Keeley died in my woodpile. That makes it kind of personal. And to me the pieces just don't quite fit."

"What in particular?"

Joe rubbed his eyes. They stung from the fire. "Oh, I don't know. I guess I can't convince myself that Clyde Lidgard just up and shot three men for no clear reason and then stayed in their camp until we found him. And I don't know why Ote Keeley came all of the way to my backyard to die."

"Joe . . ." Wacey's voice sounded high-pitched and pained, as if he were losing patience. "Clyde Lidgard was a fucking nut. You can't explain a nut. That's why he's a nut. Just let it go."

"You sound like Barnum and everybody else."

"Maybe he's right for once," Wacey said. Joe could see the pale blue reflection of the moon on the bottom of Wacey's beer bottle as Wacey lifted it to his mouth. "Trust me, Joe. It's been investigated. Everyone's satisfied. We're just Game and Fish guys. Guts and Feathers, as our critics like to say. We aren't detectives. People think we're nothing more than glorified animal control officers. Don't be a lone ranger here. You'll just embarrass the department and get yourself in more trouble, if *that's* possible."

Joe absently kicked the dirt with his toe and looked down.

"And you never know," Wacey said, "you might find a bad guy and then reach down only to remember that you lost your damn pistol again." Joe could tell Wacey was smiling at him in the dark.

"You've made your point," Joe answered sourly.

"Just go on up with your cute little family and have a nice vacation at the Eagle Mountain Club," Wacey suggested. "Besides, hunting season's just about to get hot and heavy, and you're going to be busy as hell. We both are."

"Maybe so," Joe said.

"That's what you say when you really don't agree but you don't want to discuss it anymore," Wacey commented. "I know you pretty good, Joe. You can be a stubborn son of a bitch."

"Maybe so," Joe said. Wacey grunted, and the two men stood in silence. Billowing dark clouds were low and moving fast through the sky, painting black brush strokes over stars.

"Why don't you and Arlene stay at Kensinger's?"

Wacey snorted. "Arlene's idea of high class is eighty television channels. She wouldn't exactly appreciate that place the way Marybeth would. Besides, Arlene might find a sock of mine under the bed."

Joe nodded, though he wasn't sure he could be seen in the dark.

"I'm going to work one more week before I declare my candidacy," Wacey said after a long silence. "I'm trying for a leave of absence with the state, but if I don't get it, I'll have to quit."

"What if you don't win?" Joe asked.

"I'm going to win," Wacey said, confident as always.

"But what if you don't?"

Wacey laughed and drained his bottle, then flipped it into the back of Joe's pickup where it would rattle around tomorrow. "Hell, I don't know. I haven't given it any thought at all. Maybe I'll go back to riding bulls for a living."

Wacey opened his truck door, and they looked at each other in the glow from the dome light.

"I'm not kidding you, Joe," Wacey said, climbing in. "Leave this outfitter business be. Just go back to work and have a fun vacation with your family. You've got one hell of a family, and one hell of a wife."

Wacey slammed the door, and they were in darkness again. Wacey started his pickup and the headlights bathed the peeling paint of the garage door.

Joe listened to gravel crunch and watched Wacey's taillights recede down Bighorn Road.

Marybeth was suddenly beside him, and it startled him. He hadn't heard her come outside.

"We seem to be on a lucky streak," she said, looping her arm through his. "First the job offer and now the Eagle Mountain Club."

"I might have broken that streak this afternoon," Joe said.

"What's bothering you?" Marybeth asked. "You didn't exactly get excited when Wacey told you about it."

"I am excited," Joe said flatly. "You and the kids will probably love it. And your mom, of course."

She tugged on his arm playfully. "So what's the problem?"

He started to say "nothing," but she anticipated it and tugged on his arm again. He didn't want to mention burning down the trailer and losing his gun. Still, that wasn't the problem.

"I guess I just feel bad that we live in such a dump that house-sitting seems like a vacation."

"Oh, Joe," Marybeth said, giving him a hug. "We both know this won't last forever."

Joe opened his mail while Marybeth got ready for bed. The mail was mostly junk, but there were several envelopes from headquarters in Cheyenne. There were two departmental memos, one about avoiding overtime and the other about making sure that original receipts were sent along with expense reports because credit card receipts could no longer be accepted.

When he opened the third envelope and read the letter it contained, he froze. It was written in terse bureaucratic prose and he read it three times before it sunk in. He blew a short, hard breath out through his nose in exasperation as he resisted the urge to tear the letter into tiny pieces.

"What is it?" Marybeth asked from behind a washcloth.

"Headquarters," Joe said dryly. "I've got to appear in Cheyenne on Friday for a hearing."

Marybeth stopped washing and listened.

"They're investigating the incident when Ote Keeley took my gun from me. They call it 'alleged negligence with a department-issued sidearm.' It says here that I could get suspended from the field."

Joe read the letter a fourth time to himself.

"Why now?" Marybeth asked. "That happened months ago."

"The state works in geological time," Joe said. "You know that."

"Those bastards," she hissed. She rarely said anything like that, and Joe looked up. "Just when things were going so well."

PART FOUR

E) (1) Establishment of Committee

There is established a committee to be known as the Endangered Species Committee (hereinafter in this section referred to as the "Committee").

(2) The Committee shall review any application submitted to it pursuant to this section and determine in accordance with subsection (h) or this section whether or not to grant an exemption from the requirements of subsection (a) (2) of this action for the action set forth in such application.

(3) The Committee shall be composed of seven members as follows:

(A) The Secretary of Agriculture.

(B) The Secretary of the Army.

(C) The Chairman of the Council of Economic Advisors.

(D) The Administrator of the Environmental Protection Agency.

(E) The Secretary of the Interior.

(F) The Administrator of the National Oceanic and Atmospheric Administration.

(G) The Governor of each affected State.

—The Endangered Species Act Amendments of 1982

18

Sheridan went outside to tell her animals that she'd be away for a little while, but they were nowhere to be found. Not only that, but she felt as though someone were watching her.

Sheridan's pockets were bulging with as much food as she could cram into them and still get out the door without her mom noticing. She had sunflower seeds, croutons, dry dog food, and cereal in the pockets of her skirt. It was more food than she had ever taken out to the animals, but she didn't know when she would be back to feed them again. She was very upset about having to leave the house again, this time to go and stay in the home of people she had never even met before: a stranger's home at Eagle Mountain. Mom couldn't even tell her when they would be back. Sheridan didn't care to see what Eagle Mountain was ("wealthy people share their homes all of the time!" her Grandmother Missy kept telling her. "And they have a pool!"), because she already hated it. Grandmother Missy had said that the girls at school would be envious of her, but Sheridan didn't really care about that. Grandmother

Missy liked it when other people were envious, but Sheridan wasn't sure it was all that great. Sheridan thought that taking the entire family to Eagle Mountain would be a big mistake, just as she had when she, Mom, and Lucy had stayed at the motel in town. So many things her parents did for her benefit didn't seem to help her at all. She told her mom and Grandmother Missy that. She didn't want to leave her home again, and she especially didn't want to leave Lucky, Hippity-Hop, and Elway.

But the animals didn't seem to be there.

It wasn't as if the creatures always came bounding out of the woodpile at the sight of her. Sometimes it took a while before one of them would realize she was out there. But as Sheridan walked across the yard, there was something about the woodpile that seemed vacant. The secret life was gone from it. It was just a woodpile.

She rained some seeds on the top of it and waited, looking closely for any movement. She sighed and sat under the cottonwood, her chin in her hands. Hot tears welled in her eyes. Where could the animals have gone? Could they be hurt, or worse? Did she feed them something that made them sick? Did they leave during the night and go back into the mountains? Could it be that they just didn't like her anymore? Or that they knew she was leaving and were so sad or angry that they didn't even want to see her?

"This," she said out loud to herself, "is a really bad day."

And she could not get over the feeling that she was being watched.

She shinnied around the trunk of the tree and looked at the house, fully expecting to see her mom or grandmother at the window. Or at least Lucy. But no one was there. Maybe that was it, she thought. Maybe her secret pets sensed someone's eyes on them as well.

Squinting, she looked all around her. She took in the rest of the yard, the Sandrock draw pulsing red in the evening sun, and even the roof of the house. She tucked a strand of blond hair behind her ear. But she could see no one. It was giving her the creeps, and her imagination started to wander. For the first time in weeks, she thought of the monster again. It came from somewhere deep in her mind, as if it had been there waiting for the right moment all along. Maybe, she speculated, the monster, or the monster's friend, had come back for Lucky, Hippity-Hop, and Elway.

When she stood her stomach ached. The feelings welling up inside of her were overwhelming: anger, fear, and guilt. Maybe she should have told her mom and dad about the creatures. If she had told them, possibly they would somehow still be around. Her dad could have caught them and built nice houses for them, like he did when he built the rabbit hutch. Maybe by not saying anything, she had caused the creatures to die.

She decided she would give the creatures a little more time. If they didn't come out, she would rush in the house and find her mom. She would tell her everything. When Dad came home they could take the woodpile apart, stick by stick, until they found the poor little animals. Eagle Mountain could wait.

She threw more food on the woodpile, this time harder. There was no way the animals, if they were okay, would not know she was out there.

Then she heard the familiar trill. She was suddenly joyous.

But the sound did not come from the woodpile. She stood as silently as possible, listening and smiling.

When she heard the sound again, her head swiveled toward it. Past the woodpile, past the fence, past the bushes. She found herself staring through bushy leaves at the peeling paint on the back of the garage.

She found them. They had moved, for whatever reason. The sound came from the other side of thick lilac bushes, and she crawled toward it on her hands and knees. She knew the area around their house so well that she was certain where she would find her pets: under the foundation of the garage. There were some large cracks in the concrete where the structure met the ground, and the cracks led to a large dark space under the floor of the garage. She had once probed the space with a long stick and had not been able to find the sides. That, she was sure, was where she would find them.

When she emerged from the bushes, the first thing she saw was Lucky sticking his head out of the crack and then vanishing under the garage.

"Boy, am I glad to see you," she said, emptying her pockets into the hole. "That ought to keep you guys full for a while." The relief she felt made her giddy. "I'll be back as soon as I can be, you can count on that." She felt as wildly good as she had horribly bad a moment before.

"You guys are pretty smart." She smiled, pulling her pockets inside out to get every last sunflower seed. "This is a much safer place for you."

Rather than crawl through the bushes again back into the yard, Sheridan skipped down the length of the lilacs toward the end of the fence and the corner of corral. She planned to turn and enter the yard through the same gate the monster had used.

As she turned toward the corral, she saw the face of a man in the window of the pole barn, and it stopped her cold.

The man's face withdrew from the window into the shadows of the barn and then reemerged in the doorway, so that she could now see all of him. He stood in the light but didn't step outside into the corral. He was motioning to her to come to him. He was smiling. She had been *right* about being watched.

Sheridan couldn't move. She was terrified. She didn't know whether to scream for her mom, run for the gate, or run back toward the garage. If she ran back to the garage, the man might follow her and maybe see the animals.

"Sheridan, right?" The man asked softly. He spoke just loud enough for her to hear him. "I need to talk to you for a second. Don't be afraid," the man said. "I know your dad."

He did look familiar, Sheridan thought. She had seen him before with her dad. She didn't know his name, and if she had been told what it was, she had forgotten. There were a lot of people who came to their house because it was Dad's office also. There had been a lot of men at their house when the dead man was found. She knew she shouldn't talk to strangers. But if he knew her dad and her name, was he really a stranger? She weighed going to the man against screaming or running to the house. If the man saw her feed the animals, he might tell her mom. If she ran screaming, she might embarrass her dad.

The man kept smiling and motioning for her to come.

She walked toward him on stiff, heavy legs. Her eyes were huge. She walked past the gate and ducked through the poles of the corral. Still, the man stayed in the pole barn. Sheridan suddenly realized that he was standing there so he couldn't be seen by anyone in the house, and she knew she had made the wrong decision. She turned to run, but he was on her in an instant, and he jerked her back roughly into a dark stall with him.

He swung her around and pressed her against the hay bales, and her scream was smothered by his hand. His face was so close to hers that his hat brim jammed against her forehead and his breath fogged her glasses.

"I'm sorry I had to do this, darling," he whispered when she had stopped struggling. "I really am. I wished you hadn't come around the yard that way. I didn't expect you and you saw me."

He kept his hand, massive and rough, crushed against her mouth. Her breath came in quick little puffs from her nose, and he didn't intend to let her answer.

"Before I take my hand down, there is something you have to understand, Sheridan. Are you listening?"

She tried to nod her head yes. She was trembling, and she couldn't make herself stop. She was suddenly afraid she would wet her panties.

"Are you listening?" he asked again. This time his voice was very gentle. "Are you listening?"

She said with her eyes that she was.

"You've got some secrets, don't you little girl? You've got some little friends in the woodpile, don't you? I've been watching you. I saw you feeding them."

The big hand did not move from her mouth.

"Do your mom and dad know about them?"

She tried to shake her head no. Even though he pressed her to the hay, he could tell what she was trying to say because he smiled a little.

"You're not lying to me, are you, Sheridan?"

As forcefully as she could, she tried to say no. He pressed his face even closer to her. His eyes were all she could see of his face.

"Okay, then. That's good. We both have a secret, don't we? And we're going to keep it our secret, just between us. Just between us friends. You just keep this to yourself and don't you ever say a word about this to anyone. Look at me."

Sheridan had averted her eyes toward the door, hoping her dad would be there.

"Look at me," he hissed.

She did.

"If you say one thing about this to anyone, I'll rip those pretty green eyes of yours right out of their sockets. And I won't stop there."

With his free hand, Sheridan felt him reach back. She heard a snap and a huge black gun filled her vision.

"I'll use this on your dad. I'll shoot him right in the face. I'll do the same thing to your pretty mom and your itty-bitty sister. I'll even kill that stupid dog. I'll blow her head right off. *Keep looking at me,*" he said.

She had stopped shaking; she was beyond it. She was absolutely calm, and absolutely terrified.

"I'm going to take my hand down now and let you go as soon as you can smile," he said. "Then you take that smile right into the house and never, ever tell anyone what happened here. Your little animals in the woodpile are going to heaven, do you understand? Your family won't have to go to heaven or anywhere else if you keep your little mouth shut."

He eased his hand down. Her face felt cold as the air hit it. Her lips had been crushed against her teeth, and she tasted a drop of salty blood from inside her mouth.

"Are you listening, Sheridan?"

"Yes." Her voice was thin, and it nearly cracked.

"Then smile."

She tried. She didn't feel like smiling.

"That's not a smile," he chided, his voice gentle again. "You can do better than that, darling."

She tried.

"Closer," he persisted. "Keep working on it."

Her mouth smiled.

"We can live with that," he said, stepping back. His crushing weight was now off of her. She stood up. She winced as he reached over her shoulder, but he was just brushing the hay off of her dress.

"Don't be scared of me," he admonished. He sounded like a normal person now. She was as confused as she was frightened. "Nothing bad will ever happen because we've got a deal. I won't break it if you don't. Shoot," he said, "we might even turn out to be friends someday. That'd be nice, wouldn't it?"

"Yes," she said. But she was lying.

"You might even get a little older, and I'll take you to a movie. Buy you a Coke and some popcorn." He smoothed her dress across her bottom, pressing his hand more firmly than he needed to. "You might even like it."

They both looked up when they heard her mom call her name.

"You had better go now, darling," he said.

19

The house he was looking for was located down a mud-rutted dirt road in a thick stand of shadowy, old river cottonwoods. Joe had never been down the road before, but he had often passed by the crooked wood-burned sign on a post near the county road that read:

OTE KEELEY OUTFITTING SERVICES
GUIDED HUNTS
ELK • DEER • ANTELOPE • MOOSE
SINCE 1996

The Keeley house was a pine log home that looked tired. There was a slight sag in the roof, its once dark green wood shingles now gray and furry-looking with age and moisture. In the alcove where the house slumped, there was a rusty 1940s Willys Jeep, a horse trailer, an equipment shed, and a yellow Subaru station wagon. Antlers hung above the doors of the house and the shed. Joe shut off his pickup, sat with the window opened, and listened. The heavy, damp quiet of the river bottom lay over the house and to Joe the scene seemed to be more Deep South than Rocky Mountain. Cross beams in the trees indicated that Ote had hung game animals in his yard.

Joe had checked in some fishermen early that morning, working his way upriver toward the Keeley house. He had ticketed a local ranch hand for using worms in a stretch of the river that was regulated for artificial lures only and had cited two itinerant Hispanics who were fishing without any licenses at all. Before he had left the house that morning, he had called Game and Fish Headquarters in Cheyenne to talk to the officer who had sent him the letter he received earlier in the week, Assistant Director Les Etbauer. Etbauer wasn't in yet, so Joe left a message that he would see him that afternoon for his hearing.

Joe walked by the yellow Subaru on his way toward the front door of the house and glanced inside the car. There was a child's car seat, and scattered on the bench seats and floorboards were fast-food wrappers, plastic toys, and children's books.

The unmistakable sound of a shell being jacked into a pump shotgun froze Joe in place where he walked. He was mindful of where his hand was in relation to his holster—*Damn! He was unarmed*—and he slowly raised both his arms away from his body so there could be no mistaking that he wasn't reaching for a gun.

Jeannie Keeley, Ote's widow, stood in the open front door of the house with a .12-gauge riot gun aimed at his chest. She was wearing some kind of uniform smock and a pair of faded jeans.

Using a soft voice, Joe said who he was and said he would show her his identification if she wanted to see it.

"I know who you are," she said. "I remember from the funeral."

"In that case, I would suggest you put that shotgun away somewhere safe," Joe said. "I don't even have my weapon with me." He spoke softly but there was a edge to his voice. Jeannie Keeley shrugged and stepped back inside the house and placed the shotgun in a rack near the door.

"Sorry," she said, not really apologizing. "I'm not usually home during the day so I didn't expect anybody showing up. I got a sick kid here and I've been a little jumpy since Ote died."

"I understand." Joe stood up straight, took a few deep breaths, and unclenched his muscles. He decided against telling her that he could arrest her for aiming a gun at him because he figured it would be pointless. Jeannie, like Ote before her, seemed capable of getting the drop on Joe Pickett very easily. He told her he would like to ask her some questions about Ote.

She stood in the doorway, trying to look tough, Joe thought. Her unlit cigarette bobbed up and down as she seemed to think about it, and him. She was wary of him. He read the name embroidered on her smock. She was a waitress at the Burg-O-Pardner restaurant in Saddlestring. That was the place that specialized in deep-fried Rocky Mountain oysters and one-pound hamburgers for lunch.

"I'd rather not invite you in the house," she said. "I got a sick kid in there, and it's kind of small. The house I mean."

"I don't mind staying out here," Joe said.

Inside the house, from the dark, a young girl called for her mom. Jeannie glanced over her shoulder and back at Joe.

"Oh hell," she said. "Come on in."

Joe sat down at a rough-hewn wood table in the kitchen while Jeannie tended to a girl Sheridan's age. There were four rooms in the dark house. The kitchen and dining room were crowded by the number of animal heads on the walls. Off of the dining room were a bathroom, a bedroom, and another bedroom that looked as if it were crammed full with bunk beds. Joe thought *his* house was small, and he wondered how the Keeley family managed without tripping over one another.

April, the girl with the haunted face that Joe had seen at the funeral, was in the bottom bunk of one of the beds, and Joe could see a tangle of sheets and wet, dark hair. Jeannie gave the girl a glass of something and asked her to rest and be quiet until the man went away. The girl nodded her reply. Joe could also see another child—he couldn't tell if it was a boy or girl—playing on the floor in the room. The child wore only a disposable diaper and a T-shirt that was torn and dirty.

Jeannie came back into the kitchen and asked if Joe wanted coffee. He said no and she sat down with a cup for herself. She took the cigarette out of her mouth and put it in an ashtray.

"I can't smoke on account of I'm expecting, as you can tell," Jeannie said. "But sometimes I just have to stick one in my mouth for a while. It helps."

Jeannie went on to tell Joe a lot of things he would rather not have known, like how Ote had no insurance when he died. How Ote spent every dime they made on horses, guns, outfitting equipment, and that damned truck he was buried in. How the Ford dealership in Casper where Ote bought the truck was on her case because, come to find out, Ote had missed the last three payments and they wanted the truck back and wouldn't *that* be a hoot? How Ote married her when he was home on leave from the army and she was a junior in high school and got her pregnant for the first time on their wedding night. That was three and a half kids ago. How Ote spent everything he saved in the service to buy this cabin and land in Wyoming so he could live his dream of killing things and getting away from people. He wanted to be a mountain man. He liked to say he was born 180 years too late. Ote hated people, but mainly he hated the government. Ote believed in the right to keep and bear arms. Ote told her all the time how he would die when the Feds came to get him for one thing or another. That's why he kept himself armed. That's why he showed her how to use and shoot the shotgun they kept in a rack near the door. That's why he wore a Derringer holster in his boot. Ote always thought his outfitting business would take off someday. He guaranteed a trophy to any of his clients on the promise that they wouldn't tell anyone when, where, or how they got it. He wanted to buy a float plane and expand into Alaska someday. He wanted to homeschool his kids, but she wouldn't let him because the kids drove her nuts when they were home all day, and besides, someday they would have to get jobs and go out on their own and Ote didn't know enough himself to teach anybody anything except how to butcher an elk. How Ote liked being with Kyle Lensegrav and Calvin Mendes more than he liked being around anyone else. Ote was a mean-spirited *prick* of a man. Ote thought he knew everything, but he was basically Mississippi white trash in the middle of northern Wyoming. He left her nothing, not even the damned truck. She would have to go on welfare, money from the government he hated. Wouldn't *that* make Ote spin in his grave? She thought there might be insurance and benefits through the Veterans Administration, since Ote was a veteran. She needed to pursue that. Again, money from the government he hated. Ote would keep spinning down there. Like a top. She would have to sell the house and the cars and move. Maybe she would take the kids; maybe she wouldn't. She wasn't sure. Her mama in Mississippi could take them for a while until she got her shit together. Go to Colorado, maybe. New Mexico. Arizona. Somewhere it was warmer. A good waitress could get a job anywhere.

Joe listened and watched her. He was as unprepared for this torrent as he had been unprepared for her at the door with the shotgun. She would not stop talking. She was bitter about Ote's death, but possibly just as bitter at the life he had given her and left her with. Joe could see that she could have been pretty when Ote had married her. But her features were now sharp, and her outlook was flinty. He was surprised how quiet the children were in the other room. He wondered if they were simply terrified of her. And she was going to have another.

"When he died, it was in *your* yard," she said, her eyes flashing. "He didn't even have the decency to die in his own yard. The *prick.* I had to sell his horses to pay for that funeral. I didn't know how much a front-end loader cost to rent. Why did I pay for his perfect funeral? Why? I'm so goddamned idiotic. He wouldn't have done that for me if I'd got shot. I bet he would have gotten drunk with his pals Kyle and Calvin and burned my body on a pyre like some kind of Indian woman."

Joe rubbed his neck. He stole a glance at his watch. She had been going nonstop for forty-five minutes. He would need to leave soon if he wanted to get to Cheyenne on time.

"Aren't you the guy Ote took the gun from?" she asked suddenly, grinning.

Joe said he was.

"Damn, he was proud of that," she said. "He couldn't stop talking about it for a while. Then he realized he could lose his outfitter's license. Then he got scared and depressed. You've got to understand that if Ote had lost his license, he might as well have been dead. It would have killed him. It drove me up the wall, him talking about it."

Joe looked at her as she talked, but his attention was diverted by the absolute quiet in the other room where the children were. He wanted to know what was wrong with the little girl in bed.

"Ote liked you," Jeannie said. "He bragged for a while about that gun thing, then he got scared. He said he thought you were a good man. He said you were fair and square, not like Vern Dunnegan."

Joe asked what she meant.

She shrugged. "Ote didn't tell me a lot about his business. All I know is that Ote was really mad once because Vern caught him doing something—poaching, probably—and Vern made Ote make it right with him."

"You mean a bribe?" Joe asked.

"Something," Jeannie said. "Vern made Ote do something, but I don't know what. All I know is that Ote was pretty mad about it. This wasn't a fun place to be when Ote was mad."

But she didn't know what specifically had happened.

"That's the way things work," she concluded, as if she had forgotten Joe was a warden.

"Not necessarily," Joe said.

Joe couldn't listen to her much longer. He stood and asked her if he could get a glass of water. She waved toward the sink. On the way there, he paused at the children's bedroom door. April was in the bed. She looked feverish, her hair plastered to her skull, but her eyes were calm and piercing. On the floor, a baby boy with big dark eyes turned to him. There was a look on the boy's face that suggested he expected Joe to step in and smack him. But Joe could see no bruises or injuries on either child.

He turned on the spigot and filled his glass with brackish water that came from their well. Jeannie Keeley was staring at him. He absolutely could not figure her out. She could be cool and abrupt one minute, and absolutely gushing words the next. He wouldn't have been surprised if she had stood and walked back over to the rack and pulled down the shotgun again and aimed it at him. This house and the people in it were crazy.

"Did Ote give you whatever he was going to give you to make things right?" she asked.

Joe paused with the glass nearly to his lips.

"Ote said he had something that once you saw it you would drop all the charges against him and he'd have his license back. Did he give it to you?"

"No. Did Ote tell you what it was?" Joe asked.

"Something he and the rest of the guys found. Some kind of animal."

"What kind of animal?"

She paused and screwed up her face. From the bedroom the little girl cried, "Mama."

"SHUT UP AND BE STILL," Jeannie Keeley roared without looking toward the bedroom, and there was silence.

"What kind of animal?"

"I can't remember for sure. We laughed about it, though. I had a gym teacher by that name in high school, I remember that."

"What was the gym teacher's name?"

"Mr. Merle Miller. We called him 'Killer Miller.'"

"Was it," Joe paused, searching his memory for the answer, "a Miller's weasel?" He vaguely recalled the name from a course he once took in biology. All he could remember was that the species was indigenous to the Rocky Mountain west and had been extinct for at least a century, maybe longer.

"Could've been," she said. "That sounds familiar, I think."

"Did he tell you any more about it?" Joe asked.

She reached into her smock for a book of matches. She lit the cigarette she had put in the ashtray and inhaled deeply. "Can't do it," she muttered. "I been since breakfast without a cigarette. I got to learn to quit. Ote would be pissed if he was here." Which meant she had been smoking all along.

"Did he tell you any more about the Miller's weasel?" Joe asked again, this time letting his voice rise.

"Ote never told me nothing," she said flatly.

When Joe drove out of the cottonwood trees into the sagebrush and the bright white sunlight, he could not get three things out of his mind. The first was what Jeannie had said about the animal Ote was going to give him. The second was the manic, almost deranged look she had had on her face when she told him about Ote. The last was the look on April's face when Joe first saw her in the bedroom. He had seen the expression before, but only on domestic animals. It was Maxine's expression, the Labrador look. It said: *please hit me if it will make you feel better.*

The static sound of gravel crunching stopped abruptly as his tires climbed onto the smooth pavement of the state highway. He pressed the accelerator and the engine roared. Twin spoors of dirt trailed him on the blacktop. He could not get away from the place fast enough.

He turned in the direction of the interstate highway, away from Saddlestring. The drive to Cheyenne would take six hours.

To hunt and fish in the State of Wyoming, Joe thought, people were required to buy licenses and, in some cases, pass tests that proved they knew how to use firearms and knew Game and Fish regulations. There were no such requirements for having children.

20

From the moment he walked into Game and Fish Headquarters in Cheyenne and said he was Joe Pickett and he was there to see Les Etbauer for a meeting, the atmosphere changed within the room. The receptionist looked at him warily and pushed herself away from her desk as if he were contagious. Joe noticed that two young female license agents shot looks at him the instant they heard his name, then quickly turned back to their computer monitors as if suddenly reading the most fascinating e-mails they had ever seen. The receptionist directed him down a long hallway and told him to take a seat on the molded plastic seat outside of a door. Painted on the frosted glass were the words LESLEY ETBAUER, ASSISTANT DIRECTOR.

Joe took off his hat and sat down. There wasn't much to look at. The sprawling cinder-block building had been built in the early 1960s, and the walls were painted institutional yellow and lit with industrial neon tubes. The hallway was narrow and the black-and-white checkerboard linoleum floor was scarred. It was the kind of hallway that echoed and amplified the rat-a-tat sounds of clicking heels as people walked down it. Not that there were many employees about; most of the doors in the hall were shut and there were no lights on behind the glass. He recognized many of the names on the doors as his agency superiors, but apparently they were already gone for the day. As he sat waiting for Les Etbauer, Joe realized that he felt as though he was back in grade school and he'd been sent to the principal's office. Like most of the field wardens, Joe had spent as little time as possible inside this building. This was where the agency bureaucracy was, where policy was set and regulations formed. It was here that the director met with the governor and individual legislators while they were in town for the legislative session and where laws and new regulations were hammered out and concessions were made. This was the place where hunters, fishermen, landowners, and environmentalists stormed (although they rarely made it past the front counter) when things didn't go their particular way. It was the place where all of those departmental memos came from. It was a place where they knew him, but he really didn't know them.

During the long drive to Cheyenne, Joe had had a lot of time to think. He had mulled over not only where the investigation of the outfitter murders seemed to be leading him, but also about the things Vern had said in the bar. It was the first time since this had all started that Joe had had the free time to try and put the things that he'd learned together. The conclusions he had reached unsettled him.

A man with an open collar and a short-sleeved dress shirt that stretched across his large belly approached from an office far down the hallway, and Joe looked up at him as he passed. The man stopped warily and turned around.

"You're Joe Pickett?" The man asked.

Joe nodded.

The man looked down the hall in both directions to make sure no one was coming.

"I just want you to know that there are a lot of people here who think you're getting screwed."

"Really?" Joe had not realized he had been the subject of discussion at headquarters, although the behavior of two license clerks behind the counter had hinted at that.

The man took a tentative step toward Joe and bent forward. "We hope you fight it and take it all the way to the governor," he said. "This kind of good old boy shit has gone far enough."

Joe was confused. "You seem to know a lot more about what's going to happen here than I do."

The man snorted and a smug look passed over his face. "Why do you think they'd want you here at four o'clock on Friday afternoon if the whole thing wasn't cut and dried? Think about it. If you get mad and want to protest, there's nobody to hear you until Monday morning."

"What . . ." Joe started to ask but the man turned quickly on his heel and continued down the hall. The receptionist had reappeared.

He was going to be suspended. It was simply a matter of time until Etbauer pronounced those words. He had said a lot of words, Joe thought, but not those. Joe sat and listened. His mouth was dry, and his hands were wet. He couldn't quite believe this was happening even as he sat there. In his career, he had never received either a verbal or a written warning regarding his conduct, except for when he arrested the new governor for fishing without a license. His performance reviews had always been good if not brilliant. He had done his job well, he thought, to the best of his ability and according to regulations. He had tried very hard to be honest and fair. He had not cut corners, and he had worked hard. The time he spent working was far beyond what was required of him and he never asked for overtime or compensatory time. He never cheated on expense reports. He had reported what had happened with Ote Keeley because it was the right thing to do. He had never even suspected that it would result in anything but, at the worst, a mild reprimand. After all, he had recovered the weapon and arrested Ote with an ironclad case of poaching.

But he was going to be suspended. Joe felt as though the wind had been kicked out if him.

Etbauer went on and on in a thin, nasal voice. He sat behind his desk and read aloud the report Joe had written about Ote Keeley taking his gun. When he was through reading Joe's report, Etbauer found the passages in the agency handbook that pertained to department-issued firearms and read those aloud. Joe hoped like hell that Etbauer wouldn't notice that he wasn't wearing his gun now and ask him about it.

Etbauer had a wide, flushed alcoholic face and thick, photo-gray glasses. Joe also noticed that he was balding. He didn't speak with Joe as much as speak to him. There was a quiver in his voice, and he mispronounced some of the words. It was as if Etbauer was reading aloud from a script.

Joe didn't know much about Etbauer, but he had heard things. According to Wacey, Etbauer had gone straight from the U.S. Army to the Game and Fish Department without a real job in between. Wacey had called Etbauer "the ultimate government employee," a man who had never collected a paycheck in his life that wasn't from either the state or the Federal government. He had attained his rank due to a particularly bureaucratic method known as ADV or "advanced due to vacancy." That meant that Etbauer simply put in his time and moved up as others moved out or retired. As state employees either left to take other jobs or start businesses of their own, bureaucrats like Etbauer (who no private sector employer would ever want on the payroll) simply grew in power and seniority like a tumor within the agency, amassing security and building a fine pension.

Joe had always considered individual words as finite units of currency, and he believed in savings. He never wanted to waste or unnecessarily expend words. To Joe, words meant things. They should be spent wisely. Joe sometimes paused for a long time until he could come up with the right words to express exactly what he wanted to say. Sometimes it confused people (Marybeth fretted that perhaps people thought Joe was slow) but Joe could live with that. That's why Joe despised meetings where he felt the participants acted as if they were paid by the number of words spoken and, as a result, the words began to cheapen by the minute until they meant nothing at all. In Joe's experience, the person who talked the most very often had the least to say. He sometimes wished that every human was allotted a certain number of words to use for their lifetime. When the allotment ran out, that person would be forced into silence. If this were the case, Joe would still have more than enough in his account while people like Les Etbauer would be very quiet. Joe had attended meetings where little got accomplished except what he considered the random drive-by spewing of words, like unaimed machine-gun bullets. What a waste of words, he often thought. What a waste of currency. What a waste of bullets.

Joe realized that there had finally been a pause and snapped back to the present. Etbauer was staring at him.

"I said," Etbauer asked, miffed that Joe had ignored him, "how could something like this happen?"

"Easier than you might think," retorted Joe.

Etbauer narrowed his eyes with scorn. This was not the answer he had been waiting to hear.

"I was writing out a citation," Joe said. "It's in the report. I was holding the clipboard with one hand and a pen with the other. I admit that I wasn't prepared for what happened, and I regret that it happened, and it's my fault that I let it happen."

"But he took your weapon," Etbauer said, as if bolstering his case. "He took it from you while you just stood there." Etbauer said it with disbelief, as if he couldn't imagine anyone being as stupid as Joe Pickett.

Joe stood up suddenly from his chair, reached across the desk, plucked Etbauer's name badge from his shirt pocket and sat back down. Etbauer looked at him with wide eyes, and a hint of panic.

"See what I mean?" Joe asked, holding up the name badge. "Even if you realize what's going on, sometimes you just can't react quickly enough because you're kind of boggled that it's happening in the first place."

Etbauer swallowed, trying to recover his authority. But his voice was weak: "Give me back my badge."

Joe slid it across the desk. "You thought I was going to pop you in the mouth, didn't you?" Joe asked. "And you still weren't able to do anything about it. Well, that's what happened with Ote. I screwed up, but I didn't expect it at the time. Just like you."

Etbauer's face was now bright red. He wouldn't look Joe in the eye. When he said that he had carefully reviewed the report and the evidence and that his determination was that Joe was to be officially suspended without pay as of next Tuesday, September 30, he was declaring all of it to a place on the wall behind and far to the right of where Joe sat.

In addition, Etbauer said, there had been some other very disturbing reports. Serious allegations.

"We plan to investigate whether or not there has been a serious dereliction of duty while you investigate murders that have already been solved. And there is some question of whether or not you destroyed evidence that could link the accused to the crime."

When Joe asked who had made the reports, Etbauer cautioned that "he was not at liberty to say." Joe felt a chill snake down his spine.

Etbauer continued. "Let me inform you right now that because of your recent actions and behavior, we are going to investigate whether or not you should be a suspect in the crimes themselves. Do you understand the gravity of this?"

Joe nodded. He certainly did, but he had trouble speaking.

"Me, a suspect?" he finally croaked.

"You, a suspect," Etbauer confirmed, his smile cruel. "We hope you can be cleared quickly because, frankly, if you aren't, it would cast the entire department under a black cloud, and we wouldn't want that."

Joe sighed. Etbauer was clearly a vicious, petty bureaucrat who lived for opportunities like this.

"Department policy states that you can challenge the suspension at the next Game and Fish Commission meeting, which takes place at the end of next month, by submitting a written appeal to the director. You've got three days to journal your area. Your duties will be turned over to an interim warden in an adjacent district who will be assigned on Monday."

Joe discovered that his mouth was too dry to swallow.

"You're dismissed," Etbauer said. "There's not much more I can say right now."

Joe stood. He knew it would all hit him later, but at the moment he felt both angry and oddly calm.

"At least give the Saddlestring district to Wacey Hedeman," Joe said. "He knows it pretty well, and he's a good hand."

"We'll consider it." Etbauer said, fingering the name badge Joe had snatched. "You're dismissed."

Before Joe opened the door, he turned to Etbauer.

"Have you ever done this before?" Joe asked. "Suspended an active field warden for this kind of first-time violation?"

Etbauer flushed again and looked away. Joe followed Etbauer's sight line. He was looking at a digital clock on a credenza behind him. It was 4:58 P.M.

"Anybody tell you to do this now?" Joe asked.

"Of course not," Etbauer replied, still looking at the clock.

"Nobody called you and said, 'Les, I need you to move this Pickett gun thing to the top of the pile'?"

Etbauer wheeled around in his chair. "Of course not." He was defensive. "This conversation is over."

Joe opened the door. The receptionist who had been standing outside, listening, quickly gathered herself together and escaped down the hallway, her shoes clicking like an old Royal typewriter.

"It was never a conversation," Joe said to Etbauer. "A lynching maybe, but not a conversation."

He slammed the door so hard behind him that he stopped in the hall to make sure he hadn't cracked the glass.

He found an unoccupied, unlocked office and called Marybeth at the Kensinger house. Joe still felt strangely calm, but the need to talk to his wife was urgent. He wanted her thoughts after he told her what had happened. When she answered the telephone, he asked her how she liked the new place.

"Oh, it's nice," she said, but he could tell from her voice that she was completely enraptured. "Five bedrooms, four bathrooms. A beautiful deck that overlooks the Twelve Sleep River, a Jacuzzi, a kitchen the size of our house and a dining room the size of a stadium. All of the closets are walk-in and so is the refrigerator. A breakfast bar and three fireplaces, one in the master bedroom. Mom and Lucy just love it. Right now, they're out walking Maxine and the Kensinger dog around the golf course."

Joe felt better just hearing her voice. After what he'd just been through, he needed to hear it.

"You didn't mention Sheridan," Joe said. "What does she think?"

Marybeth paused before she spoke. "I don't know for sure. She doesn't seem real excited for some reason. She didn't eat any lunch, and she didn't want to go out with Mom. She's just sitting in the living room staring out the window."

"Is it just the change of scenery?" Joe asked, thinking about how much they had moved Sheridan around from place to place in the last few years. The consistency and routine of the Saddlestring house was something Sheridan obviously enjoyed. Maybe she thought they were moving again.

"I hope that's all it is," Marybeth said. "I hope she isn't coming down with something."

Joe agreed. Then he said it: "Marybeth, the department has suspended me without pay as of Tuesday because Ote Keeley took my gun. They also suspect me of somehow being involved in the outfitter murders."

She gasped. "Oh my God, Joe."

He said nothing and neither did Marybeth. Finally, he asked if she was still there.

"Joe, what does this mean?"

"Two things, I think," Joe said, with as much confidence as he could muster. "The first is that there are some pretty powerful people who want me out of the field. The second is that it looks like you're talking to the newest employee of InterWest Resources."

"Are you sure?" she asked. "Joe, is this something you really want to do?" Her concern was genuine, and he loved her for it.

"I don't see a lot of options," he said. "I've got a family to support."

"What about the house?" Marybeth asked.

"We can stay in it through an appeal, if we decide to appeal."

"Joe . . ."

"I've got three days before I'm officially relieved," Joe interrupted. "I want to spend those three days following up on a few things I was thinking about on the ride down here. Then I'll let Vern know what the decision is. Is that okay with you?"

"Of course."

"I'll be home tonight," Joe said. "But don't wait up for me."

"I love you, Joe Pickett," Marybeth said.

"I love you, too."

Joe went downstairs into an area marked WILDLIFE BIOLOGY SECTION. He walked past a desk already vacated by a secretary, then into a maze of small cubicles and tables littered with lab equipment. It smelled of wet fur and feathers and strong disinfectant, and without any windows, it was dark down there. His boot steps seemed amplified in the empty room as he walked though the middle corridor looking for anyone who might still be working.

When he saw the woman emerge from her cubicle with a jacket folded over her arm and a handbag, he knew immediately who she was. She had that harried look about her that said she had children at day care and she was on her way to pick them up.

"Working late on Friday?" Joe asked, smiling.

"Later than I wanted to be," she said, looking him over and clearly wondering why he was down there. "Can I help you find something? I'm kind of in a hurry."

He recognized her voice.

"I'm Joe Pickett," he said. "I believe we spoke on the telephone last week."

The look on her face confirmed it. Her expression was pained.

"I'm sorry to bother you when you're in a hurry and all, so I'll get right to it," Joe said. "I appreciate what you did. It took guts and I know you could get in trouble for it. As far as I'm concerned, we're not even talking right now. I don't know your name, and I'm not going to ask."

She continued to watch him suspiciously. He could tell that she was trying to decide whether or not to simply walk away.

"Yes?" she prompted.

"Would you please show me where I can look up some information on an endangered species? Actually, it's an animal that is thought to be extinct."

Her face was a mask. "Is the species indigenous to Wyoming and the Rocky Mountains?"

"Yup."

She made up her mind and shrugged. "Oh, come on," she said. "It'll only take a minute, and then you're on your own."

She walked quickly down the length of the room into a library cluttered with reference books and journals. Joe followed. There was a computer and fax machine on one stand and a microfiche reader on another. She put her coat and handbag on a shelf while she booted up the computer, double-clicked through a series of menu screens, and pulled up a document database.

"Do you know how to operate this?" she asked.

"I do," Joe said. He thought he did, anyway.

"Key in what you're looking for. If the search turns up something, you'll get an index number and a title for the publication. The reference books are on the shelves behind you and next door in the resource room." She stood up and quickly gathered her belongings. "I'm out of here."

He called after her. "One more thing . . ."

She wheeled, obviously out of patience.

"Did anyone locate the package I sent here?"

She sighed. "Try the incinerator."

"Thank you again."

"Forget it." She sang over her shoulder as she walked away. "I really mean that. Make sure you shut off the computer and the lights when you leave, and if anyone comes down here, just leave and don't say anything."

"It's a deal," Joe said, chuckling. He liked her.

He sat and turned to the computer monitor. After taking a few moments to figure out how to move around within the document, he pulled up the find command and typed in the words "Miller's weasel."

When Joe was through reading, he drove into downtown Cheyenne and bought a Smith & Wesson .357 Magnum revolver at a pawn shop for $275. Farther down on the same block, he bought a box of cartridges for it.

21

"Hey, little school girl," the man called out as his vehicle slowed to a stop and his power window whirred down. "Do you need a ride?"

Sheridan squinted against the roll of dust that followed from the road. It was the same man who had been hiding in the horse stall. He had been traveling on the other side of the road but had crossed over the middle of the county road and stopped in front of her. Because the passenger seat was empty and the vehicle was high, Sheridan could only see his face and his hand that rested on the steering wheel. He wore sunglasses, and she couldn't see his eyes. He was smiling.

"I'm not supposed to get in a stranger's car," Sheridan said.

The man chuckled. He could seem so friendly. "I'm not a stranger, though, darlin'. I know your dad, remember? And you, too!"

Sheridan nodded yes. She was wearing a blue jumper and lace-up shoes. Her homework and reading were in her backpack. Because she was staying at the Eagle Mountain

Club, she had to take a different bus from a different place than she was used to and the bus was always late. She was the only child who got on in Saddlestring for the long ride.

"Mom is waiting for me to get off the bus," Sheridan said.

"Okay, okay. But at least come closer," the man said, still smiling. "So I don't have to yell."

Sheridan stepped up to the road but kept well back of the window. She was cautious, and her legs felt ready to run. Because the man would have to leap across the passenger seat and through the window, she thought she could easily get away if she needed to. Now that she was up on the road with him, she could see him a little better, and she could see clearly into his car. Her insides were knotted. Sheridan felt as if she might get sick and throw up. She had not been able to stop thinking about this man ever since he had pulled her into the stall, and now he was here again, right in front of her. He seemed so nice, but he had said such horrible things. And he looked at her like she was something special to him, as if by sharing the secret, they were somehow close to each other. She had never thought about any grown man in these terms before. It frightened her and made her feel guilty.

Without being obvious, she tried to steal a look down the road in both directions.

"There's nobody coming," the man said, an edge creeping into his voice. "What's the matter, don't you trust me to stay put? You think I'm going to grab you or something?"

She didn't reply. In her imagination, her dad's pickup had appeared on the top of the hill and was getting closer.

"If you were a couple years older, I probably couldn't stay put," the man laughed. "But you're safe for now." His voice dropped. "Unless of course you don't want to be so safe."

Sheridan turned her head, so he wouldn't see how scared she was.

"Let's make this quick so we can get on our way," the man said, his voice serious now. "How did you get those little weasels to come out of the wood pile?"

Sheridan said she tossed handfuls of food on the top of the pile. Like rain.

"What kind of food?"

Dry cereal, she said. Raisins, nuts, bread, sometimes bits of hamburger.

"And you just sort of sprinkled it on top, huh?" He asked. "Did they come out every time?"

No, they didn't, she said. Not every time.

The man seemed to be thinking about something. She couldn't see his eyes, but she could tell they were glaring at her behind the glasses.

"Sheridan, are there any secrets you're keeping from me?"

Sheridan went cold. "No," she lied. She hoped to God he wouldn't ask her if she knew where the weasels were now, because she wasn't sure she could answer him without showing she was lying. But he didn't ask, and like most grownups, he thought he knew everything.

"We've still got a deal, don't we, darlin'?"

Sheridan nodded, relieved they were off the subject. "A deal is a deal."

"You bet it is," he said slowly as he reached and pushed the silver button that held the glove box closed. The cover dropped open. There was something in the glove box. "Look," he commanded, in a voice that made her obey.

She couldn't see it very well. The glove box was dark, but there was something round and white in the corner of it. It was something about the size of his fist, but wrapped in red-stained white paper that looked wet.

He snapped the cover shut before she could see any better.

His voice was almost a whisper: "Have you ever seen a kitty's head after it's been twisted off, Sheridan? When you twist it, the neck breaks and it sounds like when you crack your knuckles."

Sheridan stepped back, nearly falling. She covered her mouth with her hands, horrified.

"That," he pointed toward the glove box, "could happen to someone you know real well unless you keep our secret just between us."

Sheridan found herself backing away from the truck, wanting to be as far away from what lay in the glove box as possible.

"If I can't get those weasels out, you might have to help me," the man said. "Maybe you can talk weasel language to them or something. I don't know."

He started up the motor. His voice rose as the engine raced. "Take it easy, darlin'. Wish me luck with those weasels!"

The man pulled away and drove down the road. He watched in his rearview mirror as the yellow school bus cleared the hill behind them and began to slow down for the girl. She was moving toward it. The bus door swung open, and the little girl in the blue dress disappeared from his sight. She was a cutie, that Sheridan.

He leaned over and opened the glove box and reached inside. The package was still warm, and the paper greasy. He peeled away the wrapper with his teeth. He took a big bite out of it, and dollops of ketchup spattered in his lap.

It was a triple chili cheeseburger from the Burg-O-Pardner on Main. *Damn,* it was good. That place could sure cook a burger.

He wiped his mouth with the back of his hand and looked at himself good and hard in the mirror. Despite everything, he liked what he saw.

22

The first written description of a Miller's weasel was made by Captain Meriwether Lewis in the *Journals of the Lewis and Clark Expedition,* published in 1805. The passage was not extensive. Lewis wrote, with his particular brand of spelling, that the party had encountered small colonies of the "plesant creatures" shortly after they had reached the Three Forks of the Missouri River and had followed the Jefferson River toward the Rocky Mountains. The animals, like prairie dogs, burrowed into the earth along what proved to be traditional buffalo migration routes. Their name came from Rodney "Mandan" Miller, a surveyor's assistant in the expedition, who injured his ankle by stumbling into one of the burrows. Lewis wrote that the creatures sometimes stood in tight groups on their hind legs and chattered a warning as the party approached. The Miller's weasels were, he noted, "happey little companions of the trail" and that their primary food supply was buffalo carrion. The day after a buffalo bull or cow was shot by the party for food, the weasels would gather and wait patiently until the large predators—the wolves, coyotes, eagles, vultures—were through with the carcass themselves and then would move in to finish what was left. He wrote that the weasels ate the meat, fur, and viscera of dead buffalo. As was his custom, Lewis first made a sketch, then shot several of the weasels, skinned the hides, and salted the bodies for later study by scientists back home.

It was dusk and Joe drove north, bathed in the brilliant copper light of the mid-September sun. He kept the window open so he could breathe in the sweet, dry smell of the sagebrush—covered flats that stretched like an endless rumpled quilt in every direction as he approached Waltman north of Casper. There were few other vehicles on the two-lane highway. It was just before dusk, the time of day when silent herds of deer were moving out from the secret draws and the tall sagebrush—a brief, magical time when the light was of perfect force and angle so it lit up the brown-and-white coloring of hundreds of pronghorn antelope, revealing them like beacons in the gray brush. In a few minutes, the light would change and the pronghorns, their particular illumination extinguished, would meld back into the mottled texture of the country as if they had never really been there at all.

Joe rolled down the window and turned the radio off. There weren't many places left in North America where humans could still be virtually alone and inaccessible but this was one of them. He had driven out of range of the only available radio signal several minutes before, and the "search" feature had been unsuccessfully spinning through all of the frequencies like a slot machine that wouldn't stop. He had now entered what Wacey referred to as "Radio Free Wyoming," and he would remain in it for at least the next half hour. He planned to drive straight through without stopping except for gasoline. He wanted to get home to Marybeth by midnight.

A strange, almost giddy feeling overcame Joe. He had seen thousands of Wyoming sunsets before, but for some reason, this one touched him. His emotions flitted like the radio search command from guilt to relief to outright anger. Guilt that he was letting Marybeth and his family down, relief that this chapter of his life—the long hours, the low pay, the frustration of trying to do a good job in a numbingly indifferent government bureaucracy—was over, and anger, nasty pulses of white-hot rage to which he was entirely unaccustomed, because he was a pawn in someone's game.

He tried to not dwell on the fact that this might be one of the last times he drove this pickup or wore his uniform. He wouldn't just be losing his job—he'd be losing his own self-image as well. Without a badge he was just like everyone else. He started to understand, for the very first time, why a police officer might want to turn his weapon on himself instead of turning it in. He fought against the self-pity that threatened to engulf him.

Instead, he turned his thoughts to what he had learned in the resource room.

What was known of Miller's weasels came from four primary sources: Captain Lewis' writings, the field notes of early biologists, references in pioneer journals, and a series of articles about the lastknown group of the creatures, which had been displayed at the Philadelphia Zoo in 1887 (according to the articles, they were a popular exhibit years before anyone had ever heard of the phrase "endangered species"). No more than twelve inches long and startlingly quick, Miller's weasels were more closely related to mongooses than any other North American species. They were civets, and seemed to resemble the Suricate or Stokstert meerkat of West Africa. They were omnivorous and aggressive, and they would eat eggs, snakes, mice, birds, lizards, fruit, insects, bulbs, and seeds. They would even give chase to foxes and dogs. It was estimated that at one time in the early nineteenth century, there were as many as a million Miller's weasels located within the Rocky Mountain West and Great Plains. They lived in family units as small as five or as large as 30, and they moved their colonies several times a year, following the buffalo wherever they went. They relied on the buffalo not only for carrion, but also for breaking up and churning the earth with their hooves as they grazed, thereby exposing plants, tubers, and small animals for the Miller's weasels to feed on.

American Indians considered the Miller's weasels to be good luck animals, and there were likenesses of them painted on tipi skins and beaded on clothing. The reason was simple: if there were Miller's weasels, then the Indians knew that buffalo would be nearby.

References to Miller's weasels were found in many of the journals kept by those who traveled the Oregon Trail, but no extensive or comprehensive passages. Most of the references had to do with killing the weasels wherever they could be found. It seemed that a legend had developed along the trail that Miller's weasels, despite their cuddly appearance, liked the taste of human flesh. The biologists who had analyzed the journal entries speculated that the pioneers had seen the weasels feeding on bison carcasses or perhaps digging into the numerous human graves that lined the route. There were rumors—none confirmed—that the animals were known to steal into Conestoga wagons at night and feed on human babies while they slept. Because of this legend, Miller's weasels were exterminated in every possible way. The pioneers poisoned the weasels by leaving tainted meat or oats near the colonies. They also would set bonfires on top of the animals' holes or flood these areas, then club the animals to death as they tried to escape. They were also shot, of course, on sight. Sometimes a single shotgun blast would cut down a dozen as they stood on their hind legs and yipped.

But what really led Miller's weasels down the path to extinction was the virtual elimination of the great herds of buffalo on the Great Plains. Because the Miller's weasels were dependent on the buffalo, they died out when the buffalo vanished. It wasn't until many years later that it became apparent that Miller's weasels no longer existed in America.

Was it possible that a few of the species still existed?

It *was* possible, Joe thought. Maybe the weasels had learned to eat something else. If the remaining weasels managed to change their staple diet, there were plenty of elk, moose, and deer in the mountains to feed on.

And Vern was right. If a colony of Miller's weasels was discovered, the news would hit the scientific and environmental community within hours via the Internet. It would sock the already fading town of Saddlestring, Wyoming, with a punch Joe wasn't sure it would recover from. Federal employees from various agencies, journalists, biologists, and environmentalists from all over the world would come, all dragging their own distinct and separate political agendas along with them. The ranchers, loggers, outfitters, guides, and residents of Saddlestring would be no match.

Joe had no hard evidence of the species to present to anyone yet. But when everything that had happened was viewed in a certain light, a light not unlike the sunshine that had found and exposed the antelope in the sagebrush, it all seemed to point to the fact that a species thought extinct for 100 years was alive and well in the Bighorns—and that three men who found out about them had been murdered. The murderer, according to Sheriff Barnum and the state investigators, was Clyde Lidgard. But if Clyde didn't do it—and Joe couldn't decide if he believed that—who did? And why did the people who should be the most concerned about the possibility of this discovery, Joe's colleagues, seem uninterested or at least want to steer him away?

Joe smiled bitterly in the dark.

He had only three days to try and find the answers to those questions, and he was completely on his own.

In Waltman, at a small pink general store 30 miles from anywhere else, Joe bought a half-pint of bourbon and a six-pack of beer from an old man behind the counter who had not only lost an eye but also his left arm from the elbow down. The store owner didn't bother to pin up the empty sleeve of his dirty, gold cowboy shirt, but let it flap beside him like a broken wing as he rang up the purchases. Yup, the store owner answered Joe, that pay phone outside still worked.

Outside, Joe dialed the telephone, opened a beer, and leaned against the pink building in the dark. A humming neon Coors beer sign from the window of the store painted his face a light blue.

Dave Avery, Joe's friend from the Montana Fish and Game Department, answered at his home in Helena. Joe could hear the sounds of a football game on television in the background. Joe asked Dave if he had been able to analyze the samples he sent him yet.

"Are you screwing with me, Joe?" Dave asked, his voice wary. "Is this some kind of a trick you're pulling on me?"

That meant Dave had received and tested the scat samples Joe had sent him.

"Why do you say that?" Joe asked.

Dave snorted. He was animated. No doubt he had already had a few beers that evening. "You know why, Joe. That scat had a little of everything in it. Pine nuts, vegetation, traces of cartilage, even some elk hair. It could be a fox or something, but it's way too small for that. You win this game. I can't guess that shit. I thought I could name that shit in three notes, maybe less. But I'm baffled. Boggled. Blown away."

For Joe, this confirmed he was on the right track.

"Ever hear of a Miller's weasel?" Joe asked.

"A what?" Dave asked. Then he laughed, unconvinced. There was a long silence. Dave Avery was well versed in both the current and former species of the region. "You're not kidding, are you?" Dave asked. "Did you actually see any?"

Joe told him what had happened, where he found the samples, and what he suspected. Dave kept saying "Jesus Christ" as Joe talked.

"Do you know what you might have here?" Dave said when Joe was through. "If the Feds find out, it'll get wild."

"That's the least of my worries right now." Joe said. "Now will you do me a favor for the time being?"

Dave said he would.

"Do a couple of more tests to make sure neither of us is wrong. Then lock up those samples and the analysis. Don't tell anyone what you've got or what we discussed. Just keep it under wraps for a while until I can sort things out down here."

Dave asked how long it would be before Joe got back to him.

"Three days."

Thirty miles north of Waltman and 20 miles south of Kaycee, Joe turned off of the highway onto a little-used ranch access. His tires bounced over ruts until he cleared a rise where he knew he couldn't be seen from the highway.

Joe killed the engine and swung out of the truck. There was just enough light that the sagebrush looked cottony. A jackrabbit bounded away from the road with tremendous leaps, looking twice its actual size in the headlights. Behind him, the hot engine ticked.

He stroked the checkered grip of the new revolver and raised it. He thumbed the hammer, and the action worked smoothly, rolling the cylinder. He aimed down the long barrel at the now-distant rabbit and squeezed the trigger. The .357 roared and bucked violently in his hands and a two-foot explosion from the muzzle left an afterimage in his vision. A plume of dust exploded in front of the jackrabbit, and the animal reversed direction and now bounded right to left.

Joe fired, then fired again. He kept squeezing the trigger until he realized it had clicked three times on empty cylinders. A half a mile away, the jackrabbit had hit overdrive and was streaking toward the mountains.

With his ears ringing and half-blind from the concussive reports of the big pistol, Joe stumbled back to his pickup to reload.

23

Vern Dunnegan was not in his room or in the lounge at the Holiday Inn, but Joe saw his black Suburban on Main Street in front of the Stockman's Bar. Joe parked beside it. As the front door closed behind him, Joe squinted down the length of the dark narrow room through cigarette smoke and saw Vern sitting in the back booth just as he had a few days before. Vern was alone, hunched over and staring down at a tall glass of bourbon and water that he held between his hands.

As Joe approached, Vern looked up and in that instant something passed quickly over Vern's face—perhaps a mixture of both surprise and anger. Joe barely had a chance to register the look before it was replaced by a huge, overdone grin. Joe sat down heavily in the booth and ordered a beer when the barmaid approached.

"You're up awfully late," Vern said, studying Joe carefully from behind his smile.

"I just got back from Cheyenne," Joe said. "That's one hell of a long drive."

"It's a two-and-a-half six-pack drive." Vern chuckled. "A

drive I made many, many times. It looks like you might have had a few yourself to make the hours more bearable. Gotta be careful on the highway," Vern said, smiling paternalistically. "Some of those patrolmen would like nothing better than to give a ticket to a fellow state employee and get you in all sorts of trouble."

Caught, Joe nodded. A drunk like Vern who had tried to hide it for years could be very perceptive when it came to identifying someone else who'd been drinking, Joe thought.

"You just missed Wacey," Vern continued. Vern was now in command. Whatever had passed across his face when he looked up and saw Joe was now well hidden. "We were having a little celebration."

Joe looked puzzled.

"Barnum announced today that he's dropping out of the sheriff's race," Vern said. "He's going to retire."

"You're kidding," Joe replied. He wondered what had made Barnum come to that decision. With Barnum out, Wacey was assured of winning the Republican primary in a couple of weeks. And in Twelve Sleep County, winning the Republican primary was the same as winning the general election. There were only a handful of Democrats, and few of them even bothered to vote anymore.

"So ole Wacey was pretty excited and we had a few drinks to celebrate," Vern said.

"I bet he was," Joe agreed. "Strange that Barnum dropped out."

Vern shrugged. "These things happen. Maybe he thought he was going to get whipped."

Joe recalled the conversation he'd had with Barnum earlier that week. Barnum had certainly acted as if he had already been defeated. But Joe hadn't understood it then, and he didn't understand it now. He had noticed no groundswell of support for Wacey Hedeman in the community—and very little dissatisfaction with Barnum. It seemed to Joe that voting against Sheriff O. R. "Bud" Barnum was like voting against the Bighorn Mountains.

"Politics," Vern said, as if the word alone summed up the conversation. "Stranger than fiction."

Joe sipped his beer. He wished he hadn't been drinking on the ride home. He wished his head was more clear.

"So what brings you down to the Stockman's Bar when it's obviously past your bedtime?" Vern asked.

Joe looked up. "I guess I want to accept that job you offered me with InterWest," Joe said. "I got suspended today."

Vern frowned melodramatically. "Suspended? *You?* That doesn't even seem possible."

Joe had a feeling that it wasn't as much of a surprise to Vern as Vern made it out to be. They were now playing some kind of game with each other. But in this kind of game, Joe was an amateur and Vern was All-Pro.

Joe told Vern what had happened. Vern shook his head and rolled his eyes at the right places. Joe thought for a moment that maybe Vern hadn't known. No, Joe amended, *Vern knew.* There were still plenty of people in Cheyenne that owed Vern a favor and could have tipped him off.

"So I want to work with you," Joe finished.

"Why don't you fight it?" Vern asked. "It sounds like a ridiculous overreaction by the department. You should be able to win it at your hearing."

"I don't have the time or money to go against them and I need to support my family," Joe said truthfully. "I'm not sure I have the determination I need. I guess I'm not really sure I want my job back at all if this is what they're capable of."

Vern drained his drink and ordered another for both of them. "What does Marybeth say?" The tone of the question was not kind.

"I haven't talked to her about it yet," Joe said, flushing just a bit from the implication. "I came straight here."

"Joe," Vern said after the drinks had been delivered. "We seem to have some kind of misunderstanding here."

"What do you mean?"

Vern chuckled in his most kindly way, as if he were sharing the embarrassment for both of them. "Joe, I don't think that I ever actually offered you a job. If I remember correctly, I just asked if you might be interested in something with InterWest. I believe I said I was 'testing the waters.' Don't you remember that phrase?"

"I do remember it," Joe said, trying to understand what was going on and where Vern was headed. He still wanted to trust Vern, but Vern's statement that there *wasn't* a job waiting for him at InterWest had left him shaken and wary. "But I know what I heard from you. I know what you meant."

"Look," Vern said, glancing around the bar and lowering his voice. "It's not going to happen."

Joe sat back in his seat.

"Besides," Vern said, rolling the sweaty drink slowly between his palms, "I talked to my bosses at InterWest and they now think things are just fine as they are. For a while there, they tossed it around and they asked me if you were willing to make the commitment and I had to honestly tell them at the time that I didn't think you were. They reconsidered after that and now they don't see the need for additional employees at this level and at this phase in the project. Maybe if you had come back to me sooner—or with some enthusiasm. Before this thing in Cheyenne happened. It would be pretty hard right now to convince them that you suddenly changed your mind and it wasn't connected to the fact that you got thrown out of the department."

Joe started to speak, but he caught himself.

"One of the reasons I wanted you aboard with me was because of your clean record and your sterling reputation," Vern said, sounding almost apologetic. "But lately you've been neglecting your real job and running around the county with a wild hair up your butt trying to reopen that outfitter case. Don't think nobody has noticed it. You've been the talk of the morning business coffee at the café. There's talk that you burned down Clyde Lidgard's trailer house for some reason that only you know. Now you've been suspended from the department. I really don't think there's a job for you with us, Joe. I'm sorry."

Joe was stunned for the second time that day. He couldn't believe this was happening. He didn't know what to say to Vern. This was exactly the opposite of what he thought he would be able to tell Marybeth when he got home. And his girls. And his mother-in-law. The worst thing about it was that he had not really wanted to come to Vern and ask in the first place. He had talked himself into it as he drove and drank on the highway. He had done it, he thought, because it was the most responsible thing to do. As Joe stood up, he considered raising his fist and smashing Vern in his grinning mouth as hard as he could. But he didn't. He felt too defeated for that.

"All is not lost, Joe," Vern said as Joe clamped on his hat. "Wacey might need a new deputy, you know. He's going to get rid of that McLanahan guy just as soon as he takes office. All is not lost."

Joe turned and leaned forward into the booth, with both of his hands on the tabletop, and put his face directly in front of Vern's.

"You're wrong, Vern," Joe said, nearly whispering. "All is just about lost."

"Now, Joe . . ."

"Vern." Joe cut him off. "Shut up and listen for a change."

Vern's eyes quickly confirmed that no one in the bar was paying them any attention. He looked suspiciously back to Joe.

"Vern, I lost my job and my house today. My faith in the

belief that if you do your job and you work hard and you're honest then good things will happen is real shaky right now. My family is one paycheck away from being on the street. One paycheck. Now I've lost my only prospect for another job. And to top it off, you tell me I've lost my reputation. Then you tell me that *all is not lost.*"

Vern reached up and put a hand on Joe's shoulder, but Joe angrily shook it off.

"Hey, Joe," Vern said, "it's time to start thinking a lot more about Joe Pickett and a lot less about what your family and everybody else thinks. That's what I've learned, Joe."

Vern's eyes turned hard and his lip curled back in a sneer. "Welcome to my world. The *real* world. It's a place where nice things don't necessarily happen to nice people. I," Vern said in his most grandiloquent way, "am an entrepreneur. I create wealth. I empowered this InterWest deal into being. An offer was made to you, and you passed on it when you had the chance."

Their eyes locked.

"Vern, have you ever heard of a species called the Miller's weasel?"

The corners of Vern's mouth twitched slightly, then out came the false smile. "Miller's weasels are extinct," Vern said. "They don't exist, even though every decade or so a rumor pops up that somebody saw one. Kind of like sightings of Bigfoot or something."

"Vern," Joe hissed. "If I find out you're involved in all of this, things are going to get real western."

The look Joe had seen on Vern's face when he walked into the bar passed over it again. But this time there was some fear mixed in. It was good to see.

The night had turned sharply colder and the stars were shrouded by clouds. Joe's hands were shaking as he dug in his pocket for his keys. He started his truck and began to drive to his house. He hit the brakes and cursed loudly when he realized that he was headed in the wrong direction. His family was at Eagle Mountain now, so he turned in the middle of Main Street and roared away in the other direction.

PART FIVE

Land Acquisition

Sec. 5(a) Program. - The Secretary, and the Secretary of Agriculture with respect to the National Forest System, shall establish and implement a program to conserve fish, wildlife, and plants, including those which are listed as endangered species or threatened species pursuant to section 4 of this Act. To carry out such a program, the appropriate Secretary -

(1) shall utilize the land acquisition and other authority under the Fish and Wildlife Act of 1956, as amended, and the Migratory Bird Conservation Act, as appropriate; and

(2) is authorized to acquire by purchase, donation, or otherwise, lands, waters, or interest therein, and such authority shall be in addition to any other land acquisition authority vested in him.

(b) Acquisitions. - Funds made available pursuant to the Land and Water Conservation Fund Act of 1965, as amended, may be used for the purpose of acquiring lands, waters, or interests therein under subsection (a) of this section.

—The Endangered Species Act Amendments of 1982

24

In the dining room, there was a long, dark hardwood table that could seat fourteen people comfortably. In the middle of the night, Joe sat in his robe at the foot of it under a dimmed chandelier and felt sorry for himself. Hours before, he had switched to drinking water, and he filled up a stubby cut-glass tumbler from a pitcher that was older than he was.

The Kensinger house was magnificent, but he had surveyed it with amused dispassion. The bar area alone was half of the square footage of his house on Bighorn Road. The walls were hung with original Bama and Schenck contemporary western paintings and eighteenth-century English sporting prints. Two-thousand-dollar Navajo rugs hung from ceiling beams. There was a pure stainless steel kitchen with a walk-in refrigerator/freezer, giving Joe the impression that food preparation in this place was a serious, almost clinical affair. In the book-lined den (the books were mainly leather-bound editions of sporting and history categories with stiff, uncracked spines), a powerful telescope was mounted on a tripod to study the Twelve Sleep River and the wildlife that came down from the foothills to drink from it. To Joe, the house was not built or arranged to be lived in as much as it was a stage for entertaining. Small children would kill this house, and this house would kill small children. It was a kind of rancho deluxe contemporary western living museum.

Joe sipped his glass of water and looked around the dining room in the dark. The unreality of this place, given his situation, was overwhelming.

"Can I get you anything?" It was Marybeth. She stood in the shadow of the double doors. He gestured at the half-empty pitcher of water to indicate he was okay. He looked at her as if he were seeing her for the very first time. To sleep in, she was wearing an extra-large T-shirt that extended to midthigh. The cotton cloth strained across her pregnant belly and substantial breasts, her nipples poking out like buttons. Beneath the T-shirt, her legs were firm and thin, and her toes were curled into the nap of the thick carpet. Her hair was down around her shoulders and sleep-mussed. She was lovely.

When he had first come in, he had told her everything. The kids had been in bed, and Missy Vankeuren was who knows where within the house. He had held nothing back as they sat across from each other at the dining room table: what had happened at Game and Fish Headquarters, what Dave Avery had confirmed, what Vern had said about the job and his reputation.

"One way or other, that man has made sure he still has power over you," Marybeth had said. "Vern Dunnegan may be the only person I have ever truly learned to hate."

He had told her about his plan to go back up into the Crazy Woman Creek canyon tomorrow where the outfitters had been murdered—while he still had the authority to do so. Maybe he could find something that would substantiate what he was beginning to suspect about the outfitters' murders. He had laid it out in flat, declarative sentences. When he was through, she had looked at him and had said, "That's a lot to think about," and then she had gone to bed. They had left things on a difficult, unresolved note. Now she was back.

She came from the doorway, pulled out a straight-backed chair next to him, and sat down. She reached over and slipped her hand between the folds of his robe and put a warm hand on his leg. She looked into his eyes.

"Joe, I've been thinking about everything you said."

He waited for what would come next.

"Joe, all is not lost. You have me. You have your family. You have character. That's a lot, and not many people can say that. We love you and appreciate who you are and what you've done."

He looked at her quizzically.

"Joe, you are a good man. You're the last of your kind. Don't forget that. There aren't many like you left. You have a good heart and your moral compass is a model of its kind. You need to do what you need to do. Things will work out, and we can talk about it all later. We're being tested, God knows why."

Joe was taken aback. For some reason—and he felt more than slightly guilty about it now—he thought she was going to tell him that she had had it and maybe the best idea was for her to take the children and go and live with her mother in Arizona for a while. He felt he had failed her. But she was showing that she was stronger and more committed to him, and them, than he had given her credit for. He started to speak and ask her why, but she didn't let him.

"Don't ask me, Joe. There isn't anything logical about it. There's nothing I can really explain to you other than I trust you and I'm with you until the bitter end."

"That's a lot to live up to." Joe said.

"You bet it is," Marybeth answered. "But you haven't let me down yet."

Joe thought she had never seemed as beautiful as she did at that moment.

"I'm not sure what I should say next," Joe said, flushing.

She withdrew from his robe and guided his hand under the T-shirt to her belly. He rested his hand on her and then spread his fingers. Beneath the taut flesh he could feel the baby shifting inside of her.

"We make wonderful babies," she said softly. "We're bringing good little people into the world who have a mom and a dad who care about them and love them. They know right from wrong because their parents teach them which is which, and because their parents live by example. Somewhere, there is a reward for us, Joe. We need to believe that. We won't just be abandoned."

Joe stared at Marybeth, still unsure what to say. "But right now, I just want you in my bed," she continued. "I need you there."

He followed her to a bedroom he had never even seen before and to a bed he had never slept in. In it, they made love in a warm, clumsy way that at least for a few wonderful moments made him forget where he was.

He didn't know how long he had been sleeping, but when he opened his eyes it was still dark outside. He eased out of the bed, not wanting to wake Marybeth, and padded along the cold stone tiles in the hallway. Then he realized, standing in the strange house, that he wasn't sure where the closest bathroom was. He stopped at a curtained window and brushed it aside to look outside. There was still no sign of dawn. Stars shown brilliantly in the black sky. His intention was to be in the saddle by seven and to the elk camp by noon. Beyond that he wasn't sure where he was going or how far he would go.

By the faint blue light from the moon, he saw the shadow of a lamp on a table in the hall; he bent down, turned it on, and looked at his wristwatch.

"Dad?"

The voice made him jump and spin around. He hadn't known which room the children were sleeping in. When he entered the bedroom, he saw Sheridan sitting upright on the bed, her fingers wrapped tightly around the covers.

"Honey," Joe said as he sat down on the bed, "it's three-thirty in the morning. Why aren't you sleeping?"

He couldn't see her well in the dark. She looked like a tangle of blond hair and thin limbs. He stroked her hair and eased her back to her pillow.

"I can't sleep," Sheridan said, her voice hoarse.

"Is it the new house?" he asked. "Sleeping in a new bed?"

She didn't answer, but he had the feeling that she wanted to say something. Tell him something. He petted her hair and shoulder to calm her. Something was wrong. He heard her sniff and realized that she had been sobbing. He felt her cheeks, which were moist with tears.

"You can tell me," he said, his voice gentle.

Suddenly, she sat up and threw her arms around his neck, burying her face into his chest. He assumed she must have heard some of the earlier conversation with Marybeth. Maybe she was worried about their situation . . . like he was. He told her that everything was going to be okay. He told her that she needed to get some sleep. He waited for her to tell him what the problem was. She had never been shy before when it came to talking about her feelings. Far from it, Joe thought.

Finally: "I don't like this place," she told him, crying.

He didn't tell her that he wasn't real sure he liked it either. Instead, he once again eased her back into her bed.

"Is that all?" he asked.

She paused for an inordinate amount of time. She covered her face with her hands.

"That's all," she said, meekly.

"We won't be here forever," he said, aware of the irony of that statement.

He rubbed her shoulder until he thought she had drifted back to sleep. He rose eventually and quietly walked across the room toward the hall.

"I love you and Mom," she said. "I love our whole family."

He turned at the door.

"Your whole family loves you, too, Sheridan. Now get some sleep."

25

Joe rode hard, pushing Lizzie as fast as he dared, and made it to the elk camp by midday. It was cold. Gray, scudding clouds filled a sky that seemed especially close. He dismounted in the camp, stretched, and unsaddled his horse. They had both worked up a sweat. Steam rose like contrails from Lizzie's back, and he rubbed her down with his gloved hands while she drank from the trickle of cold water that was Crazy Woman Creek in early fall. He set out some grain for Lizzie and then draped the smoky, wet saddle blanket over a branch. He would wait for Lizzie to dry and rest before he continued on.

Except for a few early rising hunters waiting for their coffee to brew in the campground before sunrise, Joe had not seen another living person since seven that morning. On his hard ride up the mountain, he had spooked a small herd of cow and calf elk and had nearly ridden on top of a coyote who was loping lazily down the same trail he was riding up.

As Lizzie rested, he carried his saddle and walked through the elk camp. He sat on a rock, pulled his Thermos from a saddlebag, and poured a cup of coffee. In addition to the new Smith & Wesson revolver he wore on his hip, he had brought his Remington shotgun loaded with double-ought buckshot. He arranged the saddle scabbard on top of the pommel so he could pull the shotgun out quickly.

Even though it was the same place he, Wacey, and McLanahan had moved in on that morning just two weeks before, it seemed very different now. The tents were gone, as were the stoves and wooden floors. The earth within the camp had been trampled flat and hard by investigators. The fireplace had been kicked apart, and the cross beams in the trees that were used for hanging elk had been dismantled. In a year or two, with plenty of snow and new grass and erosion, the elk camp would be unrecognizable, nothing more than a wide, flat place along the stream.

He spread a topographical map across his knees and studied it until he found the location of the elk camp where he now was and the creek that ran alongside it. Along the creek a few inches up from the camp, the contour lines narrowed and became dark and thick, indicating a steep and narrow canyon. The creek became a hairline. The trail, marked by dots and dashes, ended at the mouth of the canyon.

On the map, the canyon looked incredibly long and narrow. He traced it with his finger as it snaked through the heart of the mountain. But what Joe was most interested in was where the creek began, and where the walls appeared to widen. It looked like a huge bowl or depression, two miles long by three miles, all four sides rimmed by sharp cliffs. The area was in a roadless section, and the map showed virtually no access from above. The only way in, it seemed, was upstream along the creek.

Joe had never been to the bowl before. He had asked Vern about it, back when he had just started in the district, because it was such a unique topographical feature. Vern had said he had been there once but hadn't been back as it was so hard to get to. Hunters avoided it, Vern said, because, although it was remote and probably rich with game, it was one of those places where "the only way to get an elk out was with a knife and fork."

But Ote Keeley, Kyle Lensegrav, and Calvin Mendes had spent a lot of time up here scouting and hunting elk. Joe wouldn't be a bit surprised if they had felt the urge to find out what was upstream, beyond the narrow canyon. They had probably used the same topo map Joe had and could see, as he could, that the bowl could very likely be the home of magnificent elk that were rarely, if ever, hunted.

Joe looked up and searched upstream for the spot where the canyon walls began to narrow. That was where he planned to go.

26

"Why do you want to go back to the house so badly, Sheridan?" her mom asked as she gathered up the breakfast dishes from the table. Lucy had already left to go watch television. Lucy had fallen in love with all of the channels available on the satellite dish.

Sheridan had thought long and hard about a story that would work. She had forgotten her library books, she said. The books were due on Monday, she said. It was a lie, Sheridan knew. But it was sort of a good lie.

"Can't we go tomorrow?" her mom asked. "Tomorrow is Sunday."

"I've got to read the books," Sheridan said, looking to her grandmother for sympathy. "I've got to do a book report on one of them."

Missy Vankeuren laughed. She had been in a good mood ever since they had come to the house at the Eagle Mountain Club. "She sounds like me in my school days."

"Yes," her mom said, looking with disapproval at her own mother. "But it doesn't sound like Sheridan."

Mom turned back to her.

"Sheridan, you know better than to wait until the last minute to do your homework," her mom admonished as she took the dishes to the kitchen.

"Well, it's been pretty busy lately," Sheridan said, indicating the move. That would instill a little guilt, Sheridan thought. Her mom knew Sheridan didn't really like the new "vacation home," as Missy called it.

"Just use your charm to get yourself out of it," Missy said, winking at Sheridan. "Bat your eyes and make up some good story. That's what I would do." Then she smiled.

Sheridan's mom came back into the dining room.

"Well?" Sheridan asked her. "Can we go get my books?" Persistence usually paid off.

"We'll see." Her mom looked at her sternly.

"Does that mean yes?" Sheridan asked.

"It means, we'll see," her mom answered. "Now, scoot. You look like you could use a little nap."

"I'm okay."

"Are you feeling all right, honey? You're looking a little pale."

"I'm okay," Sheridan repeated, hopping down from the chair.

"She's fine," Missy told her mom with a knowing smile.

Boy, Sheridan thought, *is* she *ever wrong.*

Which meant yes, Sheridan thought, as she huddled with Lucy under a blanket on the sofa to watch Saturday morning cartoons. A second "we'll see" *always* meant yes.

Despite what she had told her mom, Sheridan wasn't feeling good. She stared blankly at the television set. She had not eaten much breakfast and her stomach hurt. Last night had been the worst night yet. In the unfamiliar bed it was almost as if that man was in it with her, he seemed so close. She could almost smell his breath. It was as if he were there watching her, waiting for her to say or do something she wasn't supposed to. Then that smile of his would turn into something else, something wicked, and in her imagination she could see him turn on his heel to hurt her family. And there was nothing she could do to stop him.

She had awful dreams. The dreams awakened her, and she had trouble getting back to sleep. In one dream, the worst, the man was in her room sitting on a chair near the foot of her bed. He was talking to her, telling her that he was her friend, but in his lap there was something round and large and wrapped in paper. Only this time, when she looked at the object, it was not the head of a kitten. It looked like Lucy's head. In the dream he began to unwrap it.

Another dream had her back in the barn, pinned again to the stall by the man as he breathed in her face and talked to her. He would do things to her mother, he had said. That he'd do things to the baby that was coming, too. *You don't really want another brother or sister around here anyway, do you?* he asked. *I can tell,* he said. *You would like it if it were only you, wouldn't you?* It made her feel bad that in the dream she had nodded her head yes. She hoped she didn't really feel that way. To prove it, she hugged Lucy, but Lucy wriggled free.

Sheridan had stayed awake after her dad had left her room, and had listened as he made coffee and shuffled around the house, gathering things to take with him. She had come close to telling him about the man and her secret pets when he was in her room. She had come *so* close. But remnants from her dreams had stopped her at the last second. After her dad had left the house, she stared at the unfamiliar ceiling and made a couple of decisions. When she made them, they felt right to her. So she wouldn't forget them in the morning, she got out of bed and wrote them down on a piece of paper with a crayon. The crumpled paper was in her pajama pocket now.

First, she would figure out a way to get back to the house so she could make sure the creatures were still there. She would feed them if she could. She prayed they would be all right.

Second, she would tell her dad everything. Something about the way he had put his hand on her face the night before made her feel that if anyone could protect her and the family, it was her dad.

Knowing what she planned to do made her feel a little better. Lucy leaned back against her, and they snuggled under the blanket. Lucy laughed at something that happened in the cartoon. Sheridan let her eyes close. Her eyes were burning. This was too much for her. All of it.

She would have to wait for her dad to come home. Then she would talk. It was time.

27

The first half mile of the canyon was easy going, even as the dark gray walls became sheer and the sky became no more than a ribbon of blue light straight overhead. There were Indian petroglyphs on the rocks, scenes of elk bristling with arrows, painted and feathered men on horseback, figures of warriors holding aloft the scalps and entire heads of other warriors. Near the petroglyphs, Joe found newer and much more stupid graphics written with a felt-tipped marker. "Ote Keeley Sucks the Big One," someone had scratched. "Kyle Eats Shit," said another. "Calvin Is a Needle Dick." Yup, Joe thought, the outfitters had come up here all right.

The rock walls eventually became so narrow that Joe dismounted and hung the stirrups over the saddle horn so they wouldn't catch on the sides. Lizzie was fidgety, her ears were pinned back, and her eyes were wide with apprehension. He led her, coaxing her to continue and keeping up a singsong, inane monologue to calm her as the walls closed in around them. He stepped from stone to stone in the stream, trying to keep his boots dry. The mare's metal shoes clattered and sometimes slipped on the creek rocks, and the back of Joe's pants were soon soaked as a result.

He wished he hadn't brought the horse into the canyon and instead had tied her up and continued by himself. The canyon was much narrower than he had anticipated, and the roots, foliage, and thick spiderwebs that covered it made it claustrophobic. The problem he had now was that they had gone too far to turn around. He would have to back her out nearly a quarter of a mile along slippery rocks. The likelihood that she would fall and injure herself—as well as block the canyon—was too great. He had to continue on and hope she would trust him.

At one point when the walls became so narrow that they were literally touching both sides of her and the brush in the canyon was so thick above them as to block out the light, Lizzie finally balked and jerked back on the halter rope, pulling Joe into the creek. Her eyes were white and wild with panic, and they partially rolled back into her head. Joe tried to stop her as she backed up, and the rope sang through his hands, scorching his gloves. She finally stopped when her shoes skated over the tops of the rocks, and she sat down with an enormous thud and splash. Her breath pistoned out of her flared nostrils. She sat quivering and let Joe approach her. He spoke softly to her saying much the same things he had told Sheridan the night before. After a long ten minutes, she awkwardly scrambled upright. Her breathing had settled to a rhythm. He wedged in beside her and could find no injuries on her except for on her flank, where a small flap of torn hide stuck out like a pink tongue. He was now wet everywhere, and getting cold. The buckskin was wet also, and the canyon smelled strongly of horse.

"We are over halfway there, Lizzie," he told her, over and over again in a kind of mantra. "We can either keep going or back our way out. Let's keep going. It's not that far now. It'll get better, I promise. It's okay. Things are just real okay. Everything is not as bad as it seems."

As the walls eventually receded, the creek became shallow and soon Joe was able to mount again and ride upstream along a sandy bank. The sky didn't seem as gray as it had earlier in the morning, and the little bit of sun that filtered through the clouds warmed and dried them.

When the canyon walls finally opened, the bowl in the mountains was even more lush and untrammeled than Joe had imagined it could be. It was a beautiful, remarkable place. Around the rim of the bowl in all directions were sheer, red rock cliffs, which provided both protection and a windbreak. Thin rivulets of water that looked like old lace streamed down the rock walls from above. Joe imagined that in the spring the waterfalls would have real volume and would fill the bowl with their roar. The old-growth trees were mossy and tall, the foliage thick. Tall grass carpeted the edge of the creek while spring-fed pools full of clean, cold water dotted the creek bottom.

Something cracked in the trees and Joe pulled his shotgun out of the scabbard in a single movement. But even before he had racked the pump, he could see that the sound had come from a huge bull elk who had seen him and was now fleeing through the trees, a shadow moving through the thick timberlike fan blades whirling in front of a light until it was gone. He lay the shotgun across the pommel of the saddle and nudged the buckskin on.

Joe knew what a unique place this was. It was like going back in time, like being one of the first to ride into a natural wonder like Yellowstone or the Grand Canyon and not really being able to believe your eyes. Few people in the modern world would ever have the chance to see what he was seeing or experience what he was experiencing.

Or so he thought.

He was nearly past the grassy rise before he realized exactly where he was. Later, when he thought about it, he couldn't really say why he had stopped or how he had found it. It was a feeling he felt on the back of his neck like the lick of a ghost. But when he reined the buckskin and turned in the saddle, he had absolutely no doubt about what was there in front of him.

He was looking at a killing field.

It was a treeless slope that started at the edge of a dark timber stand and continued down until it reached the valley floor. What was peculiar about the field, now thick with dried, tall grass, was its lack of life. There were no birds, and nothing scuttled in the grass. It was dead, and Joe wanted to know why.

The mounds were there. He counted 26 of them. But the holes on the top of the mounds were blocked with new spiderwebs or bits of brush and grass that had blown into them. As Joe walked through the field, from mound to mound, he found the things he had suspected he would. There were spent casings from .22 shells buried in the dirt, as well as shotgun shells. He bent over a dried quarter of elk that was old enough to be skeletal but not old enough that he couldn't see and smell the poison it had been laced with. It was Compound 1080, a deadly substance preferred by those who took the killing of predators very seriously.

He found several M–44 cartridges wired into the carcass of a rabbit. The devices, long illegal, were designed to automatically fire a stream of cyanide into the mouths of whatever tugged on them. The cyanide, which reacted with saliva, would kill within seconds. The cartridges had been fired.

In a kind of stunned fog, Joe gathered what evidence he could. He pulled his camera from a saddlebag and took several rolls of film. Many of the shots, he knew, would be of Clyde Lidgard quality. But he found a scattering of tiny bones pressed into the soft earth of one of the mounds, and he filled a plastic bag with them. He gathered a handful of spent .22 brass for another sack, as well as the M–44 cartridges. Then he sat on a downed tree and simply stared at the field. He tried to imagine what it had looked like when it was teeming with the last colony of Miller's weasels on earth.

It was nearly dusk when Joe cleared the elk camp in a trot and continued down the mountain. The long passage through the canyon had been made almost in a dream, and the buckskin mare seemed to sense that Joe was distracted, so she cooperated. She knew they were going home. Joe's mind was racing, and he was shaky from what he had discovered and from lack of sleep. Several times, he reached back into his saddlebags to confirm that he had in fact gathered the evidence he thought he had gathered. Already, the bowl seemed very far away.

He thought of the implications, which where huge. Terrible acts had taken place up there. They had happened right under his nose, in his jurisdiction, and on his watch. Of course there was now a conspiracy. He doubted that it had started out that way. He guessed that what had happened was a series of incidents and mistakes that had mushroomed into something both big and awful. He didn't know how everything was connected yet, and he wasn't really sure he would be able to find out. But he knew he was now in the thick of it, no matter what. He wondered who out there would surface, once the word got out.

He thought again of the killing field, which both disgusted and depressed him. He was astonished at the thoroughness of the people responsible. First they had started with Miller's weasels and then moved on to killing the outfitters. That progression indicated that perhaps they weren't yet through.

Joe loaded Lizzie into the horse trailer and put the saddle and tack in the back of the pickup. He shared the last of his water with his horse then climbed stiffly into the cab of the truck and started the engine.

When he cleared the timber, the Twelve Sleep Valley opened up below him. In the distance, he could see the early evening lights of Saddlestring like a jewelry box dumped on the prairie. Directly below him was the campground, and the winking yellow lights of hunters' lanterns and propane lamps. Between the two, miles in the distance and hidden in the folds of the foothills, was his house on Bighorn Road.

God, he was angry. He was furious at his own situation and at the people who had put him there. He was enraged when he thought of the killing field and the purposeful, deliberate way a species had been completely wiped off of the face of the earth. In all of his studies and all of the gossip he had heard over the years, this was the first instance he knew of in which there had been a purposeful and determined effort to wholly terminate a species.

It was nearly dark, and it was getting colder. An icy wind raced up the mountain from the valley floor. The sky had cleared to the horizons, but it seemed to be regrouping for later. Long, thin faraway clouds paralleled the western horizon looking like multiple red knife wounds slashed across purpling flesh.

"We have some beautiful sunsets, don't we, honey?" Sheridan's mom said.

"Yeah," Sheridan answered blankly. She had other things on her mind.

In the car, on the way to their house on Bighorn Road, Sheridan's mom had asked her to tell her what was wrong. It was just the two of them, she said, and she was getting a little worried about her big girl. She could tell that something was really bothering her, and she wanted Sheridan to tell her what it was. She said Sheridan's eyes looked very tired.

"I'm okay, Mom," Sheridan said. Her backpack was on the floor of the car. She had brought it, she said, to put her books in. But now it held a full bread sack of table scraps.

"Did you hear some of the things your dad and I discussed last night when he got home?"

Sheridan shook her head no. Her mom seemed relieved. Sheridan was glad it was nearly dark outside, because she knew her mom could read her face. It was as if her mom could tell what she was thinking sometimes. Sheridan felt guilty about not telling her mom about the creatures and the man. Mom was wonderful, and very smart, even though she could be stern. Sometimes she couldn't believe how wonderful her mother was, especially as Sheridan spent more time with Grandmother Missy. Sometimes it seemed like her mom was the adult and Grandmother Missy, Sheridan, and Lucy were the children. But her mom sure could worry, and Sheridan knew how much she would worry if she knew what Sheridan knew. Worrying wasn't a good thing for a woman who was so pregnant. This Sheridan was pretty sure of.

"I want you to feel you can tell me what's wrong, Sheridan," her mom said. She wasn't letting this go.

Sheridan had part of her problem solved. When they got to the house, Sheridan would go into her bedroom and fill her backpack with some of her own books from her bookshelves. She doubted her mom would want to look at the books to see if they were from the school library. The hard part, though, would be figuring out a way to get outside alone. She had a little flashlight in her backpack for shining under the garage. She hoped she would see them under there, and she hoped they would be all right.

"I think I don't like that house we're staying in," Sheridan said. "It seems too fancy. It seems like we're living in somebody else's house."

"I know you feel that way," mom said. "We *are* living in someone's house. Wealthy people like your grandmother do it all the time, but I realize it's new to you. But isn't it nice to have your own big room for a while? And that TV with all of those channels? What about that wonderful fireplace and all of those books on the shelves?"

"They're all right," Sheridan confessed. "But I still like our old house better."

"Sometimes change is good," her mom said.

"Most of the time it's bad," Sheridan echoed darkly.

Her mom laughed. "You can be so dramatic, sweetie."

The car slowed and her mom turned the steering wheel.

"Well, it's still here," her mom said.

Sheridan looked through the windshield. The house was very dark. It looked like her father's truck was parked where it usually was on the side of the house. But it wasn't her father's truck.

"Wacey must have gone with Dad and left his truck here when they took the horses," Mom said. "I didn't realize he was going, too." She turned off the motor.

"Anyway, let's not take all night," Mom continued. "Grandmother Missy is making lasagna, and we don't want to miss that."

Grandmother Missy had come to the conclusion that everyone in the family loved her lasagna. The fact that no one finished their dinner hadn't changed her mind. The truth was that the only person who liked Grandmother Missy's lasagna was Grandmother Missy herself.

Sheridan was behind her mother while her mom found the keys, opened the front door, and went in. Mom reached to click on the lights, but she stopped before she did so, and Sheridan bumped right into her.

Her mom didn't move.

"What? . . ."

Suddenly, her mother was bent over and her face was close to Sheridan's.

"Don't turn on the lights, honey. Just be still." Her mom's voice was urgent—and serious. Sheridan had rarely heard that tone, and it scared her.

"What's wrong?" Sheridan's eyes were wide.

"I don't know for sure," her mom said. "But I can see some kind of light in the backyard."

Sheridan couldn't speak. She looked around her mother and could see it, too. Yellow light came in through the kitchen window and swept across the ceiling. Then it flashed the other way.

Sheridan's mom guided Sheridan to the couch and sat her down.

"Just stay here for a second. I'm going to go see what it is."

Sheridan sat, clutching her backpack. She watched her mom walk through the front room and into the kitchen. Her mother's silhouette was framed by the window.

"Mom . . ."

Her mother turned. "There is a man out there by the woodpile with a flashlight. He's kicking it apart." Her voice was a tense whisper. "I think he intends to steal our firewood."

Sheridan was jolted the instant she heard that someone, a man, was in the woodpile. It came to her in a brilliant flash of panic: the truck parked outside, the fact that Mom didn't know about it, the friend of her dad's.

What was his name?

"Mom!" Sheridan screamed, hurtling off of the couch toward the kitchen, even as her mother reached over and clicked on the floodlights that illuminated the backyard.

"Get away from that wood!" her mother yelled, smacking the window with the palm of her hand as if the man were a stray dog rooting through the garbage.

Then the window shattered and there was a sharp crack outside. Her mother was thrown backwards to the floor, her head bouncing hard on the linoleum. Outside, a man was shouting.

Sheridan tossed the backpack aside and fell to her knees, sliding into her mother on the floor. Sheridan put her hands on both sides of her mother's face.

"Oh, Mom . . ."

"I'm hurt, Sheridan darling," her mother said in a clear voice. "He shot me, and I don't think I'm okay. I don't know who it was who shot me."

Sheridan wailed and buried her head into her mother's

breasts. She could feel her mother's strong heartbeat. But Sheridan's hand, which was wrapped around her mother's waist, was warm and wet.

"Oh God," her mom said, with a choke in her throat. "I can't feel anything. Everything is numb."

It had all happened so quickly that Sheridan couldn't yet grasp the situation.

Suddenly, her mother was bathed in light, and Sheridan could see her mother's face and the tears in her eyes and the blood, lots of it, spreading across the floor. Her mother looked from Sheridan to the source of the light, and Sheridan followed. "Stay where you are, you two," the man said, almost calmly. Then he withdrew the flashlight. They heard him trying to get in the locked back door.

"Somebody let me in," the man said with authority.

Sheridan's mom reached up and squeezed Sheridan's arm.

"Get away, Sheridan."

"I can't," Sheridan said. The words tumbled out as she cried. "It's all my fault this happened. He said if I told anyone he would hurt our family. He said he would hurt you and Lucy and Dad. He said he would hurt the baby." Her tears dropped on her mother's face.

"Unlock the goddamned *door*!" A loud crash accompanied the man's yell as he began to hurl himself against the back door. There was a big crack down the center of the door. Splinters flew across the floor.

"Get away *now*," her mother said. "Run out the front door and keep running. Hide and wait for your dad and Wacey to come back." Her voice was not as strong as it had been a minute ago. "Don't you stop, Sheridan."

Her mother's words rooted Sheridan to the spot. The truck outside that looked like her father's but wasn't, the man's familiar voice, and her mother's words all sprang out in sharp clarity and a surge of recognition hit her.

"But Mom, that's *Wacey* outside the door," Sheridan cried. "It was Wacey who said he would hurt us!"

But her mom's eyes were closed, and her hand had dropped to the floor. Sheridan could still feel her heartbeat though, and she looked like she was sleeping.

Sheridan said, "I love you, Mom," and then she was up and running, deftly juking around the coffee table in the living room and out the front door just as the backdoor gave way and Wacey Hedeman stumbled into the house.

29

Running like she had never run before, not even feeling the soles of her tennis shoes on the grass or the broken concrete of the walkway, the screen door slamming behind her, Sheridan ran through the front gate onto Bighorn Road, changed her mind, and turned back toward the driveway. Sheridan stopped and caught herself as she reached for the handle on the door of the car. She was not thinking clearly, and she realized she had no plan at all once she was inside the car. She could lock the doors, but Wacey could simply smash through the glass and get her. She couldn't drive away because her mom always took the keys with her and they were probably in her purse, on the floor, in the house.

So she dropped to her belly and scrambled under the car like a crab. Gravel from the driveway ground into her bare hands and jammed into the top of her trousers. A piece of hot metal that was sticking out under the car tore through her shirt and into the skin of her back.

Then she was out the other side and up again. She paused and tried to think. Either she could run out onto Bighorn

Road again and maybe be seen and picked up by somebody or she could go around the garage and into the backyard. But in the road, he could see her better, and shoot or run her down. She knew the backyard very well and the grounds around it. He might not look there first, which would give her time. These thoughts shot through her brain, and then she ran toward the garage. For a terrifying few seconds she was in the open where she could easily be seen if he was looking. Before she dropped to her hands and knees to crawl through the lilac bushes, she glanced over her shoulder.

The lights in the house were on now, and Wacey was coming out the front door. He had one hand on the screen door knob and was holding the pistol in the other. He was looking out toward the road, squinting, and she was sure he hadn't seen her vanish into the dark bushes that formed a hedge between the house and the garage.

As she weaved through the bushes toward the back—she couldn't see well but had done it so many times before—she heard him call her name. Then he called her name again.

Not really seeing but knowing, she cleared the bushes and ran across the backyard. She avoided both the light of the floodlights and the trunk of the cottonwood tree, then raced through the woodpile where the neat rows of logs had been kicked to pieces and then through the corral fence. The stall was empty and dark, and her dad's horse was gone. She pulled down a heavy horse blanket from a cross beam in the tack room and threw it over her shoulder and ran out of the stall toward the Sandrock draw and up into the foothills. She would go to the place where she once thought monsters had come from.

She heard Wacey yell her name again.

He was now out on the road.

Sheridan climbed up the draw away from the house. Cactus pierced her feet, and wild rose bushes tugged at her clothes, hair, and skin as if trying to prevent her from climbing still farther, as if trying to throw her back to where she belonged. It was hard to see where she was going so she navigated blindly, using senses she didn't know she had to tell her when to turn, when to duck, and when to step over a rock. Several times, she covered her head and arms in the horse blanket to push her way through thickets that would tear her skin or trip her.

Finally, she stopped. She could go no farther. Her chest hurt from panting, and her legs and arms were too heavy to lift anymore.

She sank to the ground, her back to a boulder on the side of the draw. She pulled the horse blanket around her and covered her mouth with it to muffle her racking sobs. Her mind was filled with the image of her mother on the floor. She put the fingers of the hand she had held her mom with in her mouth, and she tasted blood. And she listened, hoping she wouldn't hear Wacey coming after her.

Instead, she heard her name being called very clearly.

"Sheridan, I know you can hear me," he yelled. She figured he must now be in the backyard. His voice carried through the draw and certain words bounced back in echoes.

"I know you can hear me, Sheridan. You need to listen to me."

Her head emerged from the folds of the blanket.

"Sheridan, I'm really sorry about what happened. I apologize to you and to your mom. She scared the hell out of me, and I shot before I even knew who it was. Really, believe me. Please."

He sounded as if he were telling the truth, Sheridan thought.

"I called for the ambulance, and it's on the way. Your mom is going to be okay. I just talked to her, and she's going to be just fine. It looks a lot worse than it really is.

She's just worried about her little girl. She needs you to come back. She really misses you. She's real worried."

But he was a good liar. He had shot her pregnant mother, and he had come after her. The last thing her mom had told her was to get away. Sheridan believed what her mom told her. A lot more than she believed Wacey Hedeman.

"Sheridan, answer me so I can tell you're okay! Your mama needs to know."

He went on like that for a while. She listened but didn't speak or move. Her breath was finally calming, and her chest didn't hurt as much. The blanket was thick and warm, and it smelled like Lizzie and the leather of her dad's saddle. It comforted her.

His voice got harsher. He was now demanding that she answer him. There was no mention of her mother now. That meant he had been lying all along, as she had supposed. He wanted to know if she had told him everything she knew about "her little friends." He had been trying to find those Miller's weasels for two straight days, and all he could find, he said, was a bunch of goddamned turds in the woodpile.

"Get your little ass down here, Sheridan. If you don't, you're going to be in bigger trouble than you ever imagined!" He sounded crazy now.

When he said that, she resolved not to move an inch. Adults could be incredibly stupid. He had *almost* convinced her to answer before he lost his temper.

"Okay, then," he continued. "If you aren't coming down RIGHT NOW you had better stay *exactly* where you are tonight."

This was new. She listened. He was shouting. His voice was getting hoarse.

"Sheridan, there are going to be a lot of people here in a little while. Lots of lights and lots of policemen. You better not even think of coming down until after they're gone. If you do, if I see you, a lot more people are going to die. You're going to be the first one, and then I'm going to finish off your mother. JUST LIKE I'M GOING TO FRY ALL OF THESE FUCKING LITTLE WEASELS!"

It was the first thing he said that she truly believed.

She looked up, and the rock wall in front of her was glowing. Orange curls of light flickered across it, and for a moment she was sure she was witnessing a miracle.

Then she climbed on the boulder that she had been sitting under and looked down. She was amazed at the distance she had covered, and how clearly she could see what was going on below her.

The woodpile was burning, the red flames rolling into the cold night air. Wacey was in the backyard, bathed in the light of the fire. He kept looking up into the foothills and it appeared he was looking directly at her. But he couldn't see her up there, so far away on top of that rock.

He turned and went inside the house. It was too far away to see into the house, to see her mother.

30

In his pickup, Joe crested the hill on the Bighorn Road and what he saw ahead in the distance was his worst nightmare come true—something that perhaps in the past he had dreamed about, or thought about just like every father inevitably does, but something he had suppressed into a place deep in his mind. But sometimes those unthinkable possibilities, no matter how far beaten back, are unleashed at terrible moments. Like now.

His house and the road in front of it was an explosion of strobing and flashing lights. Garish blue and red emergency lights spun on the tops of Saddlestring Police Department cars and county vehicles. Orange flames rose into the clear sky behind the house, the fire so large and bright it lit up the hillside beyond.

Then, from the center of it all, a Life Flight helicopter bristling with landing lights lifted off, looking clumsy as it cleared the roof of the house, then gaining altitude once it emerged from the spoor of wood smoke that was black on black in the night sky.

For a heart-stopping moment, Joe had forgotten that his

family was at Eagle Mountain. But, after assuring himself that they seemed to be nowhere nearby, he wondered what he could be seeing.

He pressed the accelerator to the floor and sped up. The horse trailer pulled sluggishly behind him. In the few minutes it took to get to his house, a half-dozen different scenarios occurred to him: the wiring in the house had always been bad, so a short caused a fire and the Life Flight helicopter contained an injured firefighter; or a drunk hunter, mad about something, had come to his vacant house and set the woodpile aflame and gotten burned in the process; or the people who had wiped out the Miller's weasels had come after him and something had gone wrong. All of the scenarios were possible but none made any sense.

The intensity of the multiple flashing emergency lights made it nearly impossible to see where he was driving. There were vehicles blocking the driveway and lining the road in front of the house. He pulled ahead and off to the side of the road and jumped out of his pickup. He left the motor running and the door open.

Sheriff's deputies in short dark jackets and Stetson's compared notes on the front lawn. No one seemed to notice him as he approached the house. Through the front picture window, Joe could see that there were men inside, standing in the living room and the kitchen, and every light in the house was on. Joe felt he was walking through some kind of movie scene where he was invisible to everyone else in it. He saw Sheriff Barnum's hangdog face through the window talking on the telephone.

As he opened the door to go in, Wacey suddenly blocked it. He could tell by the drained, panicked look on Wacey's face that something was horribly wrong. Joe tried to step around him, but Wacey made it clear he didn't want Joe to come any farther into the house.

"Move, damn it," Joe barked.

"Joe, Marybeth's been shot."

Joe stopped. The words hit him like a hammer.

Wacey reached out and put his hands on Joe's shoulders both to steady him and to keep him in front of him.

"Joe, I was driving up the road about a half hour ago and I saw there was big fire behind your house. I saw Marybeth's car out front and the door was unlocked so I went in. I found her on the kitchen floor and there's a bullet hole in the kitchen window and the backdoor was kicked in."

Joe felt as if his insides had been sucked out. "Who . . ."

"We don't know." Wacey had a desperate look on his face that disturbed Joe even more.

"Is Marybeth all right? Why was she even here?"

"She's alive, but we don't know how bad it is yet. The Life Flight chopper is on its way to Billings right now. She should be in surgery within a half an hour."

Joe was staring beyond Wacey and into the house. The kitchen floor was covered with dark red blood. It looked like gallons of it. A county photographer was taking shots of the floor and the window.

"Joe?"

Joe looked back to Wacey.

"Joe, do you have any idea at all who might have done something like this? Was anybody gunning for you? Any problems in the field with hunters or anything?"

Joe shook his head no. He didn't want to spend the time it would take to tell Wacey what he had learned in the elk camp, not knowing if it could possibly have any significance with what had happened to Marybeth.

"Was she alone?" Joe asked. "Did she have any of the kids with her?"

"She was alone, thank goodness," Wacey said. "God, I'm so sorry this happened to you. I really am."

"Jesus Christ," Joe sighed.

"Absolutely by herself," Wacey added for emphasis. "But don't worry, Joe, we'll find out who did it. We'll probably have 'em by midnight. My guess is drunk hunters."

Joe nodded, not really listening.

"Wacey, will you help me out here?"

"You bet, Joe."

"I need to unhitch a horse trailer and get to Billings. Will you help me unhitch it and then call my mother-in-law at Eagle Mountain and tell her what's happened? I'll call her and the kids from the hospital as soon as I get there and find out what's what."

Wacey agreed, and the two of them went out to the road where Joe's pickup was. Wacey asked Joe if he was sure he was okay to drive, and Joe mumbled that he was. He was still shaken from the sight of all of that blood on the kitchen floor. Marybeth's blood.

They unhitched the horse trailer from the truck and lowered the tongue to the ground. Joe asked Wacey to corral Lizzie and feed and water her.

"Do you want me to take that saddle, too?" Wacey asked, shining his flashlight in the back of the pickup on the saddle with its bulging saddlebags and the butt of the Wingmaster shotgun still in the scabbard.

"No," Joe said. "That stays with me."

Joe ignored Wacey when he said he would be "more than glad" to take the saddle to the corrals.

As he pulled out into the road, in his rearview mirror, Joe could see Wacey leading his horse across the road and watching Joe's pickup drive away.

There had been something in Wacey's eyes, Joe thought, some glint that made him look just a bit unhinged and had made Joe want to keep the saddle and the things in it. Joe wondered why Wacey seemed so personally affected by what happened to Marybeth. Either Wacey was deeper than Joe gave him credit for—or something was going on.

Joe tried to erase the feeling he had, but it wouldn't go away. Maybe he was getting paranoid. Maybe finding that killing field and thinking about the circumstances that led up to it was making him suspicious. Maybe he just wanted to get mad at someone because he felt guilty about not being able to prevent what had happened to his wife.

He drove through Saddlestring, through four straight red lights, and out the other side. Billings, Montana, was an hour and a half away, an hour if he drove 100 miles an hour. He tried to imagine what Marybeth was thinking, and he tried to send his thoughts to her up there somewhere in the air probably right over the Wyoming/Montana border. He told her he loved her. He told her to be stronger than hell and hang in there. He told her he would be with her very soon. He told her that she couldn't die, because if she did, he didn't think he had the strength and ability to hold their perfect little family together by himself, without his anchor to the planet.

His hands strangled the steering wheel. His legs trembled strangely. He drove even faster.

31

Surgery was on the third floor. He headed up there, ignoring the shouts of the receptionist to leave his holster at the desk and sign in. The elevator was busy, so he took the stairs two at a time and burst out into the third-floor hallway breathing hard. He approached the doorway of the operating room just as a heavyset woman in a green scrub suit emerged from it, held up a rubber-gloved palm, and said, "Stop!"

"I'm the husband," he said. "My name is Joe Pickett."

The woman said she would get the surgeon but only if Joe would stay exactly where he was.

"I'll stay here for about a minute," Joe said. "If he isn't out here by then, I'm coming in."

The nurse looked him over, sizing him up. "I'll get the doctor," she said.

Joe paced. Through the thick windows covered by blinds, he tried to see what was going on in the OR. He could see movement and light; a half-dozen people in green suits like the nurse wore were standing side-by-side with their backs to him. Marybeth must be on the table in front of them. What were they doing to her? The thought of his wife in that room with all of those unfamiliar people around her disturbed him. Was she bleeding? Broken? Crying?

Joe had never liked hospitals. They brought out something mean in him. He had made an effort all of his life to avoid going in them. Even when Marybeth had been in one to have Sheridan and Lucy, he struggled with himself to be in the room with her when she delivered. It wasn't the blood or illness or weakness that turned his stomach. It was his memories of being in a hospital when he was very young, visiting his mother after she fell down the stairs. He must have been around six years old at the time. Looking out at him from her hospital bed, her face had been mottled and blue, her bottom lip was split and stitched back together, and her arms were in casts. He remembered how the nurses would smile at him like they were sorry for him instead of his mother, and how they would look at each other when he told them she had fallen down the stairs while he was sleeping. It was much later before he learned that she had never had the accident, that it was the result of a drunken fight with his father outside of the Elks Club. Nevertheless, he hated the forced quiet, the antiseptic smell, the artifice of the nurses who patted his head and looked at each other, and the doctors who thought of themselves as Olympian gods. He shivered when he heard the sounds of nurse's shoes squeaking down the hall as they walked.

A short, wiry doctor came out of the operating room and walked directly to him. The man's scrub suit was flecked with dark blood and his latex gloves were tinted pink from being immersed in it. The doctor slipped his mask down to his neck. Joe introduced himself.

"You may want to sit down," the doctor said by way of introduction.

"I'm okay," Joe said calmly. He tried to brace himself for the absolute worst.

"She's stable but still in danger," the doctor said bluntly. "The baby is lost. It might have been possible to save him, but it wouldn't have been the wisest thing to do considering his condition. We had to make a choice between saving your wife and saving a very damaged fetus."

Joe stepped slowly backwards until he could rest against the wall. Otherwise, he was afraid he might slump over. The moment passed.

"Are you all right?" the doctor asked.

Joe couldn't think of anything to say, so he nodded that he understood.

"The bullet entered below her sternum, glanced off of her rib cage, and exited her lower back. It may have injured her spine. We don't know how extensive that injury will be."

Joe appreciated the fact that the doctor was being absolutely straight with him. But he struggled with the magnitude of what he was being told. His baby—*his first son*—was lost, and his wife might not be able to walk again.

"When can I see her?" Joe asked, his voice a whisper.

The doctor sighed. He started to say something soothing and procedural but the look in Joe's eyes made him reconsider. Then: "They're finishing up in there now. She's sleeping. They should be done and have her back in bed in intensive care within the hour. You can see her then, but don't expect her to be awake."

Joe nodded. His mouth was dry, and it hurt to swallow.

The doctor approached him and put his hand on Joe's shoulder.

"There's no easy way to tell you these things," the doctor said. "Be strong, and love her back to health when she's out of here. That's the best advice I can give you."

Joe thanked him, but he really wanted to tell him to go away. He didn't want to be seen by anyone right now. He didn't want nurses clucking over him like they had when his mother was in the hospital. The doctor seemed to sense what Joe was thinking and went back into the operating room.

Joe turned and stumbled down the hallway until he found the men's bathroom. He went in it, turned out the lights, and wailed for the first time in his life.

32

Wacey knew just enough about the telephone lines in rural Twelve Sleep County to be dangerous. What little he knew he had learned from a couple of U.S. West telephone company engineers who had once needed his help. They were up from Denver to do some repairs and upgrading of the microwave station that served Saddlestring when they had run into a cow moose who wouldn't let them near the building. The microwave station was on the summit of Wolf Mountain. Between the microwave dish and the metal shack, they said, stood the moose. They showed Wacey the dent in the door of their pickup from her first charge. They had never experienced anything like it before.

Wacey had explained to them that moose couldn't see very well at all, and when panicked, they sometimes charged at whatever blur threatened them. He said it was likely that the moose had a calf somewhere up there in the bushes near the station and she was protecting her young.

He had driven to the summit with the engineers, but they never saw the cow moose. What they found instead was the stillborn body of her calf, still warm, the umbilical cord wrapped tightly around its neck. The engineers had probably appeared just after the calf had been born, when the cow was crazed with rage.

Wacey stood in the front yard of Joe Pickett's yard and looked up at the lone red light on the top of Wolf Mountain where the microwave station was. He had volunteered to stay at the crime scene until morning when Sheriff Barnum would send McLanahan or someone to relieve him. Under the front porch light, he looked at his wristwatch. Then he looked back at the mountain behind the house, where he was certain Sheridan was hiding.

While he was on the summit that spring, the engineers showed Wacey the circuitry inside of the shack and the thousands of telephone wires that fed into the main trunk line. He had noted where the trunk line emerged from the station to begin its descent into Saddlestring. He had thought at the time that a single high-powered rifle bullet into the base of the trunk line would disable the telephone system for the entire valley. It might take days to repair, but Wacey was concerned only about tonight.

He had a .30-06 in his gun rack. He would chance it that Sheridan wouldn't even know he had left.

33

It was 11 o'clock but seemed much later when Joe put coins into the telephone in the hospital lobby to call Missy Vankeuran. He had silently rehearsed to himself what he was going to say, how he was going to tell Sheridan and Lucy what had happened and try not to scare them into hysterics. It was time to be calm. It was time to be fatherly.

It took a few moments of ringing before Joe realized he had absently dialed the telephone number to his house on Bighorn Road. He found the Eagle Mountain number in his notebook and dialed. While he did, he wondered how it was possible that Barnum had already cleared the scene and left no one to watch the house. Maybe Barnum was incompetent after all. Maybe Wacey was right. Maybe Wacey would be a welcome addition as sheriff.

His mother-in-law picked up the telephone on the second ring. Her voice sounded angry and cold.

"Yes?"

"Missy, this is Joe."

First there was a pause. Then: "Oh, hello, Joe. You surprised me. I was expecting it to be Marybeth." Her reaction caught him off guard.

Joe was confused. Then he realized that no one had contacted her yet. But Wacey had said he would do it . . .

"I called your house over and over at dinner time," Missy said, speaking fast. "It was busy every time. Every time. Then all of the sudden there is no one there. Marybeth said she would be home in an hour. That was four hours ago, Joe. My dinner is ruined!"

"Missy . . ."

"I haven't cooked, actually *cooked* in ages. It took me all afternoon to make my famous lasagna. Marybeth used to love it. She said she was looking forward to it. I'm starting to think staying with her isn't such a good idea. For either of us, Joe . . ."

To Joe it sounded like Missy had a good start on the wine she must have had planned for dinner. He was angry.

"Missy, goddamnit, will you stop talking?"

Silence.

"Missy, I'm calling from the hospital in Billings."

Silence.

"Marybeth has been shot. Someone shot her when she went to the house. They don't know who did it. The doctors say she's going to make it, but the baby isn't . . ." There was more silence, and he realized that the line was dead. He wasn't sure she had heard any of it. It didn't seem possible she could have hung up on him.

He dialed again. There was no ringing. He dialed again, and a recording said that the number he was calling was not in service at this time. He tried Sheriff Barnum's office. The line was dead as well.

Joe couldn't sit. He couldn't stand still. He tried several times to read a magazine from the stack in the waiting room, but found he couldn't concentrate on the words or even remember what the article was about. He approached the nurses' station to check if he could see Marybeth yet.

The nurse was polite but annoyed. She pointed at the clock on her desk and reminded him he had asked her the same question not ten minutes before. Joe could not recall time ever moving so slowly. It would still be at least a half an hour before Marybeth would be wheeled out of the operating room.

He tried three more times to reach Missy and Barnum. Then he tried Sheriff Barnum's office again. He couldn't believe his bad luck. The phone lines all over the county were apparently down.

So he wandered the hallways, looking at his wristwatch every few minutes. The halls were all the same: heavily painted light blue cinder-block walls, dimmed fluorescent lighting, occasional black marks from gurney wheels on the tile floors, nurses at every station looking him over from behind their desks. He located the room where Marybeth would be. Her name was written on a card outside the door and the ink was still wet. She would be alone inside, he noted. She wouldn't have a roommate. He walked down the hall to the maternity ward and heard babies crying. He found himself staring at a young mother still plump and flushed from delivery. She was cradling a tiny red baby in her arms, waiting for a nurse to wheel her to her room. The scene poleaxed him. In a daze, he ascended a set of stairs to the next level.

Joe wandered aimlessly but conveyed a sense of purpose that he didn't really have, and no one stopped him. When he glanced into the rooms he was passing, he saw there were older people on this floor. People waiting to get better or die. A television set was on and Jay Leno was interviewing someone.

A Billings police officer stood casually at the nurses' station and leaned on the counter. He didn't give Joe a second glance as Joe walked past. The policeman was talking in low tones to an attractive nurse who seemed interested in what he was saying but was feigning boredom. Joe noticed the policeman's empty chair near a room at the end of the hall, and he walked past it. The card on the wall of the room read C. LIDGARD.

Joe took a few steps before it hit him. He stopped and looked down the hall over his shoulder. The policeman had his back to Joe, and he could hear the nurse giggle. Joe hesitated for a moment, then turned and walked into the room. He eased the door shut behind him.

Clyde Lidgard lay in the dark room illuminated by a small bulb mounted in the headboard. Joe hardly recognized him. Lidgard looked like he was 80 years old and was little more than a skeleton. His skin was waxy and yellow and harshly wrinkled. Webs of tubes sprang from his arms looking like the white roots of a neglected potato. His head was turned on the pillow toward the door, and the light from the bulb infused his feathery silver hair with a glow.

Joe stared at Clyde Lidgard's face as if willing him to wake up out of his coma.

"Tell me what you know, Clyde," Joe said. "Just tell me what you know."

When Clyde Lidgard's eyes slowly opened, Joe stood riveted to the floor. Lidgard's eyes were rheumy and caked with mucus. Joe wasn't sure Lidgard could even see out of them. It didn't seem possible that Lidgard was actually awake or had any idea that Joe was in the room. Maybe Lidgard normally did this while he slept.

"Can you hear me, Clyde?" Joe asked softly. He half-expected the nurse and police officer to burst in at any moment and throw him out.

Lidgard's lips pursed as if he were sucking on a candy.

"You're dry. Do you want some water?" Joe said, pouring some from a plastic pitcher into a small paper cup. He held the cup to Lidgard's lips, and Lidgard drank. His eyes followed Joe's movements.

"Do you know who I am?" Joe asked quietly.

"Warden." The response was so weak that Joe almost didn't hear it. "Warden." Joe replaced the pitcher and bent over Lidgard's face. He smelled the odor of decay on Lidgard's breath. It was the same smell a deer or an elk had after it had been shot.

"That's right," Joe said. "I'm Game Warden Joe Pickett from the Saddlestring District. You need to tell me what happened up there in that elk camp."

Lidgard's eyes closed momentarily then opened again. "I'm going to die now," Lidgard said.

"Not before you tell me about the elk camp," Joe persisted. "Not until you tell me about the Miller's weasels."

There was a tiny reaction on the corner's of Clyde Lidgard's mouth, as if he were trying to smile.

"I took some good pictures of them weasels," Lidgard replied. "But I never got to see if they turned out. Instead, I died."

Joe gave Clyde Lidgard some more water. It was still quiet in the hallway.

"You talked for a while and cleared your conscience. A huge weight lifted off of you," Joe said. "And *then* you died, feeling much better about yourself."

"I did?" Lidgard asked.

"Starting now," Joe said.

When Joe came out of the room, the policeman was still leaning over the nurses' counter, and Clyde Lidgard was dead.

The first thing Joe noticed as Marybeth was rolled out of the operating room was that, compared to Clyde Lidgard, she looked remarkably healthy. He found her hand under the sheet and squeezed it as he walked alongside the gurney. The emotion he felt when he looked at her flat bandaged belly brought tears to his eyes.

They made him let go of her hand for a moment while they situated her bed in the room, but when the nurses moved to set up the IV bottle, he went back to her. They told him they had just given her some powerful sedatives and that she would be asleep until morning.

But the drugs hadn't kicked in completely yet, because for a moment, she awakened.

"You're going to be all right," Joe said, forcing a smile. "You're going to make it and be just fine."

She seemed to be looking to him for some kind of reassurance. He hoped he was providing it.

"Marybeth, do you know who did this?"

"I couldn't see. All I know is that it was a man."

"Is there anything you can tell me?"

"What about my baby?" Her voice was thick.

Joe shook his head.

She turned her away, her eyes closed tightly as she cried. He squeezed her hands.

Suddenly, Marybeth was looking at him, frantically searching his face. Her eyes were wide.

"Where's Sheridan?" she asked. "I told her to run."

PART SIX

Like blind men building a mechanical elephant, each of the players picked up a hammer and wrench and, working separately and often secretly, fashioned gears, soldered wires, and pounded sheet metal. One built a leg, another the tail, a third the trunk. Then suddenly this creation, like a dreadful android, sprung to life, catching its builders in its gears as it lurched, uncontrolled, toward unknown destinations, without purpose, limit, or remorse.

—Alston Chase, *In a Dark Wood*, 1995,
commentary on the creation and unintended consequences of the Endangered Species Act

34

Sheridan had never been so cold, so hungry, or so alone. Once the fire down in the woodpile had died out, utter darkness had descended over the mountain. She rolled herself into a tight ball against the base of the boulder and tried to tuck the horse blanket around her body, but it was too thick and too small to cover her completely. The boulder, the dirt, and the air were all cold. She wished she had brought the backpack with her because it was filled with scraps of food. This was the first time she had ever missed dinner. She wished she could do something routine, like change into her pajamas or brush her teeth, so she could at least feel kind of normal. She didn't know what time it was, but she knew it was late. There was no moon and the cold, hard stars were relentless.

Night animals were out. Something—it sounded like a dog by the way it walked—had come down the Sandrock draw from above but had stopped when it either smelled or sensed her. With an abrupt *thump-thump-thump,* it had reversed course and crashed back through the brush up the mountain. It had scared her at the time, because for a moment she thought it was Wacey. But she was pretty sure it had been a coyote. There were lots of them up here, according to her Dad. They had eaten her puppy and her kitten, after all.

She had slept for a while, but she didn't know how long. A sharp crack—a gunshot from somewhere up in the mountains—had jarred her awake a few minutes ago. She listened for more shots but heard none. She crawled on top of the boulder again and looked down. The woodpile, now coals and ashes, glowed deep red. The lights were still on in the house but she couldn't see the man moving around inside or out. She would feel better if she knew where he was. For a moment, she thought about going back down.

She wished she had some way to defend herself if he found her. She assessed what she had—the horse blanket, a barrette, two pennies from her pockets. She didn't even have a stick. If she were in a movie, she would be able to fashion something clever out of those items to beat the bad guy. But this wasn't a movie, and she wasn't that clever. She was cold—and scared.

Then she saw the headlights coming down from Wolf Mountain. She watched them as they crossed the river and came down Bighorn Road. The pickup pulled back into the driveway at the front of the house. She heard a door slam but couldn't see who had been driving.

After a few moments, she saw someone in the house pass by the back picture window. The porch light came on and Wacey stepped out. He was carrying a rifle.

"*Yoo-Hoo!* Sheridan? Are you still with us?"

Sheridan began to cry. For a moment, she had thought the driver was her father.

"Answer me, sweetheart, so I know you're okay!" His voice was friendly, as it always was when he started out.

She was crying hard now, uncontrollably. It was as if something had released inside of her.

"It's nice and warm inside, Sheridan. I've got some hot

chocolate warming up on the stove. Hot chocolate with itty-bitty marshmallows that I found in the cupboard. *Mm-mmmmm!* You've got to be getting a little chilly up there."

She could not stop crying. She covered her face in her hands.

For a few moments, there was silence from below.

Then: "I can *heeeeear* you. I can hear you up there. Stop crying, or you'll make me feel bad. I don't want to drink all of this hot chocolate by myself."

She scrambled down from the boulder. As suddenly as she had started crying, she had stopped. She was horrified that Wacey had heard her crying. Now he knew for sure where she was.

"You sound pathetic, Sheridan. Why don't you come on down so I don't have to come up and get you?"

She pushed her way around the side of the boulder through a juniper bush so she could see down into the backyard again. He was still standing in the light of the floods. He had raised the rifle and was trying to see her through the scope but he was looking in the wrong direction, somewhere off to her left. Maybe he didn't know where she was after all. Maybe her sobs had echoed and confused him. Either way, he wasn't coming up after her. Yet.

It would be different when the sun came up.

35

It was three in the morning in Saddlestring, Wyoming, when Joe Pickett roared in from Billings. The four stoplights flashed amber, and no one was about. The last of the bars were closed, and it was too early for morning activities yet. The town was as dead as it would ever be.

Joe drove straight down Main Street and pulled around the corner from Barrett's Pharmacy. He stopped and turned off the motor and looked at himself in the rearview mirror. He expected his eyes to glow red, as if he were some kind of demon or alien. He was so tired, so drained. He had not slept in two nights and had not eaten since breakfast, now almost 20 hours ago.

And he was absolutely enraged. He knew it wouldn't be long before he would explode. The only question remaining was how many people would be involved in the blast.

Dim lights were on inside the pharmacy and Joe pressed his face to the window and looked in. In the parking lot, he had seen the pickup with a magnetic sign on the door that read HANS'S JANITORIAL SERVICE. Hans was in there all right, pushing a vacuum through the aisle that featured magazines and paperback books. Joe rapped on the window, but Hans didn't look up. He couldn't hear Joe over the vacuum. Joe hit the window again so hard he risked smashing it or tripping the alarm. But Hans, who has half-deaf anyway, didn't respond.

Joe took his flashlight from his belt and shined it through the window into Hans's face. Hans twitched and absently rubbed his mouth, not yet aware of what was annoying him. When he finally looked up, he jumped and nearly stumbled back into the best-sellers. Joe turned the flashlight on himself so Hans could see him, and he held his badge to the window. Hans stood thinking it over, his chin in his hand, then motioned Joe around to the backdoor.

"I probably shouldn't let you in," Hans said as he unlocked the door in the alley. "Bill Barrett told me never under any circumstances to let anyone in the store after hours, even him. There's all kinds of narcotics and stuff in the pharmacy."

Joe thanked him and brushed by. "It's official state Game and Fish Department business," Joe answered. "It's lucky you were here."

Hans grunted and locked the door after them.

"I gotta tell Bill Barrett about this."

"That's fine," Joe said, walking through the store to the photo counter.

"Hope you don't mind if I vacuum," Hans said. "I went hunting with Jack this afternoon, and I'm running late. Got a buck, though. Finally. Missed a nicer one. You can ask Jack about it."

"Hans, I've got to ask you something."

Hans stopped and stared at Joe. His hands shook. Joe could tell that Hans was trying to recall anything he might have done recently that could be a violation of the Game and Fish regulations.

"Don't worry," Joe assured him. "You haven't done anything wrong that I'm aware of."

Hans continued to shake.

"Do you remember a couple of weeks ago when I drove up on you and Jack after you got that pronghorn buck?"

Hans nodded his head yes.

"You asked me about whether or not I had heard of an endangered species in the mountains. Do you remember that?"

Hans nodded again.

"What do you know about it?" Joe asked. His voice was firm.

"Nothing," Hans said. "Honestly. We just heard rumors. You know, bar talk. Somebody said somebody else had found something up there."

"Who found it?"

"Somebody said it was Clyde Lidgard," Hans said.

"Vacuum away," Joe said, waving his hand. He slipped behind the counter and slid out the oversize drawer that held envelopes of developed pictures. The envelopes where alphabetized by name. Joe quickly leafed through them, finding the packets filed under "L." He found Lawton, Livingston, Layborn, Lane, and Lomiller. But he didn't find what he was looking for. Across the store, Hans fired up the vacuum cleaner. Joe slammed the drawer shut and said, "Shit!" But Hans was oblivious.

There was a stupidly simple reason, Joe thought, why Clyde Lidgard had no photos in his trailer from the two months leading up to the outfitter murders: he had not picked them up yet from the pharmacy after they'd been developed. But somebody apparently had.

Maybe, Joe thought with a grimace, he was about ten steps behind everybody else just as he had been since this whole thing had started. But maybe not.

He pulled open the drawer again and went to the back. Beyond "XYZ" he found a tab file that said "Unclaimed." In the file there were ten envelopes. Three of those were slated for pickup by Clyde Lidgard.

Joe ripped the first envelope open and slid the photos out onto the counter. They looked familiar: blurred, off-kilter snapshots of trees, clouds, Clyde's penis, a manhole cover. Then he saw what he was looking for. There were dozens of them.

The Stockman's Bar had been closed since two, but Joe drove by it just in case before he proceeded to the Holiday Inn at the edge of town. He parked under the motel's registration sign, clamped on his hat, and went in.

Like all night clerks and auditors, the man behind the desk was jumpy. He wore a greasy ponytail and thick horn-rimmed glasses. His eyes, magnified through the lenses, were enormous. He slammed a *Penthouse* magazine shut in a night auditing folder but not quickly enough that Joe didn't see it as he approached.

Joe introduced himself and showed his badge. He said a package was supposed to be sent to him at the hotel in care of Vern Dunnegan. He said he had tried to call to check on it but couldn't get through.

"Phones are out all over town," the night clerk said. "We can't get in or out."

Joe watched carefully as the clerk used his finger to go down the registry. His finger stopped on room 238.

"I can't see a note for any package," he said.

"Can you check please?" he asked. "It should have come in today. Maybe it's still in the back."

The night clerk clucked to himself and excused himself for a minute. The door behind the desk swung closed after him.

Quickly, Joe jumped up and sat on the counter. He reached across the night clerk's desk and slid out the drawer. There were two extra keys for room 238. Joe took one of them.

Joe scanned the small office as he waited impatiently for

the night clerk to return without a package. He noted the small plastic sign stuck to the wall under the clock, informing all guests that for their convenience, their room key would open the back door of the motel as well as the door to their rooms. The man finally reappeared, apologized, and Joe said good night. Once outside, Joe jumped into the pickup, wheeled around to the side wing of the motel and parked near the exit door. Using the key, he entered and took the staircase steps two at a time.

Two-thirty-four, two-thirty-six, *two-thirty-eight.* No one in the hallway. Joe pulled the Velcro safety strap from around the hammer of his .357 Magnum and turned the key in the lock. He stepped inside and shut the door after him. No lights were on.

Joe stood still for a moment, waiting until the objects in the room gradually took shape around him. It was a suite with a wet bar and some stools. A dark couch with clothes piled on it. Buckaroo prints mounted on the walls. A large-screen television. Two interior doors that he guessed led either to the bathroom or to the bedroom. Someone coughed, and he turned toward the room on the left. He walked across the carpet and eased the door open.

It smelled of stale bourbon and cigarette smoke inside. He couldn't see anyone, but he could sense there was more than one person in the bed. Pointing the revolver toward the bed with his right hand, he searched the wall in back of him with his left for the light switch.

Table lamps on either side of the bed came on, and Joe swung the revolver around until the front sight was squarely on Vern Dunnegan's sweaty forehead. Vern had thrashed in the sheets when the lights came on but was now sitting up in bed staring dumbly at the big black hole of the muzzle. An older, skinny woman with streaked blond hair clutched the blanket to her mouth. Her eyes were smudged with liner on the outside and road-mapped with red inside. She muffled a squeal.

"Joe, for Christ's sake," Vern said, his voice choked with sleep and anger. "What in the hell are you doing here?"

"I'm looking for you," Joe said. "And I found you."

The woman was beside herself. She was trembling and looking from Joe to Vern.

"What's your name, ma'am?" Joe asked. He recognized her as a barmaid at the Stockman's Bar.

"Evelyn Wolters."

"Evelyn," Joe said. "If you don't get out of that bed right now, you're going to have Vern Dunnegan's brain splattered all over you."

Evelyn Wolters shrieked and dove out from the covers. She had long pendulous breasts that swung from side to side as she scooped up her clothing from the floor.

"Evelyn, do you know Sheriff Barnum?" Joe asked.

She nodded her head yes very quickly.

"Good. Then get your clothes on and get in your car and drive over to his house as soon as you can. Tell him to get out to Joe Pickett's house right away with every deputy he can find. Can you do that?"

Evelyn said she could.

"Aren't you going to check with me?" Vern asked her, thoroughly disgusted.

Joe stepped aside so she could run past. She didn't reply to Vern as she left the room. Vern and Joe stared at each other in silence, only the sounds of Evelyn Wolters getting dressed in a hurry—grunts punctuated with the snapping of elastic—breaking the quiet. Vern's face was flushed, and his eyes were narrowed into slits. Joe had never seen him so angry.

The door slammed in the front room, and Evelyn was gone.

"Joe, what the fuck is going on here? You don't really want to do this. Joe? Do you? This isn't like you at all."

Joe thumbed back the hammer on the Smith & Wesson. The cylinder turned from an empty chamber to one filled with a hollow-point bullet. Little muscles in Vern's temples started to throb.

"Well, Vern, I don't know about that," Joe said, his voice betraying his rage. "Maybe you just haven't seen me on a night when my wife gets shot, my baby son dies, and one of my daughters is missing."

Vern shook his head. His famous chuckle rolled out. "Joe, you don't think I had anything at all to do with any of that, do you? I was closing down the Stockman with Evelyn when one of the local boys who'd been out at your place came in and told me about Marybeth being shot. He said Wacey told him to come find me and tell me what had happened out at the Pickett house. Soon after that, Evelyn and I packed it up and came here." Vern paused and shot Joe a look that was both petulant and accusatory. "Frankly, Joe, I don't know how you could even imply that I might have been involved in all this stuff that you've been going on about."

"Shut up, Vern. You're so deep into this you'll never get out."

"Joe, I . . ."

"SHUT UP!" Joe barked. His finger tightened on the trigger—Vern saw it and even though his mouth was still open, no sound came out.

"Here," Joe said, tossing the envelopes with Clyde's photos in them on the bedspread. Vern was confused until he shook one set of the photos out. He flipped through each of them, his stubby fingers snapping each photo down on the bed as if he were dealing cards.

"They're lousy pictures," Joe continued. "Just like all of Clyde Lidgard's work. If you didn't know what you were looking for, you wouldn't even know that all of those brown, furry things sticking out of the ground were the last Miller's weasels on earth."

Vern returned the photos to the first envelope and took out the next set.

"Of course, the negatives are somewhere else so don't even consider that option," Joe said.

Vern seemed to get smaller in the bed as he looked through the photos. A look of utter defeat passed over his features.

"Now I know the majority of these photos are so bad you can't recognize anything in them. But Clyde did manage to take some pretty good ones of you and Wacey up there in the woods. In one you can even see a package of M–forty-four cartridges sticking out of your knapsack."

Vern neatly put the photos away, keeping his head down. When he raised it, he looked wounded.

"Where did you find all of this?" Vern asked. "How did you know where to look?"

"Barrett's Pharmacy," Joe said. "Clyde Lidgard told me all about it. He told me everything."

"Clyde Lidgard?"

"I'm not here to talk," Joe said. "You are the one who needs to talk. But right now, Vern, you have about twenty seconds to get dressed because we're going to walk out of here to go find my daughter."

36

Joe drove out of town on the Bighorn Road with his right hand on the steering wheel and his left hand on his lap holding the .357 Magnum, still cocked, aimed at Vern's big gut. The sky was beginning to lighten to the east, and the stars were not as brilliant as they had been. It was a cold, clear morning and there was no other traffic on the roads. Joe felt like he and Vern were alone in a world of their own making.

They were headed back toward Joe's house. Joe figured that if Marybeth had told Sheridan to run, there was a chance his daughter might still be somewhere not too far away from the house. It was a place to start anyway.

Vern wore a pair of baggy sweatpants, a T-shirt, slippers, and a bathrobe. Joe had not given him any more time to dress. When Vern had opened the closet to get his clothes, Joe had seen the butt of a handgun on the top shelf. Joe had ordered Vern to close the damned door and put on something from the dresser.

"I could use a drink right now," Vern said. "That would help."

"Shut up."

"I'm really sorry this turned out the way it did, Joe. I'm sorry you had to even get involved in it."

"Shut up."

"I'm an entrepreneur," Vern said, his voice rising. "I'm terribly misunderstood. I'm an endangered species just like you. I'm sorry about not being able to give you that good job when you finally wanted it. Especially now that it's available again. I bet you didn't know that, did you?"

Joe snorted. Vern just kept trying, Joe thought. He didn't quit.

"It's hard to believe how this all turned out," Vern moaned. "How screwed up everything got."

"Speaking of screwed, did Les Etbauer at headquarters owe you one?"

"He *still* owes me a couple," Vern sighed. "I got him that cushy job and covered for him a couple of times when he was too drunk to function."

Joe grunted. He had thought it must have been something like that.

"A lot of people owe me," Vern said. "Some of those favors could be called in on your behalf, if you would just ease up on me a little bit. We don't *have* to be on opposite sides, here."

Vern looked over as if to gauge if Joe had softened some.

"Joe, what I'm saying here is that we could either get you your old job back or you could work for InterWest. Your choice. I can call Etbauer if you want me to. Even Wacey could hire you if I told him to. You've got lots of options, Joe. We really don't have to go through with all of this."

"Shut up, Vern," Joe gritted out, through clenched teeth.

"In fact, Joe, you owe me, too. How do you think you got the job after me? Do you realize how many guys wanted this? Wade, from Pinedale. Charley Gardener over in Rock Springs—"

"Shut the fuck up."

"Christ, Joe," Vern whined. "You could at least be civil."

The explosion of the pistol in the closed cab of the pickup was deafening, and the only thing louder than the ringing in Joe's ears was the high-pitched cursing of Vern as he searched himself frantically for the wound. There was a now a hole in the truck door the size of a quarter, just a few inches from Vern's belly.

They drove in silence for a few moments. The truck smelled sharply of cordite. It also smelled of urine because Vern had wet himself.

"How did Wacey get involved in this?" Joe asked calmly.

"Jesus, this is really embarrassing," Vern said, looking down in his lap. He clutched his thighs with his hands to keep his legs from shaking.

"How did Wacey get involved in this?"

Vern rubbed his face and sighed. "Getting Wacey in this deal was the single most stupid fucking thing I ever did. But he was the one who told me about that idiot Clyde Lidgard. He said Lidgard had talked to him about some little creatures he saw up in the canyon. Wacey knew about the pipeline, of course, and he had heard about Miller's weasels just like everybody else had. He told Clyde to keep it a secret, that it was some big government secret that just he and Clyde could know about. Clyde liked that shit. Then Wacey told me about it."

"So you and Wacey and Clyde went up there and wiped out the weasels," Joe said. "But unfortunately you didn't wipe them all out, and Ote Keeley and his buddies found what was left."

Vern nodded. Joe thought Vern figured he had nothing more to lose by talking.

"Ote must have hoped that if he delivered a Miller's weasel to you that you would drop the charges on him,"

Vern said. "That was how you got involved in this whole stupid fucking mess."

Joe grunted.

"I always thought of you and Wacey as *my boys*," Vern said, his voice cracking. "My protégés. Wacey was always a little hotheaded, but he was determined and he was tough. You were the straight-arrow. A little slow at times and you fucked up now and then, but basically you were a stand-up kind of guy. Now look what's happened: Wacey has gone over the edge and you're pointing a gun at me. I'm disappointed, Joe, at the way things turned out. How did they ever go so wrong?"

"Who killed the outfitters?" Joe asked.

Vern sighed, rocking his head back as if he were in pain. "Wacey killed the outfitters. Then he killed Clyde. He's a goddamned lunatic hothead. He likes to be the one in control. I had no idea he could be like that. That was never supposed to happen with the outfitters. He said they were drunk when he rode up on them, and they showed him a couple of the weasels they had dug up and they mouthed off. Wacey said one of 'em went for a rifle."

"So Wacey told Clyde Lidgard to stay up there and guard the camp until we showed up?"

Vern nodded.

"I wondered why Wacey slept so hard the night before we went into that camp," Joe said. "And how he could just walk right up to that camp like he owned the place. It's because he had spent the night before that up there and he knew exactly what we were going to find."

"Wacey made sure Clyde got shot," Vern confirmed.

"What was in it for Wacey?"

Vern slumped against the door of the truck. It was as if every question knocked him farther down. "He wanted in the worst way to be the sheriff, if you can believe that. He wanted to be the big shot."

"I believe it."

"I told Wacey I had some things on Barnum that would make Barnum drop out of the race. Barnum, back in the old days, liked Indian women. He used to hit on them when they were drunk and brought into jail. He's got a couple of grown kids on the reservation he pays support for. Nobody knew that but him and me. And eventually Wacey. That was part of the deal before it went so sour.

"That's how it started," Vern said, his voice small. "All I wanted to do was make a lot of money and all Wacey wanted was to be the sheriff. All I wanted were the big bucks I know I deserve after all of those years of working for the state. I was so close, too. The clearances were issued and that pipeline was just humming toward Saddlestring. But things got out of hand because of Wacey. All I ever wanted was a ton of money. Then Wacey went fucking nuts trying to cover up everything. The more he tried to cover it up, the worse it got. I warned him off of going after your daughter, but he was absolutely convinced that she knew about some living Miller's weasels. He kept saying if he could find those weasels and get rid of them that this whole thing would be over."

Joe had suddenly lost his concentration.

"What?" he yelled.

Vern looked scared. "You didn't know about your daughter?"

"Know WHAT about her?" Joe quickly switched the revolver from his left to his right hand and shoved the barrel into Vern's nose, pinning Vern's head against the passenger window.

"Jesus, Joe!" Vern honked.

"WHAT?"

"That Wacey thought she was keeping a couple of them as pets!" Vern said his eyes fixed on the gun barrel. "That's why he figured out a way to get you people out of your house and up to Eagle Mountain—so he could find those weasels. He told me this morning that he was going to head up to your place today to look for them."

Anguished, Joe pushed harder on the pistol. "Wacey went after my daughter?"

"Please, Joe . . . ," Vern pleaded, eyes bulging and blinking.

"Did Wacey shoot Marybeth, Vern? Did he? Is that what happened? He was up there looking for weasels and instead he fucking shot my wife?"

Vern started to sputter out a reply but Joe, already knowing the answer, cut him off. "That son-of-a-bitch was my *friend,*" he said, more to himself than to Vern. Joe thought about how Wacey had blocked Joe's entrance into his own house earlier and how he had hustled Joe back out onto the road. Wacey had told the cop to find Vern and tell him Marybeth had been shot. Wacey had made a point of telling Joe he would stay and watch over everything. Wacey had seemed unnerved. *Wacey.*

"Shit," Joe said, finally looking at the road and jerking the truck back in his lane after it had wandered. "Sheridan was right after all. There *are* monsters out there."

37

When dawn breaks over the Bighorns, it breaks hard and fast and with cascades of bright sunlight gushing over the mountains like a broken dam. A shaft of sunlight burst through the windshield of the pickup.

Joe pulled over in a stand of mountain ash about a half a mile from his house. He shut off the motor and stuffed the keys in his pocket.

"Get out," he told Vern. "We're going to walk the rest of the way. I don't want him hearing us drive up. Shut the door easy."

Vern started to walk down the road bed, and Joe waved him into the ditch on the shoulder. Joe holstered his pistol and pulled his shotgun from behind the seat. He pumped a shell into the chamber. In his slippers, Vern gingerly stepped down from the road into the ditch. Frosted reeds in the ditch lit up with morning sun, and Vern's feet crunched through a skin of ice.

"This water's cold," Vern said.

Joe nodded and motioned with the shotgun for Vern to start walking.

"I look like a clown," Vern mumbled. Already his sweatpants were wet from the frost. A red "O" from the muzzle of Joe's revolver was still visible on Vern's nose.

"You *are* a clown," Joe said. "Now stay in the ditch and don't say anything when we get close. The only way to keep your life is to help me find my daughter."

Vern moaned. "Then we're through, right?"

"Then we're through."

Neither told the other what they meant by that.

Sheridan untwisted herself from beneath the horse blanket. The sun was coming up. She was surprised to see that the blanket was covered with frost. She stood and tried to rub some feeling into her legs, arms, and face. She was no longer hungry—she was beyond that.

The night had been long and terrible. She was dirty and she felt featherlight. Everything hurt. There seemed to be scratches, bruises, or imbedded thorns all over her body.

She could finally see what was around her, but she knew he could, too.

Rather than crawl on top of the boulder where she might be seen, she pushed her way through the juniper bushes on the side of it again. She tried not to rustle the bushes too much.

Wacey was not in the backyard. That meant he either was in the house or was already stalking her. She couldn't believe she had actually fallen asleep. She hoped she hadn't slept too long.

Then beyond the house, up Bighorn Road, something caught her attention. It was the glint of morning sun reflecting off of the glass of a windshield. It was a green truck way down the road, a green truck just like her dad's and parked in some trees. And in the foreground, between the house and the truck, there was movement in the ditch. Two men, walking in the tall weeds. The first man was big in a long flowing robe. Behind him was her dad!

Sucking in her breath, Sheridan scrambled out from around the boulder and started to run down the mountain.

Wacey stood at the broken kitchen window sipping from a cup of coffee that he had just brewed. When he saw a flash of color on the mountain, he stepped back and picked up his binoculars from the table. He focused.

Sheridan Pickett, blond hair streaming in the sun, was racing down the hill like her pants were on fire.

"Damn."

He had been beginning to believe that maybe she wasn't up there after all, that maybe what he'd heard crying in the night was a cougar or a coyote. They sounded the same as kids sometimes.

The next business would not be pleasant at all. But like burning the Miller's weasels, it needed to be done.

Boy, he thought, he had sure sunk low. He had gone from killing three heavily armed hunters to shooting an unarmed woman. Now he was waiting for a seven-year-old. Strangely, it wasn't all that hard to do. He would make a damned good sheriff, he thought. He had a good understanding of the criminal mind.

Wacey placed the cup on the table. He started to reach for the .30-06 but decided that if she saw him come out with a rifle now, she might turn and run right back up the mountain. He didn't feel like chasing her or possibly missing her with a long shot. She was remarkably fast for a girl her age—especially one with glasses, he thought. Instead, he would wait until she got to the backyard. Then he would step out and run her down. He knew of a sump hole at the base of Wolf Mountain where some hunters had once trailed a wounded elk. The animal had gotten caught in the sump and sunk out of sight, much to the hunters' dismay. It would be a perfect place to throw a body. He would weight her down with rocks.

He waited until she ran through the back gate before he stepped out on the porch.

When she saw him, she froze in place. Her green eyes were so *huge.* He tried his best smile on her as the screen door slammed behind him.

What he didn't understand was why those eyes had moved off of his face toward the side of the house. He followed them.

"Wacey," Vern said in his deep voice, "it's over, buddy. Our deal is done and we had better get the hell out of Dodge while we still can."

Wacey turned toward him, confused. Vern looked like he just got out of bed and had walked all of the way from Saddlestring.

"You look real stupid, Vern," Wacey said. "What'd you do, piss your pants?"

Joe came around from the other side of the house near the garage. Wacey's back was turned to him; he was facing Vern. Sheridan was out in the yard. Her clothes were tattered and she was smudged with dirt and blood.

"What are you *doing* here? What are you saying?" Wacey asked Vern, his voice high-pitched. "I wiped out the rest of the weasels, and we're almost home free." He gestured toward Sheridan and spoke to her.

"Don't you move, darlin'."

Sheridan stood absolutely still. But Joe knew she could see him. *Don't give me away,* Joe silently implored.

"Let's get out of here while we can," Vern said to Wacey. "They know about the weasels, and Barnum's on the way now."

"How in the hell did that happen?" Wacey demanded, almost in falsetto.

"I'll tell you in the car," Vern said, shaking his head from side to side.

"Tell me now."

Vern sighed. "Clyde Lidgard woke the fuck up and told everybody what happened. Somebody found some pictures he took up in the mountains with both of us in them." His voice cracked again, like it had in the pickup. "Remember Clyde and his *goddamned camera*? We've got to get out of here NOW!"

"Not yet," Wacey said, reaching down for his 9mm pistol. "I've got to finish up here."

Joe thought Wacey would turn on Vern. But the pistol started to raise toward Sheridan, started to arc up from the holster as Wacey held it with a stiff arm, started to flush up into the air like a pheasant exploding from the brush into the sky, and Joe heard his daughter start to scream . . . *How could Wacey, the same Wacey who had shared coffee with Joe on so many mornings while they watched the elk come down from the mountains to eat hay in a rancher's meadow, the same Wacey who scrunched in between Joe and Vern on the bench seat of Vern's Game and Fish pickup, the same Wacey who, with that goofy laugh, recalled riding both bulls and buckle bunnies at the National College Rodeo Finals in Bozeman—how could this be the Wacey who was now leveling his 9mm pistol at Joe's older daughter?*

With the shotgun, Joe shot Wacey's arm off at the elbow.

The blast spun Wacey around until he was facing Joe. Joe had never seen terror in Wacey's face before. Wacey's disembodied forearm, with the fist still gripping the pistol, flew end over end through the air and dropped to the ground near the base of the cottonwood tree.

Joe racked the shotgun and, with two more lightning blasts, blew both of Wacey's knees back in the wrong direction. Wacey buckled to the pavement on top of himself, howling.

Vern stood stock still with his palms out and his mouth open. His robe was spattered with Wacey's blood.

Sheridan rushed to Joe, and he bent to catch her. He didn't know she could squeeze his neck so hard. She was sobbing, and he kissed her and hugged her back.

"Your mom is okay," he told her, picking her up and rocking her as if she were an infant. "I saw her last night and she's okay."

"I was so worried about her," Sheridan sobbed. "It's all my fault."

"No it isn't, darling," Joe said, wincing. "Don't ever think that. Don't ever say that. You are such a brave girl. You are such a hero. Your mom will be proud of you."

"Is he dead?" she asked.

"I'm sorry you had to see all that," Joe said to Sheridan. "It makes me kind of sick."

"He deserved it. Nobody ever needed it more than him."

He lowered her to the grass when he noticed that Vern had bent over and dug the pickup keys out of Wacey's pocket and had started to walk away.

"Where do you think you're going?" Joe asked.

"We're through, remember?" Vern said over his shoulder. "I did my part. And shit, you sure did yours. I forgot what a wing shot you were." Out came the chuckle.

"Don't take another step, Vern," Joe cautioned. "We're waiting for Barnum now. You're going to prison."

"We're through, Joe. We had a deal." Vern was angry. "Remember that one you owe me." He never stopped trying.

On the porch, Wacey moaned. He was alive, but blood was pouring out of him. His legs were grotesquely bent backwards underneath him.

"Stop, Vern," Joe said. He didn't yell, but he knew Vern could hear him.

Vern continued to walk along the back of the house.

"Honey, turn your head," Joe said sternly to Sheridan.

"No, I want to see this," Sheridan said.

"Turn your head!"

Sheridan reluctantly obeyed.

Joe raised the shotgun and waited until Vern was far enough away that the shot pattern wouldn't be tight. Then he shot him in the hip. Vern dropped like a rock.

"Jesus!" Vern cried, writhing on the ground. "I can't believe you *shot me in the ass*!"

"It was the least I could do," Joe said. "If you try to get up, I'll shoot you again."

Joe found Wacey's pistol in the grass, and tucked it in his belt. He walked back to the porch and squatted on the pavement. Wacey was balled up with his back against the door. His good arm was pulling a smashed leg to his chest. His wounded arm, now a hamburger-like stump pulsing gouts of arterial blood, flopped about like a broken wing. Wacey's eyes were wide, and his mouth was fixed in a waxy snarl.

"Can you hear me, Wacey?" Joe asked.

Wacey grunted and nodded through the pain.

"Wacey, the only reason I didn't kill you for what you've done to my family is because if you were dead, you wouldn't think about it much," Joe said. "Do you understand what I'm saying? I want you to be able to think about what you've done to my family, and to me, and to those outfitters. Not to mention the Wyoming Game and Fish Department."

"Get an ambulance!" Wacey hissed through chattering teeth. "I'm bleeding to death!"

"Do you understand what I'm saying?" Joe asked again, calmly.

"Yes! Goddamn you!" Wacey spat. He was trembling violently.

"No," Joe said, standing. "*Goddamn* you *to hell,* Wacey. And take Vern Dunnegan along on the same horse."

Joe picked up Sheridan and carried her around the house and through the front yard to Bighorn Road. He put her down near the gate.

"Dad, look," Sheridan said, pointing down the road toward Saddlestring.

Evelyn had done what she said she would. County sheriff's vehicles were roaring down the road from town, Barnum's Blazer in the lead with the siren and lights on.

Joe leaned his shotgun against the picket fence and stepped out onto the gravel road. Sheridan stayed with him. She was his shadow. He guessed that she might be his shadow for a very long time.

PART SEVEN

. . . Wilderness is the raw material out of which man has hammered the artifact called civilization.

No living man will see again the long-grass prairie, where a sea of prairie flowers lapped at the stirrups of the pioneer . . .

No living man will see again the virgin pineries of the Lake States, or the flat-woods of the coastal plain, or the giant hardwoods . . .

—Aldo Leopold, *A Sand County Almanac,* 1948

Epilogue

Spring.

Or at least what passed for spring in Wyoming, a place with only three legitimate but not independent seasons: summer, fall, and winter. Spring was something that occurred in other places, places where flowers pushed up from the soil during May when it warmed, places where leaves budded and opened on hardwood trees, places where flowers exposed themselves like sacrifices to the sun. Places where it was unlikely that after those leaves and flowers emerged, 10 inches of heavy, wet, and unpredicted snow would fall and would cynically, sneeringly, kill every living thing in sight and stop all movement.

Through the slush, Joe drove home on the Bighorn Road from the Crazy Woman Campground and thought that in his entire life in the Rocky Mountains he had never really experienced what spring was in other places, or truly appreciated what it stood for.

To him, and to the big game animals he was in charge of, spring was a particularly cruel natural joke: a season created and devised to remind living beings that things were often not what they seemed and that they had no real power or influence over it no matter how well educated, technologically advanced, or intuitive they had become. It was a season designed to remind the living that it wasn't safe to presume anything.

Dawn.

He entered the house as silently as he could, taking off his Sorel packs in the mudroom and exchanging them for his fleece slippers, hanging his parka, muddy Wranglers, and red chamois shirt on the nail in exchange for his robe, and tossing his Stetson onto the closet shelf.

It was Sunday, and it was his job to make pancakes.

He had left the house very early in response to a cellular telephone request from the campground, where the Defenders of Nature group had called him in a panic to report that "a hyped-up black or grizzly bear" was rooting around their tents. He had responded and arrived at the camp and quickly determined that the bear was actually a moose and that the moose was gone. The Defenders of Nature were dissatisfied with his conclusion, and they had tried to convince him that the snuffling sounds they had heard around their dome tents meant danger and not mere curiosity, but with a flashlight Joe had shown them the moose hoofprints and the still-steaming moose excrement near the fire pit, evidence that had led to his determination. The Defenders were outraged at the sudden heavy snow, and they seemed to blame Joe for it since he was a local. The Defenders—based in Arlington, Virginia, and encamped for nearly two weeks to monitor Miller's weasel recovery efforts and wholly suspicious of anybody or anything local (this was, after all, the backward land of miners, loggers, ranchers, developers, and hunters)—had grudgingly accepted Joe's hypothesis and had returned to their $800 sleeping bags.

With a whisk, Joe mixed eggs, flour, baking soda, and buttermilk into a bowl. He tested all of the heating elements to make sure the ones he replaced were now working. He greased the cast-iron skillet and set it on the stove to warm up.

Once the remains of the Miller's weasels had been confirmed, just about everything that Vern Dunnegan had predicted would happen was taking place in the mountains of Twelve Sleep County.

A moratorium on any kind of activity or recreation was quickly handed down by federal judges following scores of faxed legal briefs by dozens of environmental groups. Friend of the Court briefs appeared from organizations headquartered in Europe, Canada, Greenland, and Asia. The listing of Miller's weasels as an endangered species was petitioned for and granted in record time. The God Squad was convened to ram it through. Biologists, scientists, journalists, and environmentalists descended on Saddlestring, occupying every hotel and motel room as well as the campgrounds. Teams of agents from the U.S. Fish and Wildlife Service helicoptered in to the site of the killing field and beyond, and they soon discovered two more small colonies of Miller's weasels. Studies showed that the creatures had, in fact, evolved from subsisting almost entirely on buffalo to a diet of primarily elk. One of the colonies was dubbed the Cold Springs Group and the other the Timberline Group and the names became well-known in the media. Several networks broadcast the find live via satellite trucks during the evening news. It was, by one celebrity reporter's account, the "feel-good story of the year."

The heads of the Environmental Protection Agency and Department of Interior flew into the Saddlestring Airport in

Air Force Two and were photographed sneaking up on the Cold Springs Group with binoculars. Television viewers delighted in videotaped footage of Miller's weasels standing upright and chirping on their dens with their backs to one another. The Wyoming legislature, after a nasty floor fight, declared the Miller's weasel the "Official Endangered Species of Wyoming," beating out grizzly bears, Wyoming toads, and transplanted wolves.

Joe worked very hard to avoid being interviewed by anyone. The murder of the outfitters, the injuries and threats to his family, the death of Clyde Lidgard, and the arrests of Wacey and Vern were treated as sidebar stories that had led to the discovery of the Miller's weasels—if they were mentioned at all.

One of the colonies, the Timberline Group, which was made up of 18 Miller's weasels, died out literally in front of the cameras, and a nation mourned their loss. Autopsies revealed that the animals had contracted a viral infection, probably from one of the researcher's dogs. The Cold Springs Group declined from 28 animals to 13 for no traceable cause. A debate was raging whether the remaining Miller's weasels should be transplanted to a breeding facility or left alone. Biologists were in a dither over what to do. An additional 80 square miles were added to the newly designated Miller's Weasel Ecosystem. Everyone had an opinion, including the Wyoming Game and Fish Department, which was fighting in the courts for "custody" of the remaining animals.

The *Saddlestring Roundup* newspaper estimated that the discovery of the Miller's weasels had resulted in at least 400 local jobs lost in the lumber, grazing, agriculture, and recreation industries. Every day there were stories of families who were simply dropping off their house keys at the bank as they left town.

* * *

The trials for Vern Dunnegan and Wacey Hedeman had been postponed until summer. The rumor in town was that they had turned on each other and each was willing to implicate the other for every count of the charges. Vern had become a kind of far-right-wing media darling and was often interviewed in his cell talking about the Endangered Species Act. He was so glib and so capable of usable sound bites that his opinions were quoted by both sides of environmental controversies.

Wacey, however, had been shunned. A story leaked out from the federal detention facility in Cheyenne that Wacey had attacked a group of prisoners who were chiding him about his former profession and his new handicap and referring to him as "The Lone Arm of the Law."

Assistant Director Les Etbauer resigned from the Wyoming Game and Fish Department the day after Vern was arrested. The official statement from the department was that Etbauer had committed a serious lack of judgment when he suspended Joe Pickett and that Warden Pickett's position had been restored immediately with no further action required. There was even a commendation and a small increase in salary for Joe. Etbauer was then immediately hired as a consultant to the governor to serve as a liaison between the state and various federal land management agencies. Sheriff O. R. "Bud" Barnum won reelection with 87 percent of the vote with the remaining 13 percent going to write-in candidates that included pets, Marshal Matt Dillon, and two votes for Joe Pickett.

Joe had followed the news reports of how the pipeline that InterWest Resources had been building was capped and abandoned 50 miles from the western slope of the Bighorn Mountains. Despite congressional investigations, no credible evidence had been found linking InterWest with the webs Vern had spun on their behalf. InterWest eventually merged with CanCal to help build a single natural gas pipeline to Southern California, but market conditions were such that analysts were predicting that the project might be put on hold for years.

Marybeth came in from her walk with an armful of Sunday newspapers. She planned to start taking Maxine with her again in a couple of months, once she had built up her strength. Now though, she was walking with the aid of a cane and with a painful limp. The rigors of holding the Labrador back were too much for her. Marybeth's progress from wheelchair to walker to crutches to assisted walking on her own had all occurred before the doctors had said it would be possible. They marveled at her strength—and at her will. A full recovery was predicted. Joe had never doubted it.

Once they had moved back into the house from the Eagle Mountain Club, Missy Vankeuran had fled back to Arizona, saying she was needed to lend support for her new husband's run for the U.S. Senate.

There were now three children at the table for pancakes. Sheridan, now eight, and Lucy, now four, shared the table and the family with April Keeley, their foster child. It had been Marybeth's idea, and she had pursued it, even while she was in the wheelchair, after she had learned that Jeannie Keeley, Ote's widow, had left the county after she had given birth, taking only the baby with her. The youngest child had died of pneumonia. April, the sick child Joe had seen at the Keeley's home, had been left behind in Saddlestring. She was between Sheridan's and Lucy's ages, and she was slowly discovering that she could trust both of them. Marybeth had explained to Joe that April Keeley, likely to be a bundle of problems, would be the focus of all of the love and mothering that had been stored in her for the new baby. April was beginning to open up to Marybeth and Joe, although she was painfully shy and ashamed of her situation. Marybeth spent hours with her. Lucy was of course a little jealous, but Sheridan seemed to understand.

During the first month and a half when Marybeth returned home from the hospital, the situation had been difficult for all of them. Joe, Marybeth, and Sheridan had all been through separate but connected ordeals. Marybeth focused her hate on Vern Dunnegan, and Sheridan raged about Wacey Hedeman. Marybeth tried to explain to Joe how she felt about losing a child, how the feeling would never go away, how she would forever blame herself as a mother for allowing it to happen. There were many long nights when Joe held Marybeth while she cried. There were other nights when he held Sheridan.

Joe knew that he would never really fathom the depths of feelings both Marybeth and Sheridan had about what had happened. All he could do, he concluded, was what he did: be there and listen.

Joe had become concerned that both of them would be bitter, but it hadn't happened. Instead, they had become even closer as a family.

After breakfast, Joe and Sheridan put the remaining pancakes and bacon into a sack and went outside into the backyard. They walked around the house and sat in two lawn chairs facing the back of the garage. The morning had become warm, and the sun was out. Yesterday's snow was already melting. Muscular rivulets of runoff rushed down the Sandrock draw.

Sheridan broke off pieces of the pancakes and bacon and scattered them on the ground near the foundation of the garage. Joe cut up a couple of small chunks of meat from the haunch of a road-killed cow elk he had stored in the freezer and tossed them out. It didn't take long for the Miller's weasels to zip out of their den and clean up the food. Joe and Sheridan exchanged conspiratorial smiles while they watched.

There was a good reason why the Miller's weasels had moved from the woodpile to the roomy cavern beneath the garage. It turned out that, while Sheridan had been right about Lucky being a male and Hippity-Hop being a female, she was wrong about their "son," Elway. This spring, Elway had produced 10 babies (Joe had learned from the biologists in the canyon that the young were called "kits"), and eight had survived.

The kits were fascinating to watch because, although they were a quarter the size of their parents, they were just as fast when they shot out from beneath the foundation, grabbed food in their forepaws, and flashed back into the den. When Joe pointed a flashlight into the den, the weasels were a mass of writhing, chirping, long, brown bodies equally annoyed at the intrusion. The kits would sometimes come out into the sun and try to stand on their hind legs like their parents, and Joe and Sheridan would laugh as the kits would lose their balance, fall over, and scramble upright again until they could hold the famous pose.

"They're getting big," Sheridan said, nodding at the kits and tossing small pieces of food.

"Yes they are," Joe replied.

"Dad, what do you suppose would happen if anyone found out about these little guys?" Sheridan asked. He could tell she had been contemplating the question for a while. Joe had been amazed when Sheridan told him the entire story about the weasels, and she and Joe had promised each other not to tell anyone. As far as anyone knew, the Miller's weasels that Ote Keeley had brought down the mountain with him had died in the woodpile fire, just as Wacey said they had.

"Well, I don't know for sure," Joe answered. "I'm pretty certain that what we're doing isn't legally the right thing.

There's some biologists who would go berserk if they found out. A lot of other people, too."

"But aren't they the people who are at the colonies where the Miller's weasels keep dying?" Sheridan asked.

Joe chuckled. "That's them," Joe said.

Sheridan dutifully scattered the remains of the food near the den.

"You're doing this for me, aren't you?" Sheridan asked.

Joe nodded. "Yup."

Sheridan settled back into the lawn chair.

"You know, Dad, these critters remind me of our family," Sheridan said. "They were in great danger, and now they're doing okay. They're a family again."

Joe nodded. This was the kind of conversation that made him uncomfortable.

"We're sort of like them, aren't we, Dad?"

Joe reached over and squeezed Sheridan's hand. "Sheridan, sometimes we see things in animals that aren't really there. It's called transference, if that makes any sense."

Sheridan was studying him now. "That's okay, isn't it?" she asked.

"As long as we admit it to ourselves, I think it's okay," Joe said. "I think there are a lot of people who say they do things for animals when they're really doing it for themselves. They see things in animals that might not really be there. I think sometimes that hurts the animals in the end, and it hurts other people, too."

Sheridan thought it over. "Transference," she repeated.

"There are people on both sides of the issue who think animals are more valuable than people are," Joe said. "That's what's happening here."

Joe stopped speaking. He thought maybe he had said too much.

Joe was well aware of the fact that by keeping the Miller's weasels and not reporting their existence, he was breaking more regulations and laws than he could count.

And he knew that what he was planning to do with the creatures could probably land him in a federal prison. He could be accused of playing God. It could be construed as scandalous behavior by the Defenders of Nature—an offense worthy of at least a death sentence. He didn't try to justify his reasons, even to himself. He *was* playing God, after all. He was making a judgment simply because he thought it was the right one, and one that might somehow benefit his daughter.

"How long can we do this?" Sheridan asked. "Help the Miller's weasels, I mean."

"As long as you want to," Joe said. "As long as you feel it's important to you."

"They might be ready in a couple of weeks," Sheridan said, holding back a tear. She was admitting something. "We probably won't have any snow after that."

Joe told her about where he would want to transplant the animals. He had found a small, protected valley high in the Bighorns miles away from roads or trails. The valley lay in a natural elk migration route, and it was filled with mule deer. It was about 10 miles from the perimeter of the Miller's Weasel Ecosystem.

She sniffed and asked him if she would ever see them again.

"This summer," Joe promised, "you and I will put the panniers on Lizzie, and we'll horsepack into the mountains together. I'll take you to where the weasels are if you promise never to tell anyone about it."

"Of course, I promise," she said. "I can keep a secret."

He laughed. "I know you can."

And now
an exclusive excerpt from

Savage Run

the next Joe Pickett novel

by acclaimed mystery writer
C. J. Box

Available from

The Berkley Publishing Group!

1

Targhee National Forest, Idaho
June 10

On the third day of their honeymoon, infamous environmental activist Stewie Woods and his new bride Annabel Bellotti were spiking trees in the Bighorn National Forest when a cow exploded and blew them up. Until then, their marriage had been happy.

They met by chance. Stewie Woods had been busy pouring bag after bag of sugar and sand into the gasoline tanks of a fleet of pickups that belonged to a natural gas exploration crew in a newly graded parking lot. The crew had left for the afternoon for the bars and hotel rooms of nearby Henry's Fork. One of the crew had returned unexpectedly and caught Stewie as Stewie was ripping off the top of a bag of sugar with his teeth. The crewmember pulled a 9mm semiautomatic from beneath the dashboard and fired several wild pistol shots in Stewie's direction. Stewie had dropped the bag and run away, crashing through the timber like a bull elk.

Stewie had outrun and out-juked the man with the pistol and he met Annabel when he literally tripped over her as she sunbathed nude in the grass in an orange pool of late afternoon sun, unaware of his approach because she was listening to Melissa Etheridge on her Walkman's headphones. She looked good, he thought, strawberry blond hair with a two-day Rocky Mountain fire-engine tan (two hours in the sun at 8,000 feet created a sunburn like a whole day at the beach), small ripe breasts, and a trimmed vector of pubic hair.

He had gathered her up and pulled her along through the timber, where they hid together in a dry spring wash until the man with the pistol gave up and went home. She had giggled while he held her—*this was real adventure,* she'd said—and he had used the opportunity to run his hands tentatively over her naked shoulders and hips and had found out, happily, that she did not object. They made their way back to where she had been sunbathing and while she dressed, they introduced themselves.

She told him she liked the idea of meeting a famous environmental outlaw in the woods while she was naked, and he appreciated that. She said she had seen his picture before, maybe in *Outside Magazine*?, and admired his looks—tall and raw-boned, with round rimless glasses, a short-cropped full beard, and his famous red bandana on his head.

Her story was that she had been camping alone in a dome tent, taking a few days off from her freewheeling cross-continent trip that had begun with her divorce from an anal retentive investment banker named Nathan in her home town of Pawtucket, Rhode Island. She was bound, eventually, for Seattle.

"I'm falling in love with your mind," he lied.

"Already?" she asked.

He encouraged her to travel with him, and they took her vehicle since the lone crewmember had disabled Stewie's Subaru with three bullets into the engine block. Stewie was astonished by his good fortune. Every time he looked over at her and she smiled back, he was pole-axed with exuberance.

Keeping to dirt roads, they crossed into Montana. The next afternoon, in the backseat of her SUV during a thunderstorm that rocked the car and blew shroudlike sheets of rain through the mountain passes, he asked her to marry him. Given the circumstances and the supercharged atmosphere, she accepted. When the rain stopped, they drove to Ennis, Montana, and asked around about who could marry them, fast. Stewie did not want to take the chance of letting her get away. She kept saying she couldn't believe she was doing this. He couldn't believe she was doing this either, and he loved her even more for it.

At the Sportsman Inn in Ennis, Montana, which was bustling with fly fishermen bound for the trout-rich waters of the Madison River, the desk clerk gave them a name and they looked up Judge Ace Cooper (Ret.) in the telephone book.

Judge Cooper was a tired and rotund man who wore a stained white cowboy shirt and an elk horn bolo tie with his shirt collar open. He performed the ceremony in a room adjacent to his living room that was bare except for a single filing cabinet, a desk and three chairs, and two framed photographs—one of the judge and President George H. W. Bush, who had once been up there fishing, and the other of the judge on a horse before the Cooper family lost their ranch in the 1980s.

The wedding ceremony had taken eleven minutes, which was just about average for Judge Cooper, although he had once performed it in eight minutes for two Indians.

"Do you, Allan Stewart Woods, take thee Annabeth to be your lawful wedded wife?" Judge Cooper had asked, reading from the marriage application form.

"Anna*bel*," Annabel had corrected in her biting Rhode Island accent.

"I do," Stewie had said. He was beside himself with pure joy.

Stewie twisted the ring off his finger and placed it on hers. It was unique; handmade gold mounted with sterling silver monkey wrenches. It was also three sizes too large. The judge studied the ring.

"Monkey wrenches?" the judge had asked.

"It's symbolic," Stewie had said.

"I'm aware of the symbolism," the judge said darkly, before finishing the passage.

Annabel and Stewie had beamed at each other. Annabel said that this was, like, the *wildest* vacation ever. They were Mr. and Mrs. Outlaw Couple. He was now *her* famous outlaw, although as yet untamed. She said her father would be scandalized, and her mother would have to wear dark glasses in Newport. Only her Aunt Tildie, the one with the wild streak who had corresponded with, but never met, a Texas serial killer until he died of lethal injection, would understand.

Stewie had to borrow a hundred dollars from her to pay the judge, and she signed over a traveler's check.

After the couple had left in the SUV with Rhode Island plates, Judge Ace Cooper had gone to his lone filing cabinet and found the file. He pulled a single piece of paper out and read it as he dialed the telephone. While he waited for the right man to come to the telephone, he stared at the framed photo on the wall of himself on the horse at his former ranch. The ranch, north of Yellowstone Park, had been subdivided by a Bozeman real estate company into over thirty 50-acre "ranchettes." Famous Hollywood celebrities, including the one who's early-career photos he had recently seen in *Penthouse*, now lived there. Movies had been filmed there. There was even a crackhouse, but it was rumored that the owner wintered in LA. The only cattle that existed were purely for visual effect, like landscaping that moved and crapped and looked good when the sun threatened to drop below the mountains.

The man he was waiting for came to the telephone.

"It was Stewie Woods, all right." He said. "The man himself. I recognized him right off, and his ID proved it." There was a pause as the man on the other end of the telephone asked Cooper something. "Yeah, I heard him say that to her just before they left. They're headed for the Bighorns in Wyoming. Somewhere near Saddlestring."

Annabel told Stewie that their honeymoon was quite unlike what she had ever imagined a honeymoon to be, and she contrasted it with her first one with Nathan. Nathan was about sailing boats, champagne, and Barbados. Stewie was about spiking trees in stifling heat in a national forest in Wyoming. He had even asked her to carry his pack.

Neither of them had noticed the late-model black Ford pickup that had trailed them up the mountain road and continued on when Stewie pulled over to park.

Deep into the forest, Stewie now removed his shirt and tied the sleeves around his waist. A heavy bag of nails hung from his belt and tinkled while he strode through the undergrowth. There was a sheen of sweat on his bare chest as he straddled a three-foot thick Douglas Fir and drove in spikes. He was obviously well practiced, and he got into a rhythm where he could bury the 6-inch spikes into the soft wood with three heavy blows from his sledgehammer; one tap to set the spike and two blows to bury it beyond the nail head in the bark.

He moved from tree to tree, but didn't spike all of them. He attacked each tree in the same method. The first of the spikes went in at eye level. A quarter-turn around the trunk, he pounded in another a foot lower than the first. He continued pounding in spikes until he had placed them in a spiral on the trunk nearly to the grass.

"Won't it hurt the trees?" Annabel asked as she unloaded his pack and leaned it against a tree.

"Of course not," he said, moving across the pine-needle floor to another target. "I wouldn't be doing this if it hurt the trees. You've got a lot to learn about me, Annabel."

"Why do you put so many in?" she asked.

"Good question," he said, burying a spike in three blows. "It used to be we could put in four right at knee level, at the compass points, where the trees are usually cut. But the lumber companies got wise to that and told their loggers to go higher or lower. So now we fill up a four-foot radius."

"And what will happen if they try to cut it down?"

Stewie smiled, resting for a moment. "When a chainsaw blade hits a steel spike, the blade can snap and whip back. Busts the saw-teeth. That can take an eye or a nose right off."

"That's horrible," she said, wincing, wondering what she was getting into.

"I've never been responsible for any injuries," Stewie said quickly, looking hard at her. "The purpose is to save trees. After we're done here, I'll call the local ranger station and tell them what we've done. I won't say exactly where we spiked the trees or how many trees we spiked. It should be enough to keep them out of here for decades, and that's the point."

"Have you ever been caught?" she asked.

"Once," Stewie said, and his face clouded. "A forest ranger caught me by Jackson Hole. He marched me into downtown Jackson on foot during tourist season at gunpoint. Half of the tourists in town cheered and the other half started chanting, 'Hang him high! Hang him high!' I was sent to the Wyoming State Penitentiary in Rawlins for seven months."

"Now that you mention it, I think I read about that," she mused.

"You probably did. The wire services picked it up. I was interviewed on *Nightline* and *60 Minutes. Outside Magazine* put me on the cover. My boyhood friend Hayden Powell wrote the cover story for them, and he coined the word 'eco-terrorist'." This memory made him feel bold. "There were reporters from all over the country at that trial." Stewie said. "Even the *New York Times*. It was the first time most people had ever heard of One Globe, or knew I was the founder of it. Memberships started pouring in from all over the world."

One Globe. The ecological action group that used the logo of crossed monkey wrenches, in deference to late author Edward Abbey's *The Monkey Wrench Gang*. One Globe had once dropped a shroud over Mount Rushmore for the president's speech, she recalled. It had been on the nightly news.

"Stewie," she said happily, "You are the real thing." He could feel her eyes on him as he drove in the spiral of spikes and moved to the next tree.

"When you are done with that tree I want you," she said, her voice husky. "Right here and right now, my sweet, sweaty . . . *husband*."

He turned and smiled. His face glistened and his muscles were swelled from swinging the sledgehammer. She slid her T-shirt over her head and stood waiting for him, her lips parted and her legs tense.

Stewie slung his own pack now and, for the time being, had stopped spiking trees. Fat black thunderheads, pregnant with rain, nosed across the late-afternoon sky. They were hiking at a fast pace toward the peak, holding hands, with the hope of getting there and pitching camp before the rain started. Stewie said they would hike out of the forest tomorrow and he would call the ranger station. Then they would get in the SUV and head southeast, toward the Bridger-Teton Forest.

When they walked into the herd of cattle, Stewie felt a dark cloud of anger envelop him.

"Range maggots!" Stewie said, spitting. "If they're not letting the logging companies in to cut all the trees at taxpayer's expense, they're letting the local ranchers run their cows in here so they can eat all the grass and shit in all the streams."

"Can't we just go around them?" Annabel asked.

"It's not that, Annabel," he said patiently. "Of course we can go around them. It's just the principal of the thing. We have cattle fouling what is left of the natural ecosystem. Cows don't belong in the trees in the Bighorn Mountains. You have so much to learn, darling."

"I know," she said, determined.

"These ranchers out here run their cows on public land—our land—at the expense of not only us but the wildlife. They pay something like four dollars an acre when they should be paying ten times that, even though it would be best if they were completely gone."

"But we need meat, don't we?" she asked. "You're not a vegetarian, are you?"

"Did you forget that cheeseburger I had for lunch in Cameron?" he said. "No, I'm not a vegetarian, although sometimes I wish I had the will to be one."

"I tried it once and it made me lethargic," Annabel confessed.

"All these western cows produce about five percent of the beef we eat in this whole country," Stewie said. "All the rest comes from down South, in Texas, Florida, and Louisiana, where there's plenty of grass and plenty of private land to graze them on."

Stewie picked up a pinecone, threw it accurately through the trees, and struck a black baldy heifer on the snout. The cow bolted, turned, and lumbered away. The rest of the herd, about a dozen, followed it. The small herd moved loudly, clumsily cracking branches and throwing up fist-sized pieces of black earth from their hooves.

"I wish I could chase them right back to the ranch they belong on," Stewie said, watching. "Right up the ass of the rancher who has lease rights for this part of the Bighorns."

One cow had not moved. It stood broadside and looked at them.

"What's wrong with that cow?" Stewie asked.

"Shoo!" Annabel shouted. "Shoo!"

Stewie stifled a smile at his new wife's shooing and slid out of his pack. The temperature had dropped twenty degrees in the last ten minutes and rain was inevitable. The sky had darkened and black coils of clouds enveloped the peak. The sudden low pressure had made the forest quieter, the sounds muffled and the smell of cows stronger.

Stewie Woods walked straight toward the heifer, with Annabel several steps behind.

"Something's wrong with that cow," Stewie said, trying to figure out what about it seemed out of place.

When Stewie was close enough he saw everything at once: the cow trying to run with the others but straining at the end of a tight nylon line; the heifer's wild white eyes; the misshapen profile of something strapped on it's back that was large and square and didn't belong; the thin reed of antenna that quivered from the package on the heifer's back.

"Annabel!" Stewie yelled, turning to reach out to her—but she had walked around him and was now squarely between him and the cow.

She absorbed the full, frontal blast when the heifer detonated, the explosion shattering the mountain stillness with the subtlety of a sledgehammer bludgeoning bone.

Four miles away, a fire lookout heard the guttural boom and ran to the railing with binoculars. Over a red-rimmed plume of smoke and dirt, he could see a Douglas fir launch like a rocket into the air, where it turned, hung suspended for a moment, then crashed into the forest below.

Shaking, he reached for his radio.

2

Eight miles out of Saddlestring, Wyoming, Game Warden Joe Pickett was watching his wife Marybeth work their new Tobiano paint horse, Toby, in the round pen when the call came from the Twelve Sleep County Sheriff's office.

It was early evening, the time of night when the setting sun ballooned and softened and defined the deep velvet folds and piercing tree greens of Wolf Mountain. The normally dull pastel colors of the weathered barn and the red-rock canyon behind the house suddenly looked as if they had been repainted in acrylics. Toby, a big dark bay gelding swirled with brilliant white that ran up over his haunches like thick spilled paint upside down, shone deep red in the evening light and looked especially striking. So did Marybeth, in Joe's opinion, in her worn Wranglers, sleeveless cotton shirt, and her blond hair in a ponytail. There was no wind, and the only sound was the rhythmic thumping of Toby's hooves in the round pen as Marybeth waved the whip and encouraged the gelding to shift from a trot into a slow lope.

The Saddlestring District was considered a "two-horse

district" by the Game and Fish Department, meaning that the department would provide feed and tack for two mounts to be used for patrolling. Toby was their second horse.

Joe stood with his boot on the bottom rail and his arms folded over the top, his chin nestled between his forearms. He was still wearing his red cotton Game and Fish uniform shirt with the pronghorn antelope patch on the sleeve and his sweat-stained gray Stetson. He could feel the pounding of the earth as Toby passed in front of him in a circle. He watched Marybeth stay in position in the center of the pen, shuffling her feet so she stayed on Toby's back flank. She talked to her horse in a soothing voice, urging him to gallop—something he clearly didn't want to do.

Persistent, Marybeth stepped closer to Toby and commanded him to run. Marybeth still had a slight limp from when she had been shot nearly two years before, but she was nimble and quick. Toby pinned his ears back and twitched his tail but finally broke into a full-fledged gallop, raising the dust in the pen, his mane and tail snapping behind him like a flag in a stiff wind. After several rotations, Marybeth called "Whoa!" and Toby hit the brakes, skidding to a quick stop where he stood breathing hard, his muscles swelled, his back shiny with sweat, smacking and licking his lips as if he was eating peanut butter. Marybeth approached him and patted him down, telling him what a good boy he was, and blowing gently into his nostrils to soothe him.

"He's a stubborn guy—and lazy," she told Joe. "He did *not* want to lope fast. Did you notice how he pinned his ears back and threw his head around?"

Joe said *yup*.

"That's how he was telling me he was mad about it. When he's doing that he's either going to break out of the circle and do whatever he wants to, or stop, or do what I'm asking him to do. In this case he did what I asked and went into the fast lope. He's finally learning that things will go a lot easier on him when he does what I ask him."

"I know it works for me," Joe said and smiled.

Marybeth crinkled her nose at Joe, then turned back to Toby. "See how he licks his lips? That's a sign of obedience. He's conceding that I am the boss. That's a good sign."

Joe fought the urge to theatrically lick his lips when she looked over at him.

"Why did you blow in his nose like that?"

"Horses in the herd do that to each other to show affection. It's another way they bond with each other." Marybeth paused. "I know it sounds hokey, but blowing in his nose is kind of like giving him a hug. A horse hug."

"You seem to know what you're doing."

Joe had been around horses most of his life. He had now taken his buckskin mare Lizzie over most of the mountains in the Twelve Sleep Range of the Bighorns in his District. But what Marybeth was doing with her new horse Toby, what she was getting out of him, was a different kind of thing. Joe was duly impressed.

A shout behind him shook Joe from his thoughts. He turned toward the sound, and saw nine-year-old Sheridan, five-year-old Lucy, and their seven-year-old foster daughter April stream through the back yard gate and across the field. Sheridan held the cordless phone out in front of her like an Olympic torch, and the other two girls followed.

"Dad, it's for you," Sheridan called. "A man says it's very important."

Joe and Marybeth exchanged looks and Joe took the telephone. It was County Sheriff O. R. "Bud" Barnum.

There had been a big explosion in the Bighorn National Forest, Barnum told Joe. A fire lookout had called it in, and had reported that through his binoculars he could see fat dark forms littered throughout the trees. It looked like a "shitload" of animals were dead, which is why he was calling Joe. Dead game animals were Joe's concern. They assumed at this point that they were game animals, Barnum said, but they might be cows. A couple of local ranchers had grazing leases up there. Barnum asked if Joe could meet him at the Winchester exit off of the interstate in twenty minutes. That way, they could get to the scene before it was completely dark.

Joe handed the telephone back to Sheridan and looked over his shoulder at Marybeth.

"When will you be back?" she asked.

"Late," Joe told her. "There was an explosion in the mountains."

"You mean like a plane crash?"

"He didn't say that. The explosion was a few miles off of the Hazelton Road in the mountains, in elk country. Barnum thinks there may be some game animals down."

She looked at Joe for further explanation. He shrugged to indicate that was all he knew.

"I'll save you some dinner."

Joe met the sheriff and Deputy McLanahan at the exit to Winchester and followed them through the small town. The three-vehicle fleet—two County GMC Blazers and Joe's dark green Game and Fish pickup—entered and exited the tiny town within minutes. Even though it was an hour and a half away from darkness, the only establishments open were the two bars with identical red neon Coors signs in their windows and a convenience store. Winchester's lone public artwork, located on the front lawn of the branch bank, was an outsized and gruesome metal sculpture of a wounded grizzly bear straining at the end of a thick chain, it's metal leg encased in a massive saw-toothed bear trap. Joe did not find the sculpture lovely but it captured the mood, style, and inbred frontier culture of the area as well as anything else could have.

Deputy McLanahan led the way through the timber in the direction where the explosion had been reported and Joe walked behind him alongside Sheriff Barnum. Joe and McLanahan had acknowledged each other with curt nods and said nothing. Their relationship had been rocky ever since McLanahan had sprayed the outfitter's camp with shotgun blasts two years before and Joe had received a wayward pellet under his eye. He still had a scar to show for it.

Barnum's hangdog face grimaced as he limped aside Joe through the underbrush. He complained about his hip. He complained about the distance from the road to the crime scene. He complained about McLanahan, and said to Joe sotto voce that he should have fired the deputy years before and would have if he weren't his nephew. Joe suspected, however, that Barnum also kept McLanahan's around because McLanahan's quick-draw reputation had added—however untrue and unlikely—an air of toughness to the Sheriff's Department that didn't hurt at election time.

The sun had dropped below the top of the mountains and instantly turned them into craggy black silhouettes. The light dimmed in the forest, fusing the treetops and branches that were discernable just a moment before into a shadowy muddle. Joe reached back on his belt to make sure he had his flashlight. He let his arm brush his .357 Smith & Wesson revolver to confirm it was there. He didn't want Barnum to notice the movement since Barnum still chided him about the time he lost his gun to a poacher Joe was arresting.

There was an unnatural silence in the woods, with the exception of Barnum's grumbling. The absence of normal sounds—the chattering of squirrels sending a warning up the line, the panicked scrambling of deer, the airy winged drumbeat of flushed Spruce grouse—confirmed that something big had happened here. Something so big it had either cleared the wildlife out of the area or frightened them mute. Joe could feel that they were getting closer before he could see anything to confirm it. Whatever it was, it was just ahead.

McLanahan quickly stopped and there was a sharp intake of breath.

"Holy shit," McLanahan whispered in awe. *"Holy shit."*

The still-smoking crater was fifteen yards across. It was three feet deep at its center. A half dozen trees had been blown out of the ground and their shallow rootpans were exposed like black outstretched hands. Eight or nine black baldy cattle were dead and still, strewn among the trunks of trees. The earth below the thick turf rim of the crater was dark and wet. Several large white roots, the size of leg bones, were pulled up from the ground by the explosion and now pointed at the sky. Cordite from the explosives, pine from broken branches, and upturned mulch had combined in the air to produce a sickeningly sweet and heavy smell.

Darkness enveloped them as they slowly circled the crater. Pools of light from their flashlights lit up twisted roots and lacy pale yellow undergrowth.

Joe checked the cattle, moving among them away from the crater. Most had visible injuries as a result of fist-sized rocks being blown into them from the explosion. One heifer was impaled on the fallen tip of a dead pine tree. The rest of the herd, apparently unhurt, stood as silent shadows just beyond his flashlight. He could see dark heavy shapes and hear the sound of chewing, and a pair of eyes reflected back blue as a cow raised its head to look at him. They all had the same brand—a "V" on top and a "U" on the bottom divided by a single line. Joe recognized it as the Vee Bar U Ranch. These were Ed Finolla's cows.

McLanahan suddenly grunted in alarm and Joe raised his flashlight to see the deputy in a wild, self-slapping panic, dancing away from the rim of the crater and ripping his jacket off of himself as quickly as he could. He threw it violently to the ground in a heap and stood staring at it.

"What in the hell is wrong with you?" Barnum asked, annoyed.

"Something landed on my shoulder. Something heavy and wet," McLanahan said, his face contorted. "I thought it was somebody's hand grabbing me. It scared me half to death."

McLanahan had dropped his flashlight, so from across the crater Joe lowered his light onto the jacket and focused his Mag Light into a tight beam. McLanahan bent down into the light and gingerly unfolded the jacket, poised to jump back if whatever had fallen on him was still in his clothing. He threw back a fold and cursed. Joe couldn't see for sure what McLanahan was looking at other than that the object was dark and moist.

"What is it?" Barnum demanded.

"It looks like . . . well . . . it looks like a piece of *meat*." McLanahan looked up at Joe vacantly.

Slowly, Joe raised the beam of his flashlight, sweeping upward over McLanahan and following it up the trunk of a lodgepole pine and into the branches. What Joe saw, he would never forget. . . .